THE ALB

A NOVEL

LUIS ROUSSET

authorHOUSE®

AuthorHouse™
1663 Liberty Drive
Bloomington, IN 47403
www.authorhouse.com
Phone: 833-262-8899

This is a work of fiction. All of the characters, names, incidents, organizations, and dialogue in this novel are either the products of the author's imagination or are used fictitiously.

Published by AuthorHouse 10/16/2020

ISBN: 978-1-6655-0330-3 (sc)
ISBN: 978-1-6655-0329-7 (hc)
ISBN: 978-1-6655-0328-0 (e)

Library of Congress Control Number: 2020919663

Print information available on the last page.

This book is printed on acid-free paper.

ACKNOWLEDGEMENTS

This novel, The Alb, could not have been written without the support and encouragement of my wife Mariza. I am grateful for her patience and useful commentaries to the story.

I would also like to thank the following persons for their assistance in proofreading my manuscript, suggesting changes and improvements:

Ms. Vicky Adler;
Mrs. Lorraine Jarboe, LTC, IRR, US Army
Mrs. Lydia R. de Paula
Dr. Hugo Mendonça, MD.

CONTENTS

Part 3: Conclusion

PROLOGUE

Methinks, by most, 'twill be confess'd
That Death is never quite a welcomed guest.
When I leave here, let come what must.
What do I care about it now, if hereafter
men hate or love, or if in those other spheres
there be an Above or a Below?
Faust, Part I

Daybreak comes late in the deep valleys, high up in the Peruvian Andes, the first sun rays barely clearing the snowy peaks closing the river gorge of the Colca Valley tributary. In the subdued luminosity of the early morning, he could just see the outline of the camp tents, the night fire long extinguished. He would have to deal with the single posted sentinel first, quietly to avoid warning the others.

A few years earlier, before the *Sendero Luminoso*, or Shining Path, had been dealt with and terrorism practically eradicated in Peru, an unprotected campsite like this would have been impossible. However, peace had returned to the area, and people had grown careless. He dragged himself silently, crawling along ground covered by moss and short grass, stopping frequently to listen and to ensure his stealth, slowly coming closer to the unsuspecting watchman, using boulders and natural depressions to conceal his approach. Finally, he reached a point a few feet behind his unsuspecting target. From there, in a quick final rush, he could fall on his prey.

The man was smoking. He could see the brief glowing of the cigarette as the tobacco fumes were inhaled. He got up and sprang, covering the remaining distance in a flash, grabbing his victim with a hand over the mouth and pulling his head back against his chest. He used the knife on his other hand to slash deep, from left to right, opening the man's throat in a single swift movement before allowing him any reaction. He held on to the watchman's head, bending slightly forward in an almost tender gesture, as if supporting someone not feeling well, waiting for the finally gurgling sounds to cease and the initial blood spurt to subside. He laid the body gently on the ground, placing it on his side, not letting it drop to avoid even the tiniest noise. Next, he would have to deal with the camp visitor, a local shepherd who had arrived the day before with his llamas and asked to bivouac for the night. His llamas would be put to good use. The visitor had set his meager possessions on the other side of the camp. He started going around the tents until he spotted the visitor lying down on his bedding. He walked slowly, paying attention to keep to the back of the sleeping Indian. When he was a few feet away, the man's keen senses and light sleep warned him of some danger. He started getting up, still dazed by the abrupt waking, and turned in the direction of the noise. The killer jumped him, pushing him down with his superior weight, having neither the time nor opportunity for a more subtle or technical attack. He stabbed up, just below the ribs, while pressing a hand over his victim's mouth to stifle any cries. The Indian struggled for a few seconds and was then still.

He got up, looking around slowly to see if anyone had been alarmed by the fight. Satisfied that all was quiet, he unslung the shotgun he had been carrying and went to the tent, occupied by the company's geologist and the driver. The need for silence was over, and so he entered the tent and shot both men in the head. They never woke up. He went out again. The Peruvian archeologist and his female assistant were coming out of their tent, alarmed by the noise. He shot them both as well, reloaded the shotgun, and calmly shot each one again in the head.

He dragged the two bodies back to their tents and went to fetch the shepherd's body, which he placed in the third tent. He exchanged his clothing with the shepherd's and placed his wallet and his current passport in his pocket. He stopped a moment to take deep breaths and to bend down, increasing the flow of blood to his head to clear it. He went looking for the gallons of extra fuel for the Land Rovers and doused the bodies and the tents with diesel. He set fire to each tent and carefully watched the result of his work, assuring himself that the flames would consume everything. In the rarefied air of the Andes, the fire burned fiercely but without producing much smoke. Only then did the full realization of his acts hit him. He was sick and started to vomit, dizzy from the effort at this high altitude and from the emotion of the killings.

The day was finally breaking, and it was time to leave. He had a long way to go. His plan was to cross the mountains to reach Cusco, rent or steal a car to travel eastwards, and eventually cross into Brazil and drive to the town of Porto Velho on the Madeira River. From there, he could take passage on a boat going to Manaus or Belem and finally start a new life. First, he had to collect the maps and documents of the Peruvian archeologist. He would need these to reach the ancient Inca burial site and its treasure trove. He tied his pack, blanket, and extra bundle on the backs of two of the sturdiest llamas, and after a final look at the burning tents, he started walking toward the gorge wall for his steep climb out of the valley.

PART 1

A Peruvian Adventure

CHAPTER 1

Manhattan, June 2012

I woke up and slowly began to notice things, still a little dizzy with sleep. I heard the women talking elsewhere in the apartment, my wife Olivia and my daughter's nanny, Claudia. It was Monday, I realized with a shock. I had to get up and get ready for work. After our wedding and our move to New York, my Brazilian wife decided to start college and study economics. We engaged the services of a nanny to take care of Larissa while Olivia was out attending classes. Claudia was also Brazilian. My wife wanted to make sure Larissa learned to speak Portuguese at an early age. Claudia lived somewhere in Queens, but during the week, she stayed with us in one of the three bedrooms of our Upper East Side apartment. On weekends, she went home to be with her sister and family.

I had slept too much. Married life was making me lazy, I suppose—too much of a good thing. This was my second marriage. The first had been a disaster, and had I almost ruined my second chance with my lack of good sense. I met Olivia during a job in Brazil. The detective company I owned with my partner, Tony, had been hired to investigate the murder of an American oil executive there. I fell in love with Olivia the first time I saw her. Crazy, I know, but true. She worked in the same oil company in a small town northeast of Rio, where the offshore oil exploration in Brazil is centered. Olivia came from a wealthy rural family in that corner of the country. She was much younger than me, a fact I had used as an excuse to avoid a firm commitment—a huge mistake, I realized after returning to New York. I couldn't live without her. I had almost lost her, and honestly, I don't know what I would have done if I had. In the end, Olivia took me back. I still don't know why. She was so gorgeous, intelligent, well educated, and rich. I cannot fathom what she saw in me. But I'm not complaining. I'm just silly happy.

"Good morning, ladies." I embraced and kissed Olivia. Our daughter, Larissa, was sitting on a highchair, being fed by the nurse. She smiled at me and extended her arms to be picked up. Olivia stopped me.

"Alan, please, let Claudia finish feeding Larissa. If you start playing with her now, she'll stop eating. She needs her food. You can play with her all you want afterward. Please, wait."

"Oh well, fine. I can wait a little to go to work. What about you?"

"I'm leaving. I'm already late for the first class. I'll take the car, okay?"

"Sure, I won't use it. I'll take the subway to work."

"Don't come back late, love. Remember that we are having dinner with your sister, Jessica, tonight."

"I don't expect to be late. There is nothing important at work today—just meeting a potential new client. I should be back early."

"Great. I should go. You can stay and have fun with our daughter." Olivia kissed me and Larissa and left. I stayed behind a few moments longer, talking to Claudia and playing silly with Larissa.

My partner, Anthony Galliazzi, greeted me when I arrived at our detective firm, Leary & Galliazzi, on Third Avenue. The company had expanded since our job in Brazil. We now employed two younger detectives, both graduates from the John Jay College of Criminal Justice, but our workload kept growing. We might soon be forced to take on additional help.

"Good morning, Alan. How was the weekend?"

"It was great. We took Larissa to the zoo in Central Park and... what? Why are you smiling?"

"Oh, nothing. I was comparing Alan Leary before and after. You clearly do not realize the difference between the sad fellow just back from Brazil and the new one always content with life. Surely, your wife did you a world of good to you. Besides, it is funny to watch the transformation—from envied ladies' man to domestic daddy."

"Christ, is it really that bad?"

"Bad? No, definitely not, much to the contrary. People envy you now for a totally different reason. You are obviously so happy and satisfied with life, but enough of that. As you know, we have a very important meeting with this lawyer, Mr. Anton Deville. His client, a very rich and important fellow, disappeared in Peru in April of this year—a very strange and tragic event. You must have read something about the case. It was front-page news just about everywhere."

"Sure. I read about it. John Engelhard is a major shareholder and CEO of a mining conglomerate, with mines in North and South America, as well as in several other parts of the world. He vanished during a visit to one of his company's exploration camps in Peru."

"Precisely. During the exploration work, his geologist stumbled upon an Incan site. It was a significant archaeological find, rich in artifacts and gold. John Engelhard decided to travel to visit the site firsthand. During the night, his bivouac camp was intruded upon by person or persons unknown, and everyone was killed. They found a body with John's wallet and documents. For a time, they thought he had also been killed. However, DNA analysis revealed the body belonged to somebody else. It was the body of a local native who had stopped to pass the night at the camp."

"That's right, Tony. I remember the details now. Very mysterious case. The treasure was taken. There was some talk that Engelhard planned to rob the site, but he certainly didn't need the money, and his company was doing extremely well. The value of the gold, though very large, had no significance in the face of Engelhard's personal fortune. Why would he jeopardize his assets and position to steal the gold?"

"That's Mr. Anton Deville's opinion. Anyway, he wishes to discuss the possibility of hiring us to investigate the case. He is willing to spare no cost to find out what truly happened. He obviously has deep pockets. Money is no obstacle to him. This could be very important to our company. If we are successful, it would bring us a lot of exposure."

"Yes, I do realize it. Let's see what Mr. Deville has to say this afternoon."

Mr. Anton Deville was a peculiar man. Short with dark curly hair and a thick body that conveyed the impression of strength and muscle rather than fat. He wore a dark suit and a vest, not the most comfortable attire for a New York summer. He clung to a cane, a fancy one with a pommel of carved ivory, probably old and expensive, which I didn't think he needed for support. It was an additional item completing his odd look. Deville didn't seem American, or European for that matter. In spite of his looks, he spoke English flawlessly, with a subtle Southern accent. His slightly curved nose gave him a Middle Eastern appearance, perhaps Palestine. He spoke with a deep but not unpleasant voice, clearly enunciating every word and phrase and eschewing all colloquialisms.

After the usual formal introductions, we sat around the table in the meeting room table to discuss the Engelhard case. Deville directed his introductory words to my partner, Tony, to whom he had previously talked on the phone.

"Mr. Galliazzi, you know why I asked for this meeting today?"

"I do indeed, Mr. Deville, and we are ready to do everything in our power to assist you."

"Thank you. But first, I would like to say a few words about my client and friend, Mr. John Engelhard. You must understand that John is a very successful and wealthy person. His personal fortune is counted in the billions. When he vanished in Peru, he was under no financial or emotional stress. His company is solid, with a stable market, and has no notable debts."

"I understand, Mr. Deville," Tony answered.

"The idea of John killing those people to steal the gold is preposterous. He had nothing to gain, and he was mentally stable before he disappeared."

"Let me interrupt you a moment, Mr. Deville. You have been referring to John Engelhard in the present tense. Do you have any evidence that he is still alive?" I asked.

"I have nothing concrete Mr. Leary, but I am certain he is alive."

"How can you be so sure?"

"It's hard to explain, Mr. Leary. It's a gut feeling. We have been close, John and I, for such a long time, and I know him so well. I think I developed what you can call a sixth sense about him. Trust me when I say that he's alive."

"Okay, let's assume you are right. It has been two months since he vanished. If he's alive, why has there been no contact from him or his abductors?"

"I have no answer for that," Deville replied.

"Accepting that other person or persons are responsible for those killings, why would they spare only John?"

"One possibility: to be spared, John revealed to the criminals that he was a wealthy person, or they already knew," answered Deville. "Thus, he became more important to them alive rather than dead."

"Fine, but why have they not made contact to demand ransom in the meantime?"

"The Inca artifacts have a value several times their intrinsic value in gold. However, disposing of them is a complex process. I have heard that there are a few buyers, in Europe and the Middle East, who specialize in stolen and archeological objects. You can imagine how difficult it must be to conclude this sort of business. First, the pieces must be moved from Peru to Europe, a very complicated endeavor. With all the airport controls presently in place, it must be impossible to transport the pieces by air. They would have to be smuggled by sea."

"So?" I asked. "How does that justify the lack of communication?"

"Perhaps the thieves want to get rid of the pieces before proposing their ransom. Maybe they do not wish to run the risk of calling attention to themselves before concluding the business with the artifacts."

"Yes," I conceded. "It is a possibility."

"What do you want us to do?" asked Tony?

"I would like you to send a detective to Peru to visit the area and the crime scene. Talk to the authorities in that country. Gather clues about the perpetrators. In short, do everything possible to solve the crime and find John."

"You realize that what you are asking may prove to be a very long process, without guarantee of success, don't you?"

"I do, but it doesn't matter. As I said before, I'm willing to spare no cost. I'll pay you a generous bonus if you find John. If you find him alive, I'll double it."

"Very well, Mr. Deville, we accept the case," Tony said. "I'll have my secretary draft a contract to submit to for your approval. If you agree with the terms, we can start immediately."

"I think the trail's gone by now," I said, "but what you propose could help us in finding out what has happened and in clearing this case."

"You established quite a reputation for yourself, Mr. Leary, when you solved the murder of the American oilman in Brazil. I trust you will do as well in this case," Deville said.

"Thank you. I'll do my best."

"I know you will, Mr. Leary."

"I'm going to need information on John Engelhard, a copy of his passport, and a recent photo."

"Here." Deville scribbled a note on his business card. "This is the name and the phone number of John's secretary, Helen. I'll instruct her to give all the information you need and copies of any necessary documents. You can call her in my name and make an appointment to see her. John's office is not far from here, by the way. You may walk there."

"Then we are settled," Tony said. I'll have someone bring our contract to you later today."

"Thank you for seeing me and for taking the case. I'll feel much better now that I know the matter is in good hands." Deville excused himself, and Tony accompanied him to the elevators.

"What do you make of this, Alan? It's a very good opportunity for us, don't you think?"

"Frankly, Tony, I find the whole story very strange and a little fishy. I'm not at all convinced that Engelhard is still among the living. I do not swallow Deville's theory. In the end, this may turn to be a wild goose chase. But hey, it's a paycheck, and obviously, Deville has deep pockets. By the way, he's a very peculiar looking fellow."

"Yeah, definitely," Tony concurred.

"Did you notice his eyes?"

"No, why?"

"They seem to bore into you. Very intelligent, and they don't miss anything. He's always looking around, paying attention even to the minutest details. It's very intense."

"You are right. But we have a good contract in our hands. Let's try to make the best of it. When can you travel to Peru?"

"In a couple of days. I have to talk to Olivia first."

Tony smiled. "Amazing!"

"What?"

"In the past, you could have traveled the very next day, and you didn't need the green light from anyone. Now …"

I shook my head, embarrassed. "Ah, don't kid me. I'm quite happy with my new situation."

"I know you are, Alan. I'm just pulling your leg. Anyway, we have to check the information on this John Engelhard before you go. I'm going to call this Helen and send Patrick to collect the material."

"Good, Tony. I'll let you know my travel plans after I have the opportunity to talk it over with my wife and analyze the material brought by Patrick."

CHAPTER 2

A Family Dinner

My sister, Jessica, and I had always been very close. She was my confidant, the person with whom I discussed my successes and failures, the voice of reason who uncovered problems and provided wise counsel. I had the habit of dining with her practically every week. We had our preferred restaurants and hangouts where we would meet to talk and update each other. This changed after I married Olivia. To my amazement, Jessica and my wife took to each other instantly. The two became BBFs, and I was relegated to the next immediate circle of friendship. I'm not complaining. I was actually glad that my wife and my sister got along so well.

Jessica was enchanted with our daughter, Larissa. She and her husband, Nicholas, had not been blessed with children, and clearly, her niece fulfilled an important need. Besides, Larissa was indeed a lovely two-year-old child. Am I a conceited father? Please, be kind to me. I just can't avoid being deeply enamored of my beautiful daughter. Anyway, the special situation between my wife and my sister forced a change in our old habits. Jessica and I did not meet out of the house, as we did before. Now, she invited us for dinner at her home once almost every week, obviously *avec* Larissa.

I wonder what would happen if my daughter couldn't come. Would we continue to be invited? I jest, of course.

The single hitch in this arrangement was that I didn't get along with my brother-in-law that well. He was not a bad or disagreeable person. Nicholas was a very successful corporate lawyer, and he knew it. He was just a little too poised, if you know what I mean. But one has to make concessions, and I did my best to be social and treat my brother-in-law courteously and with feigned warmth.

Jessica lived nearby, her Park Avenue apartment a short cab ride or a healthy walk. In that lovely summer, as afternoon turned to evening, we decided for the latter. Larissa loved to go out. The weather was just fine for that, and I felt great strolling with my daughter and wife. Larissa walked a little, but mostly, I carried her. While holding her, we kept these wonderfully silly and long baby/parent conversations. We also took her stroller along for when we both got tired and to carry all the items required by my daughter when she went out. Larissa was my first and only child. Having had no previous experience, I was amazed by the amount and diversity of things that such a small person demanded.

I greeted the doorman when we arrived at my sister's building. Jorge was from Puerto Rico, and he usually covered the day shift.

"Hi, Jorge. How are things?"

"Fine, thank you, Mr. Leary."

"Has Mr. Nicholas arrived yet?"

"I don't believe he has. I haven't seen him this afternoon."

"Please telephone upstairs to let my sister know we have arrived and are coming up."

Jorge called my sister's apartment, and we proceeded to the elevator.

When we opened the elevator door on my sister's floor, she was already waiting for us at the apartment entrance.

"Hi, guys. Come right in." She spotted Larissa. "Oh, look how cute she is. I think she looks so pretty in this pink dress. Here, let me pick you up."

"Eh, Jess …"

"Yes, Alan."

"Do you think you could offer me something to drink after you finish playing with Larissa?"

"What do you wish, Alan?"

"A beer would be nice."

"They are all in that small fridge in the kitchen. You know where the glasses are. Help yourself."

See what I mean? Maybe it wasn't even the next immediate circle of friendship. More like the third or fourth.

"You must be all hungry. Dinner will be served shortly. Nicholas has phoned to tell me he will be home in ten minutes."

Nicholas arrived on schedule, and dinner was served. As usual on such occasions, we chatted about unimportant family themes, skipping serious subjects or politics.

Nicholas asked me, under the guise of starting a conversation, "How's the investigative business these days, Alan?"

"Oh, I can't complain, Nick. The office is doing well, and we have quite a bit of activity going on. We secured a very interesting case yesterday. Perhaps you heard of this fellow who disappeared in Peru under strange circumstances, John Engelhard?"

"Sure, who hasn't? It was all over the media. I don't believe they know what happened yet."

"No, they don't. We have been hired to investigate."

"Well, Alan, I'm impressed. Who hired you, his company?" my brother-in-law asked.

"Actually, we were sought by his attorney and friend. Maybe you know him, Mr. Anton Deville?"

"No, the name doesn't ring a bell, but it should. The name is not common. How do you pronounce his family name, like French *de Ville*?"

"Something like that. Here, let me show you his card."

Nicholas took the card and examined it. "That's odd."

"What?" I asked.

"First, I'm sure this guy doesn't practice law in New York. With such a name, I would certainly know him. Second, he has a peculiar sense of humor."

"How so, Nick?"

"Did you see the name of his group, Light-Bringing Associates?"

"Yeah, and?"

"You know, Alan, the name Lucifer comes from the Latin contraction of *lux*, light, and *fer*, a suffix indicating movement or transport. So another way of saying Light-Bringing Associates is Lucifer Associates."

"Jesus, really? A morbid sense of humor, I would say. Besides, he does look kind of … creepy."

"Isn't this a paradox? The lord of darkness being called light-bringer," my sister asked.

"You have to remember that he was once an angel who revolted against

God and was cast away from grace. Light-Bringer was how he was referred to when he was an angel. The name stuck, even after his transformation."

"Alan, I don't like this," Livy said. "I think you should keep away from this person. What a sinister thing to use the name of: you know what."

"Ah, honey, have no fears. This is just an idiotic prank of this Anton fellow. In any case, I won't be dealing with him. He's just paying us to elucidate the case. I won't even be near him, okay. I have to go to where the crime occurred."

"Are you going to Peru?" my sister asked.

"I shall have to."

"I've never been in Peru," Livy said. She looked at me, and her face lit up. "I would love to go there sometime. Apparently, it's a beautiful and interesting country."

"And historical too," my sister added. "The Spanish conquerors, the Incas, so full of tradition."

"And rich," Nicholas mentioned. "Minerals, precious metals, the fisheries—the country has a lot going for it."

"I would love to visit it. Can I go with you, love?" Livy asked.

"Sorry, baby, some other time. I have to work. I would not be able to give you any attention. Besides, you have your studies and Larisa."

"When do you have to go? I only have one test to take the day after tomorrow, and then it's summer break."

"I would be more than glad to keep Larissa," Jessica said. "We have lots of space in this apartment. Claudia could move in to help me."

"Eh, girls, stop, okay? This is no game. I don't know what I will find in Peru. It could be dangerous."

"Another reason for me to come along. You shouldn't go alone."

"Oh, come on, Livy. I would love to take you with me. You know I would, but I can't. I promise, we will go together after this job is over."

"Spoilsport. We will discuss this later." Olivia was angry and stopped talking.

Great, now my wife was mad at me. Why did I have to bring this matter up at dinner? Stupid, stupid me.

The dinner finished in a less-than-happy mood. Olivia was still clearly annoyed by my refusal to allow her to accompany me to Peru. Hopefully, after we got home, I would be able to talk things over and change her mind.

CHAPTER 3

Findings

The following morning, Olivia was still mad at me. No measure of reasoning had convinced her to give up the idea of accompanying me to Peru. It was frustrating. I dislike saying no to her. Actually, this was a first. I think it could be counted as our first fight, and I hated it.

I entered the kitchen, where Olivia and Claudia were gathered around Larissa and bent down to kiss my wife. "Good morning, honey."

"Hum, *bom dia*."

Gosh, Portuguese. I must be in big trouble.

"Ah, don't be like that, Livy, please."

"Why do you have to be so infuriatingly stubborn in this case, Alan? It's not like you."

"Livy, I'm going to get Larissa a clean bib," Claudia said, excusing herself to get away from our discussion.

"I'm only trying to protect you, baby. I don't know what I will find in Peru. I am investigating a multiple murder. It could become … no, it will be dangerous. Besides, what's the point of you coming? You'll have no opportunity to visit or see interesting places. It will be work the whole time."

"It's because it might turn dangerous that I should go."

"Sorry, I lost you there, honey. Do you care to explain?"

"Alan, think on all we've been through to be together. All the trouble and the pain we had to suffer, you and I."

"You don't have to remind me. I was an idiot, and I'll regret my stupidity forever."

"Look, I'm not talking about guilt or pinning faults on any of us. It's just that, after what I went through, I would never overcome losing you a second time. If something were to happen to you, God forbid, I don't think I would survive. I couldn't continue living without you."

"That's nonsense, sweet but nonsense nevertheless. You would have to continue living for Larissa. I would expect you to. Our daughter needs her mother."

"You are missing the point, Alan. She needs her father as well, and I love her beyond everything." Livy got up and embraced me. "But what would I do without you? Please, Alan, please …"

I was lost, all my good arguments and reasoning forgotten. Then I remembered the perfect excuse.

"There is no time to get you a visa. Lorna set an interview for me at the consulate this morning. You won't be able to do anything before the weekend, when I travel."

Livy smiled. "You are forgetting a very important point. I am Brazilian. I do not need a visa for Peru."

Darn. How could I have forgotten that important detail? "You do realize you are always getting me to do things against my better judgment, don't you? Good grief. I expected this to improve after we got married."

Livy rested her face on my chest and whispered with a smile on her face, "That's because you love me, silly."

Tony greeted me when I arrived at the office. "How did it go at the consulate this morning?

"No problem. I'll get my passport back with the visa tomorrow. Did you send Patrick to talk to Engelhard's secretary?"

"I did better than that. I invited Helen to come to our office this afternoon, and she accepted. I thought you might wish to talk to her also."

"That's great. Sure, I have lots of questions for her." I picked the phone and dialed our assistant Lorna's extension. "Hi, Lorna, could you do me a favor? I need an extra ticket to Peru. That's right; it will be in the name of my wife. Okay, thanks a lot."

Tony was surprised. "Are you taking your wife with you? Don't you think it may get a little rough down there?"

"Look Tony, would you care to explain this to my wife yourself? I should warn you as a friend. Olivia has a temper when people try to stop her from doing what she wishes. But, as you are a brave ex-NYPD cop, you may have the courage for that."

"No, thanks, man. It's yours and your wife's decision."

"It's silly, I know. More than that, it's totally stupid. I tried to dissuade her, but she stood steadfast on her decision to come along, and I finally gave in. I'm not strong enough to oppose that girl."

Helen Crawford turned out to be an elegantly dressed, attractive lady in her late thirties. She had an air of efficiency and professionalism. She was polite and agreeable but direct, clear, and thorough in her answers.

"It's a pleasure to meet you, Helen," both Tony and I said. "We must thank you for agreeing to come see us. Please, excuse us the trouble."

"No trouble at all, gentlemen. My office is very close to this place. I understand you have questions concerning my former boss, John Engelhard."

"Correct. If you can help us, we would be glad if you share with us all you know about Mr. Engelhard. How old was he? Was he married? Did he have any children or other heirs? Where is he from? Family? Friends? In short, everything you can possibly tell us about him.

"Very well. Let me try to summarize what I know. First, I have made copies of his most important documents to give you—birth certificate, passport, social security, credit cards, and so on." She gave me an envelope. "You'll find a folder inside where I have arranged everything. I shall leave it with you."

"Thank you, Helen. This is going to be very useful."

"John was forty-three years old. He was very young for the level of wealth he managed to accumulate. According to the latest evaluation of our chief accountant, his current net assets exceed four billion dollars."

Tony whistled. "He was that rich?"

"Indeed. He never married or had any children. There have been quite a number of lady friends, but I do not think he became seriously attached to anyone. He was born in a small town, Dixon, Illinois, right in the middle of the Corn Belt area. He told me he left the place very young to try his luck in the big city."

"Did he leave living parents—brothers, sisters, or other relatives?"

"I have never met another member of his family. John was a very serious and a bit of an introverted person. He did not confide in others. I don't know about relatives, living or deceased. You would have to go to Dixon to find information about his family."

"We will do that. So he was a very reserved person."

"Extremely. Not impolite, mind you, just a quiet individual who didn't talk much and didn't share his private matters with others."

"We understand that he built himself a mining empire, with properties and interests in several countries."

"John's capacity for foreseeing changes in the metals market was uncanny. It was a gift. He was rarely wrong, if ever, in predicting commodity price variations. People were impressed with his acuity."

"Was the group doing well when he disappeared?"

"Yes, it was. Horizon Mining is very solid. John had a policy of reinvesting profits. Consequently, the group has very low financial liability. Practically, the single large outstanding bank loan is the one taken for the development of his iron ore project, in Kazakhstan."

"Tell us about it, please."

"It is an extensive project comprising the mine itself, a new railway, and a deepwater port. Construction is well underway, and it should be completed in the next three years."

"Who will profit by inheriting all this?"

"I do not know. Naturally, after he is officially declared dead, we'll be able to see who he has nominated as heir, if any."

"You think he's dead?"

"What other explanation would there be? It has been more than two months since the incident occurred, and there's been no contact demanding a ransom. No, he's dead all right. It's very unfortunate. He was a great man."

"Anton Deville thinks differently. He has the firm belief that John is still alive."

Helen frowned and shook her head. "That man ..."

"I take, from your reaction, that you are not fond of him."

"Not fond? No, I deeply dislike that person."

"Why?"

"You met him. You saw the type. I find him ... well, creepy. There is no other adjective that comes to mind."

"We agree that he lacks an empathetic personality. Still, he's the one hiring us. Could you elaborate a bit more on the cause of your dislike?"

"The influence that he had over John was astonishing. Sometimes, I think John feared him. At the very least, he was very uncomfortable in his presence. I cannot fathom the kind of power he had, to be given a proxy with full powers to act in John's name, in the case of his impediment or absence. Today, he became the de facto CEO of the group."

"We suppose that Horizon Mining has other directors, in addition to John."

"Yes, indeed. We have a vice president of finance, Robert Burn, and another for mining and operations, Eduardo Peña. But John was the linchpin of the whole structure. I fear that without him, the company will sail into rough waters."

"If we may ask, what are your future plans now that your boss is gone?"

"I have to wait a few more weeks to see how this develops. I don't think I'll remain in the company for a long time, though."

"Please, consider staying longer, if you could. It's important for our work to count with a good contact in the group. If you permit us, and if you wish, we can ask Mr. Deville to keep you in the company."

"Please, don't. I wouldn't like to owe him any favors."

"Very well. We won't do it, then. But allow us to thank you once again for coming here and for your help."

"Please, don't mention it. It was my pleasure. I'm quite willing to render all the assistance I can if it helps to clarify this sad affair."

"What did you think? Alan," Tony asked after Helen departed.

"I liked her. She's a very nice lady and provided useful information."

"Yes, she did, but she also raised a lot of additional questions."

"We have to keep digging to see what we can get. I'm thinking of sending Patrick to Dixon to try to meet someone of his family. And I'm hopeful you'll be able to bring us a clearer picture once you talk to the people in Peru and examine the available evidence."

"Yes, let's hope so."

CHAPTER 4

Lima, Peru

We arrived in Lima on a Sunday morning. By the time we cleared immigration and customs, it was almost nine in the morning. I usually sleep well during long flights, but Livy was excited with the voyage and the adventure. She kept awakening me with silly things:

"Alan, wake up, love. You ever hear of the Mile-High Club? No? You know, people that do it in planes?"

"Go to sleep, Livy, please." She can be immature at times, which is part of her charm. Patiently putting off my wife's advances, I used the flight time to rest a bit and to review the material we had received from Helen.

We were welcomed at the airport by a member of the Policia Nacional del Peru, or PNP for short, inspector *Jefe* Jorge Vilar. An advantage of having worked for a long time in NYPD is that you end up making acquaintances in the police forces of several foreign countries. When you do not have a contact, you have a friend who has one. Tony had called a person he knew in PNP and was referred to inspector Vilar of its crime division, or DININCRI, who was charged with the investigation of the crime involving John Engelhard.

We shook hands, and I introduced my wife. Vilar looked at Livy and me, and from his smiling expression, I could guess the thought crossing his mind. Livy looked younger than her age. She'd be turning twenty-two the upcoming September. Without make-up, dressed in jeans and flat shoes, she looked more like eighteen or seventeen. He must have been thinking, *Wife my foot, more likely a much younger lover, an affair.* After the initial formalities, Vilar took hold of our suitcases to lead us to his car and drive to our hotel in Lima.

We had booked a suite at the Lima Sheraton in the neighborhood of Miraflores. After checking in, we thanked inspector Vilar. He promised to come back Monday morning to take us to the headquarters of PNP. Livy was going at full steam, and as soon as we got to our room, she decided to take a shower and change to visit the Museo del Oro, which keeps a large collection of Inca gold pieces. I was glad to come along. I was curious to see the type of articles that had been stolen at the Colca Valley. We hired a hotel car with driver to take us there and back.

The gold pieces at Museo del Oro are housed in a large underground vault in a house in the city's outskirts. The ground floor is reserved for a collection of ancient weapons, but that is not so interesting. The gold artifacts are a different story. I was amazed by the wealth and variety of objects on display. The exhibit had several rooms with glass-covered shelves lining the walls and cupboards in the middle, all filled with myriad objects—jewelry, cups and utensils of all sort, headpieces, and even knives, everything in gold, many pieces encrusted with precious stones. To think that this represents only a tiny fraction of the gold and silver taken by the Spanish conquerors and shipped to Spain in the sixteenth and early seventeenth centuries. I had a much stronger sense now for the treasure stolen from the Inca site. Only the knowledge of John Engelhard's immense fortune kept me from the conclusion that he was the one who had committed the murders to run away with the gold.

I took Livy for dinner at a seafood restaurant near the coast, recommended to us by the hotel.

"You know what this reminds me of?" Livy asked.

"No, honey, what?"

"Of that first dinner we had in Macaé, on the same day you arrived in the office of the drilling company. Do you remember?"

"How could I forget that, Livy? It's one of my fondest memories."

"Would I scandalize you if I said that I wanted to make love to you that same night?"

"No, actually, I felt the same."

"Then you did your best to hide your feelings."

"I had to, honey. I had just arrived in the place and been introduced to you, who was an employee of the company I was working for. It was complicated."

"Are you happy now, Alan?"

"It would be very difficult, no, actually impossible to find someone happier than I am. I have everything I care for in life, which is you and our daughter."

"I'm very happy too, you know? Let's have a second one."

"Second what?"

"Second baby, silly, a boy this time. What do you think?"

I smiled. "Can you hang on to that thought until we finish this job and go home?"

"We could start today. You do realize that it takes time to produce a baby, don't you?"

"What about college? Won't that be difficult to accommodate with your studies?"

"Nah, I had no problem with the first, and we do have help. We have Claudia and your sister. Besides, it's a good idea to have all your babies at once and be over with it. We'll be young parents to enjoy and guide our children as they grow older."

"Anything to make you happy, honey. If it's that what you wish, I'm all for it," I said.

"It's not only me, Alan. You must wish it also."

"I do, I do. I'll be thrilled with a second child." I bent forward to kiss Livy. "By the way, what was that nonsense in the plane? Don't you think the hotel is a much better place to do it—more comfortable and private?"

"Yes, it is. But then we wouldn't have done it in the plane, during the flight. Ah, well, we still have the trip back."

"Livy, you are impossible. Sometimes I have the impression that I'm married to a teenage girl."

"Don't start, Alan. This talk of young girl–old man pisses me off. You know what I think of this nonsense."

"Sorry, honey. Let's get our check and retire to our hotel, shall we? I am beginning to feel the effects of the long trip and today's activities."

"Fine, let's go back to the hotel."

The next morning, punctually at nine o'clock, inspector Vilar came to our hotel to drive us to PNP at Avenida España. We had finished breakfast and we met him in the lobby.

"Good morning Mr. and Mrs. Leary."

"Good morning to you, Inspector. I'm ready to leave."

"Very well. I have a car waiting outside. Are you coming with us, Mrs. Leary?"

"No, Inspector," I answered in Livy's place. "My wife is getting a car from the hotel to do a little sightseeing."

"Then let me suggest an alternative. Our office is not far from Lima's historical center. Mrs. Leary should come with us. I'll ask one of our female officers to show her the churches and the cathedral where the Spanish conqueror Francisco Pizarro is buried. Are you fond of art, Mrs. Leary?"

"Absolutely, Inspector. I appreciate art, paintings in particular. But I do not wish to impose on you. It would be asking too much to have someone from your office act as my chaperon."

"No trouble at all, Mrs. Leary. We are very proud of our cultural inheritance, and we love showing it to visitors."

"Thank you then, Inspector. You are very kind."

"You are welcome."

"If you like paintings, you are going to enjoy your tour. When Lima was made capital of the Spanish vice kingdom in South America, the Jesuits sent artists and painters from Europe to decorate their churches. Some of these painters are said to have trained with Rembrandt himself, and in fact, the works of the Limeña school do resemble the early-seventeenth-century Flemish masters. I'll make sure they take you to see the Convento e Museo de San Francisco, where there are a large number of those paintings."

A meeting room had been set apart, previously, in the second floor of the museum, for my briefing. Olivia had left with the female inspector assigned to show her downtown Lima. I would see her again when I returned to the hotel. Jorge Vilar introduced me to some of his colleagues and to inspector Pedro Nuñes of PNP in Arequipa, the town near Colca Valley, where the initial investigation had been conducted. The meeting space had been set as a data room, with maps and photos of the crime area pinned to the wall. A projector had been provided. After the initial formalities and exchange of business cards, we took our seats to start discussing the available evidence. The police had gathered a considerable amount of material, and Vilar began explaining the facts and his interpretation of what had taken place in that Colca Valley encampment.

A team from Horizon Mining exploring for minerals in a canyon near the Colca River, accidentally stumbled on an Inca burial site. As they are instructed to do in these cases, they immediately informed the authorities who dispatched an archeologist, Dr. Edgard Mateo of the Museo de la Nacion, to study the new discovery. Three guards were also sent to secure the site. Due to its remote location, the site was considered of low risk, and the authorities felt it wise not to appoint a larger number of guards to avoid calling the attention of the local native population. Dr. Mateo and his young assistant started to study and catalog the archeological objects. Again, to avoid undesired attention, they did not hire local workers. They were helped by the three guards, a geologist of the exploration team who had remained at the site, and his helper/driver.

The exploration team had also communicated the discovery of the Inca grave to the company's headquarters in New York. They had to justify the interruption of the geological work. Upon learning of the story, Mr. John Engelhard had immediately decided to visit the site himself. This was the first curious point in the investigation. Why this sudden interest from Engelhard? As far as the police knew, pre-Colombian history was not one of Engelhard's interests. His team had kept permanent contact with the head office by satellite. It's not known what amount or type of information they conveyed to Engelhard. They must have told him of the gold objects found. Could that have attracted Engelhard's interest? Anyway, the crime took place soon after Engelhard arrival at the site.

There was a second very interesting point in the investigation. On the night when the killings took place, the site was left with a single guard. One of the guards had a family problem and decided to go to Arequipa. The second guard went with him to keep him company and to take turns with driving. The murders were committed with great stealth by the killer—first the remaining guard and then a native bivouacking at the camp. Only after the elimination of those two did he use a shotgun to finish off the other. It would have been extremely difficult, in other words, impossible, to have succeeded in executing this had the three guards been present. No one outside the camp could have known in advance of the absence of two guards. It was a last-minute decision. Could it have been a coincidence? The police doubted that.

The crime was clearly committed by one person, maximum two. They thought that a larger number would have left other evidence. Besides, how would a larger group have arrived without calling the attention of camp members? How would they have arrived at the site? They had not found tire tracks, other than the ones belonging to the camp vehicles.

After the long explanation, they projected pictures of the area of the crime and the surroundings and of the camping place with the burnt tent remains. They exhibited photos of the carbonized remains of the six bodies found. The ones killed outside had been dragged from the place where the murders were committed and placed inside the tent to be burned. Two of the victims, the Indian and the guard, had been killed with a knife; the other four had been murdered with a shotgun. Their remains had been found in one of the burnt tents.

The third curious point in the investigation was the difficulty in getting identifying data on John Engelhard. The New York police had found no medical records or dental data. Either those records had been suppressed or Engelhard had been an extremely healthy person, without ever having a cavity to treat. Obviously, the police had considered this very odd. DNA analysis identified the body, in which fragments of Engelhard's documents and wallet had been found, as belonging to the bivouacking native.

Their conclusion? They were convinced that John Engelhard had committed the crime himself. This sounded crazy in view of Engelhard's vast fortune. Nevertheless, they couldn't come to any other conclusion. They were flabbergasted but had no better explanation. They were hoping that my investigation might help cast some light onto the matter, and they would wait until its conclusion to issue their final report.

I had some questions to pose, but I had to concede the logic of their conclusion.

"What exactly was taken from the tomb? Have you an estimated value of the stolen pieces?" I asked.

"To better answer your question, we have set a meeting for you with professor Carlos Townsend of the Museo de la Nacion, this afternoon. He is a specialist in Peruvian pre-Colombian culture. Professor Townsend worked together with the deceased archeologist Edgard Mateo. He has a file with photos and descriptions of the items that were taken. He'll be able to better explain their value and archeological importance," Inspector Jorge told me.

"Very good. Thank you."

"Now, if you have no further questions, may I suggest we proceed to have lunch before visiting professor Townsend?"

CHAPTER 5

An Afternoon at the Museum

The Museo de la Nacion was housed in a large concrete building, very modern and with architecture of arguable taste. Professor Townsend occupied a small room on the second floor. He was waiting for us in the company of a white-haired older gentleman, introduced to us as Dr. Roberto Tello of the Museo Nacional de Arqueologia, Antropologia e Historia of Peru. We squeezed ourselves, Inspectors Jorge and Pedro and I, as best as we could in the small space provided by Townsend's office. Luckily the day wasn't very warm, and after we got seated and took off our jackets as suggested by Townsend, it wasn't too bad. Olivia had not accompanied us, having previously left with a lady police inspector to visit the old downtown center of Lima. The small room could not accommodate everyone had she remained with us. Townsend had set apart a few folders with photos of the relevant aspects of the tomb and of the objects found therein.

"Professor Townsend, thank you for receiving us, today," Jorge said. I'll talk in English because it will be easier for our American friend, Mr. Alan Leary. As I have previously explained to you, Mr. Leary arrived from New York to investigate the Colca Valley murders, in which your colleague and friend, Dr. Edgard Mateo, lost his life. Mr. Leary is interested in the objects removed from the tomb."

"Could you, please, describe to me the articles that were taken and give an idea of their value, Professor?"

"In total, there were twenty-three gold objects of varying sizes—some small like earrings, necklaces and the like, others fairly large. The biggest piece and also the heaviest was a gold staff five feet long. Edgard didn't have the opportunity to weigh them, poor fellow. I estimate, however, that they weighed close to twenty-five pounds altogether."

"Then, at current gold prices, this was worth approximately half a million dollars?" I said.

"You are correct, Mr. Leary. However, their archeological value is harder to estimate. Those were pieces that any museum would love to have. Authentic pre-Colombian gold objects are rare and extremely difficult to obtain. I guess—and this is a conservative estimate—that their historical value would be more than ten to fifteen times their weight in gold."

"I see, it's a hefty sum, but seven and a half million dollars is still nothing to a man who owns a fortune of four billion dollars," I said.

"I won't contradict you, Mr. Leary. Here, take a look at these photos. They will give you a better idea of the objects."

Professor Townsend gave me the folders that he had set aside on his table, and I examined the photos of several objects—jewelry, cups, a few pieces that looked like belt buckles, what seemed to be a ceremonial knife, a crown-shaped adornment, and the above-mentioned staff. "Very impressive," I said.

"As valuable as the gold pieces were, unfortunately, the thief or thieves took away an item that raised our curiosity and which should have no value for them."

"What was that?"

"It was a white tunic that we called the Alb of Viracocha."

"You care to explain that, please?"

"Viracocha was the most important deity in the Inca pantheon of gods. He was seen as the creator of all things, the substance from which all things were created, and intimately associated with the sea. According to the myth, he rose from Lake Titicaca, Bolivia, to bring forth light from darkness. He made the sun, moon, and stars and made mankind by breathing into stones."

"That's very interesting. Please continue."

"He wandered the earth disguised as a beggar, teaching his new creations the basics of civilization, as well as working numerous miracles. For that, he took the form of a man dressed in a white robe, like an alb, secured round the waist. Viracocha eventually disappeared across the

Pacific Ocean by walking on the water, and he never returned. Before that, he left his alb to one of his sons, Manco Capác, who is credited with founding Cusco and the Incan culture."

"And you believe this tunic found in the Colca site to be Viracocha's alb?"

"No, Mr. Leary. This is just a legend with no basis in fact. What called our attention was the quality of the robe. It was very finely woven in a type of linen fiber, very unusual."

"We were discussing this subject before you arrived. Dr. Tello is an expert in pre-Colombian fabrics and textiles. I asked him to examine the photos and Edgard's report on the tunic."

"That's right," Roberto Peña said. "I had never seen anything like it. According to Edgard, it was so well made that it looked as if it had been woven in a modern loom, which is obviously impossible. So you see, it was natural to associate it with the legend; it was white and so fine."

"I understand."

"According to the myth, the alb protected whoever owned it from Supay, the god of death and ruler of the Uku Pacha, or inner world. Supay is the Inca equivalent of the Catholic devil. The person wearing the alb was invisible to him, and his soul could not be carried away from the land of the living."

"Interesting myth. So you think the alb was taken because the robber believed the legend?"

"No, most probably, it has been used to wrap some of the gold pieces. By now, it must have been destroyed, and that's unfortunate. It was a very precious archeological item."

"And that's all that we can tell you, Mr. Leary," Townsend said. "We hope the information is useful for your investigation."

What I had learned didn't contribute much to the investigation, but I didn't wish to sound ungrateful for the time they took to explain about the artifacts. "Indeed, it is. Although it didn't shed light on who committed the crime, at least I have a much better understanding of the stolen objects. It provides a clue on motives, as well. I must thank you again for your patience and assistance."

"Don't mention it. It has been our pleasure."

"I have a more mundane question. Is there a souvenir shop in the museum? I would like to pick a small gold charm for my wife. Perhaps some Inca figure, one of the mythological gods you mentioned."

"The museum does have a souvenir shop, but it sells only silver or gold-plated objects. If you need something in gold, you would have to buy it elsewhere. Luckily, I know just the place—a jewelry shop that specializes in such things. I'll be glad to take you there."

"Oh no, I couldn't possibly let you do that. Your offer is extremely kind, but I cannot abuse your hospitality."

"Nonsense. The shop is very near where I take my bus to go home. It's a fair walk from this building, and you have a car. So it's a trade. You give me a lift to my bus stop, and I'll show you the place."

"Ah, fine. In this case, we have a deal."

CHAPTER 6

The Hotel in Miraflores

Inspector Vilar drove me back to the hotel. He had made reservations for Olivia and me to travel to Arequipa the next day. The flight left at two in the afternoon, and he would come to take us to the airport at noon. That would give us plenty of time to catch our plane. It was a short domestic flight, and we could arrive at the airport half an hour before departure. He bade me a good rest and went away. I went up to my room. Olivia had already arrived.

"How was your day, sweetie? Did you enjoy yourself?" I asked, embracing her.

"Oh, Alan, I had a fantastic time. I saw so many things. The lady they assigned to accompany me was an angel, very *simpatica*, as they say here. Her first name was Violeta, a flower name. You have to thank Inspector Jorge for his kindness in detailing her as my chaperon."

"You can do that yourself honey. We'll be seeing him again tomorrow. He's coming to the hotel at noontime to take us to the airport. We are going to Arequipa."

"Fine, we have to come back to Lima again sometime soon. There is so much to see."

"Well, I'm going to take a shower and change, and then we can go out for a stroll and have dinner. And we have tomorrow morning as well. I'll be free. We can go around, do some sightseeing."

"Great. Let me show you what I bought." Olivia extracted from a shopping bag a cream-colored woolen garment of indistinguishable shape. "Isn't it beautiful?"

"Hum, it's very soft. What is it?"

"It's a vicuña poncho. I'm afraid I spent too much. It was very expensive, but the material was so gorgeously soft, much more than alpaca or cashmere wool. It is just the thing for those cool New York evenings, and I was totally taken by it. Here, let me put it on for you to see how it looks." Livy proceeded to slip the garment over her shoulders, passing her head through a central collar. "How do I look?"

"Incredibly beautiful, as always," I said.

"Flatterer."

"It's the absolute truth."

Livy kissed my face. "You are biased. This is what I bought for Larissa." She proceeded to display all the items she had procured for our daughter, every one of them indispensable, in her opinion.

"I also have something for you," I said, extending my hand holding the small charm box.

"How cute. It's beautiful," Livy exclaimed, inspecting the tiny gold object. "Thank you, honey."

"It's an image of the Inca goddess of flowers, young maidens, and sex: Chasca Coyllur. You can wear it on a chain or attached to a bracelet. You decide what you prefer, and I'll get it later for you."

Livy embraced me. "Alan, you are so nice to me. I'm so touched you took the time to buy the charm. Now, I'm ashamed."

"Why?"

"I didn't get you anything."

"That's okay. I'm not keen on local things. You can buy me something after we get back to New York. I thought that you should have a souvenir of Lima. You wanted so much to come. I need to apologize for giving you a hard time before bringing you along. Can you excuse me?"

"Stop, Alan. You are going to make me cry." She squeezed me tightly and put her face on my chest. I cannot think of a better method of forgiveness.

"Thanks, baby. Let me take a shower and call Tony. I need to brief him on developments. After that, we can decide what to do."

I called Tony's home to report the result of my meetings in Lima. He also had news for me. "I sent Patrick to Dixon with instructions to gather all the information available on John Engelhard and his family."

"Good idea, Tony. Was he able to get the information?"

"Some, but guess what? John Engelhard—the true one that is—passed away in 1918, a victim of the Spanish influenza."

"How is this possible?" I asked, surprised.

"Simple. The man in Horizon Mining, its CEO and main shareholder, was not who he said he was. He was an impostor."

"I see. This explains the difficulty experienced by PNP in obtaining his medical and dental records. The plot gets thicker and thicker."

"Yeah," Tony agreed. "It's a baffling situation."

Livy had been also busy on the phone talking to my sister to get news from our daughter.

"Livy, I'm ready. What would you like to do? We could ask the concierge to recommend us a good restaurant, or we could stay and dine in the hotel. Their restaurant seems very nice."

"Let's eat here, Alan. I don't want to go out."

"Fine, if that's what you want, I'll call their extension to reserve us a table. Are you ready to go?"

"I am. We should retire early. We have more important things to do," Livy said with a malicious smile.

I wondered what.

CHAPTER 7

Arequipa

The flight from Lima to Arequipa was a short one. It lasted an hour and a half, and by four thirty in the afternoon, we were unpacking in your hotel room at the Libertador Arequipa.

Arequipa is the second-largest city in Peru, and it is beautiful. Its old downtown is built out of a unique white volcanic rock, which gives the city a majestic aspect, especially around sunset, when the changing colors of the sky are reflected on the buildings. Flying into Arequipa, I could see the inhospitableness of the landscape, a vast desert surrounded by volcanoes and deep gorges. The vegetation of the green area around the city is maintained by irrigation water provided by the river traversing its valley. Arequipa's low buildings are of typical Spanish colonial architecture with wrought-iron balconies. It's a spectacular feeling when you cross a street and are presented with the sight of the cone shape of the snow-capped volcano Misti looming on the distant horizon. Actually, Arequipa lies in the shadow of three volcanoes, but it's the perfectly conical Misti that draws attention.

We wouldn't have time to properly explore the city and its monuments and charms. But as soon as we were settled, Livy and I decided to get a hotel car to take us to the city center for a quick stroll around the historical area. The beauty of old Arequipa is undeniable. Unmarred by modern construction and tall buildings, it preserves its original Spanish architecture, with low dwellings and narrow streets, which lead to wide plazas surrounded by covered walkways with arches. We were impressed by what we saw—the main square or Plaza d'Armas and the convent of

Santa Catalina. The city is a wonderful example of the blending of colonial architecture with local conditions. Many of the colonial palaces and houses still stand. The churches are particularly beautiful and are a delight to wander round.

However, we wouldn't be able to explore the inside of those churches and palaces. We had to return to our hotel for a meeting with inspectors Jorge and Pedro, scheduled to happen before dinner. We had to discuss our actions for the next days and the continuation of the investigation.

When we got back to our hotel, inspectors Jorge and Pedro were already waiting for us in the company of a woman we didn't know.

"Ah, here you are, Mr. and Mrs. Leary. I hope you have enjoyed your brief reconnaissance of our city," inspector Pedro said, getting up to greet us.

"It's beautiful," Livy answered. "It's a pity we won't have the time to explore it better."

"Some other time, perhaps. Alan, this is Ms. Anna Maria. She works for Horizon Mining, in Arequipa. Anna has graciously lent us the jeeps for our trip to the Colca campsite."

"Nice to meet you Anna Maria," both Livy and I said, shaking hands with the newly arrived lady.

"Likewise, Mrs. and Mr. Leary."

"What if we drop the formality?" I added. "Mister That, Inspector This. I think we know each other well enough to use our first names," I said, thinking more of Jorge and Pedro, in whose company we had been traveling.

"Perfect, Alan. From now on, we shall use our first names only," Jorge agreed for us all.

"May I ask what you do for Horizon, Anna?"

"We have a small office in Arequipa to support the exploration teams on the field. Actually, it's just a messenger boy and me. I manage Horizon's local account and petty cash, to pay people we hire locally—supplies, fuel and car maintenance—things like that."

"I see. Do you have many cars? You must have a garage and people to service those."

"Actually, we hire the services of a mechanical shop where the vehicles are kept and serviced when in Arequipa."

"Were you informed of the return from the campsite of the two guards with one of your jeeps?"

"I was, indeed. The garage manager phoned to inform me of the fact. He did it only because they were not authorized to use the jeeps, when needed. All our geologists and drivers have credentials to requisition the cars. We have six Land Rovers, used by the two exploration teams, the one in Colca and the other one near Puno. Usually, they just take the cars and the required fuel. The user must then send me a weekly report. We are connected by satellite with the teams on the field, you see? Sometimes they neglect to do it, and I complain."

"Do they forget to do it often?"

"More than I like, really. Recently, we had a company inspector who took one of the jeeps without letting me know or writing a report on its use."

"Is that so? Tell me about it, please."

"I felt that he had been impolite. He had the right to use it, but it would have cost him nothing to inform me. If people don't follow the rules, it becomes very difficult to keep track of things. I sent a written complaint but was told to just let it drop."

"Oh? To whom did you complain?"

"I sent a report to Mr. Peña, care of Helen Crawford. Why? Do you think this is important?"

"In an investigation like this, every small detail is important, Ana. Did he return the jeep?"

"All are accounted for. Obviously, it's a little more complicated to check who used which."

"Why is it complicated?"

"They are all the same color and bear no individual markings or numbers. The only distinction is their license plates."

"But, if you wanted, could you check which jeeps each one has used—say, during the few days preceding the date of the murders and a few afterward?"

"Absolutely. It will take some time. I do not keep that information on file. I just send the reports to our head office and destroy the originals. May I ask why you need it?"

"Just my detective instincts making sure that the pieces are set on their correct square."

"Fine, I'll do it. I'll email it to you when it's ready."

"Perfect. I appreciate it."

"I want to talk about our trip to the campsite, tomorrow. Are you feeling well, Olivia," Pedro asked?

"Yes, I am. Why do you ask?"

"No headaches? Feeling tired?"

"No, I'm fine."

"I see that you and Alan are in top shape. I'm asking because Arequipa is close to 8,000 feet above sea level. Many persons begin to suffer the effects of altitude at this point. Tomorrow, however, we will be climbing above 14,000 feet. The campsite itself is at a 13,400-foot level. At those heights, everyone feels the effects of oxygen deprivation, no matter how physically fit."

"Perhaps my wife should stay in Arequipa. It will be a working trip, anyway. We shall have no time to enjoy the sights or anything like that," I said.

"Over my dead body. Don't even think of leaving me behind," Livy said, her eyes flashing.

Pedro smiled. "Not to worry, Olivia. We are checking out of this hotel. You must come with us."

"Fine then." Olivia exhaled, mollified by the realization that she wouldn't be left behind and was going with us. She gave me one of those *you are going to get it later* looks.

"The trip from Arequipa to Chivay, which lies at the beginning of the Colca valley, takes approximately three hours, by the main route, the *Carretera Inter-Oceanica*. Tomorrow, however, we are making a detour. We will take a secondary road passing between the Chachani and Misti volcanoes. It's quite a scenic way and a lot more interesting than following the main Carretera. Unfortunately, it does add up some distance and travel time. We will be rejoining the main road at a locality called Patahuasi. Someone from our Puno exploration team is meeting us halfway to collect mail and some supplies."

"Very well.

"Once we reach the Colca, we have to travel at least another three hours to reach the campsite. The last stretch of the road is little more than a track. The local population calls it a *sendero,* a trail to follow with their llamas to reach the high pastures. After the discovery of the Inca tomb, the Province government sent a dozer and some men to widen and improve it. They didn't do a good job. It's a narrow, winding, dangerous route. It must be covered slowly and carefully."

"I understand. Still, I must see the site where the crime was committed."

"Undoubtedly, but we won't be able to return to Arequipa. I made reservations for us at the hotel Las Casitas del Colca, in Chivay. We'll spend the night there and return to Arequipa the next day. Then you may decide what to do next."

"After we come back, we can discuss the next steps in the investigation," I said.

"I suggest you eat light and, if possible, refrain from drinking alcoholic beverages. And try to rest well tonight."

"Will do."

"I think you should try our green coca leaves tea. It's a proven help to alleviate the effects of high altitude."

"Coca tea, isn't that habit-forming?" Livy asked.

"Not at all. The concentration of active alkaloids is very low, and it tastes delicious. Would you like to try?"

Pedro asked a waiter to bring and serve us the tea. At the beginning I had some misgivings in spite of Pedro having told us it wasn't habit-forming. I tried it, and it did taste good. I ended up drinking two cups of the stuff.

We excused ourselves and left to pack our things and follow the advice of eating light and consuming no drinks that night. As I expected, Livy was still mad at me with my suggestion of keeping her from the trip to Colca. As soon as we were alone, she complained about my misguided notion of telling her what to do.

"Alan, you are not my father. You are my husband, and in that first night when we met in Brazil, I was quite firm in explaining that I would never allow you to control me. I'm certain you remember—no caipirinhas, frankly, Alan."

To the non-advised, I should explain that a caipirinha is a Brazilian cocktail, mixing strong sugar cane rum and lime juice. When I met

Olivia, she was eighteen, the minimum legal age for drinking in Brazil. We were having dinner, and she asked the waiter to bring her one of those caipirinhas. I made the mistake of trying to prevent that, suggesting that she should have a soft drink instead. She looked so young then. She still does, actually. She let me have it for attempting to treat her like a child. She does have a temper when she gets annoyed. It's part of her charm, really. I do love her, despite her rare temper tantrums.

"I'm sorry, honey. I was being overprotective. I won't do it again. Promise."

"Hhm, fine."

CHAPTER 8

The Voyage to the Colca Campsite

We left our hotel in Arequipa around six in the morning in two Land Rovers, loaded with supplies for the campsite. Livy and I, inspectors Pedro and Jorge, and Anna Maria who, had decided to accompany us, shared the space in the two cars. It was Anna's chance to visit the exploration camp, which she hadn't done yet. A company driver traveled with us for one of the cars. Pedro and Ana would take turns driving the other. Livy took one of the front seats, the most comfortable and with the best view. We had no time for a proper breakfast before leaving. The hotel had made us snacks and gave us two thermoses, one with coffee and the other with coca tea, to take along. There would be no gas stations or much of anything else on the way from Arequipa to Chivay.

Arequipa is a city that seems to have grown a lot in recent times. Its outskirts are covered by vast, grey, arid shantytowns. Leaving the irrigated area around the city, we were soon in the middle of the Peruvian desert, and then we began to climb. The road was unpaved but remained in good conservation, in a place where it never rains. The landscape around us was stark and beautiful, with all shades of brown, yellow, orange, and ocher. Occasionally, we passed patches of flowered shrubs, their vibrant colors rendering life to an otherwise barren expanse. Our driver rewarded Livy's delighted surprise every time we encountered one of those patches with their local names: the yellow *chite* flowers, the pink *conchos de flor*, red *carboneros*, and the the national flower of Peru, the beautiful and bright red, orange, and violet *cantuta* blossoms. Shortly, we were in the middle of two volcanoes, the Misti to our right and the Nevado de Chachani to the left. Just shy of 20,000 feet, the Chachani is the highest mountain near Arequipa. We kept going higher and higher. I felt my ears popping and had to constantly swallow and yawn to equalize the pressure.

It was a fantastic day, luminous with a blue sky without clouds. Even in summer, we were warned that the temperature would drop drastically in the night. Now, during the Southern Hemisphere winter, it could get bitterly cold at our destination. Livy would have the opportunity to put her vicuña poncho to good use. Unfortunately, I hadn't come prepared for that. Fortunately, they told us we could find warm coats and sweaters in the Chivay street market.

Pedro gave to Livy and to me tablets that we should place under the tongue. The tablets were a type of drug that mildly accelerates your heartbeat, thus promoting a faster oxygen metabolic exchange and helping compensate its lower partial pressure in high altitude. In spite of all that—the medicine, the coca tea, and the light evening meal on the eve of the voyage—I felt a strange sensation as we got out of the car at a stop near 12,000 feet Pedro and Anna were switching places driving the jeep, and I wanted to stretch my legs and attend to other natural demands. I was shocked with the lightheaded sensation and even a tiny bit of nausea. Livy fared better and was less affected. I was told to avoid making sudden movements, walk slowly, and control my breathing.

After crossing the summit on our current route and reaching the Peruvian *altiplano*, we came to a division in the road. A sign indicated the way to Puno to the right, where the jeep from the other camp was waiting for us. After the formal greetings and transfer of parcels, we continued our way on the left branch of the road, toward Patahuasi, the Carretera Inter-Oceanica, and the Colca Canyon.

Four hours after we left Arequipa, we reached the town of Chivay at the threshold of the Colca Canyon. Built by the side of the Colca River, upstream from the canyon, Chivay is a small village. Its single attraction is the hotels that cater to tourists visiting the canyon. Its market had nothing to offer in terms of clothing. We asked around and were referred to a shop where we bought warm pajamas, two alpaca wool pullovers for Livy and myself, and a one-size-too-small jacket for me. We profited from the stop to eat part of our snacks, and after resting for a few minutes, we proceeded on our journey, crossing to the right margin of the Colca.

Following the river downstream, we entered the canyon, where we were amazed by its raw grandiosity. The Colca Canyon is a beautiful part of Peru, offering stunning scenery. Its walls lack the ochre and yellow shades of the Grand Canyon. They are greener at some spots, especially where the local population has carved plateaus for cultivation, a millenary practice preceding Christian times. Mostly, they are grey and dark, dropping precipitously into the deep, menacing chasm. The canyon runs for over 160 miles, and the average distance from the peaks of the mountains to the river below is 11,150 feet. It was thought to be the deepest canyon in the world, although it is now generally accepted that the Cotahuasi Canyon, also in the region of Arequipa, is deeper. On our way, we passed a few small settlements, and at the one called Madrigal, we left the canyon floor. We drove on a narrow road, climbing along the contours of a deep ravine. Soon, the road became very precarious, no more than a track. On several occasions, one of us had to step out and help the driver negotiate a particularly difficult spot. And always looming on our left side was the precipitous drop to the ravine bottom, at this hour, still shrouded in shades. I was curious with the track we were following and asked Anna Maria for details.

"How in God's name did your people find this goat track up the side of the canyon, Anna?"

"I'm no geologist, Alan. But, in this specific case, the area was sufficiently promising to justify preliminary drilling, not by the type of equipment capable of perforating the rock to great depths but rather by auger drills—you know, the ones that look like a screw and are common at construction sites. Hand labor and bulldozer work was used in tougher spots to widen a preexisting track, allowing it to be tackled by four-wheel-drive vehicles. Obviously, this side of the canyon, which is actually a seismic fault line caused by a very active nearby volcano, the Sabancaya, facilitated the access. It would have been very difficult—impossible, actually—to climb through here if not for the existence of this fault. We would have been forced to look for a way in elsewhere."

"It's very impressive, Anna Maria. One doesn't realize the amount of work associated with making a mineral discovery." A normal person has no idea of the amount of work, money, and financial risk involved in making a mineral discovery, not to count the years required to bring it to production. This was an example—carving a way into the wilderness to move in equipment and geologists to confirm the find.

"Indeed, Alan. It's a high-risk activity, one at which Engelhard was extremely successful."

As we climbed, the space between the gorge walls began to widen. They were a good 300 feet apart when Pedro called our attention to a condor flying nearby. We were so high up that we could look at the huge bird almost horizontally.

"You are lucky," Pedro said. "I have never seen one so close. There is a known spot on the rim of the main canyon where tourists go to try to spot condors. But there, the canyon is wide, and the birds are usually soaring far away. This one is so close. I feel like I could almost touch it."

"Wow," Livy exclaimed. "Look at that! It's so ... so majestic. Such a large bird, gliding without any apparent effort, and so close. It's incredible."

"It's truly fantastic to see it so close," I agreed.

We spent a few moments there, mesmerized by the unusual sight, before continuing our trip.

Finally, we reached the top and descended to a green and open landscape with small hills. After a while, we were driving on a field with no indications of a road or track. We crossed an area with widely scattered tall cactus-like plants. The queen of the Andes, we were told, shows a spectacular flower spike emerging more than twenty feet from a dense cluster of bayonet like leaves. I noticed that a few plants had the central stem covered with small yellow flowers and learned that blooming was a rare occasion, which happened once every one hundred years, more or less.

We left the area behind us and traveled in the general direction of a low rock outcrop for what seemed like a long time. When we finally drew close to the outcrop, it proved to be the top portion of the far wall of a much shallower ravine than the one we had crossed. The campsite was on the ravine floor. We had arrived at our destination. Again, the jeeps entered a small track carved on the mountain wall, one that I would have never found on my own but which the driver detected easily. He started descending into the ravine bottom.

We were welcomed at the camp by sergeant Rodrigues, a short, dark man with clear local native aspect, and the officer commanding the PNP detachment presently occupying the site. Horizon Mining had not yet indicated a substitute geologist; nor had it retaken the exploration work. The objects in the Inca burial site, the ones not taken by the thief, had been sent to the Museo de la Nacion, in Lima. The single remaining staff member from that institution was a photographer charged with recording on film the inscriptions found on the walls of the burial chamber.

"Let's walk, Alan. I want to show you the exact places where the murders were committed," Pedro told me.

I dragged myself out of the jeep and started following him with Jorge and Livy not far behind. I had developed a splitting headache, and each step demanded a serious effort.

"This is where the guard was murdered," Pedro said, indicating a spot on the ground. "The man was sitting in this spot, in front of a fire, where he could see the trail to the tomb entrance and the camp tents. The assassin approached him from the back with great stealth and slit his throat. Bear in mind, this is a confined and well-protected valley with steep walls on both sides. Most probably, there was no wind, and the nights here are extremely quiet. It's easy to catch any noise, even if very faint. The killer showed an impressive stalking skill and cold blood."

"I can see that. He wasn't telling me anything new. I had been trained in the special forces."

"After killing the guard, the murderer went around the camp to the place where the Indian was sleeping. He surprised that one, as well. In that case, however, we found evidence of a struggle. Obviously, the native's senses were keener than the guards. But it didn't help him. The assassin prevailed and stabbed him to death. Let's go look at the spot where it happened."

I strode after Pedro.

"Are you feeling well, Alan?" Pedro asked. "You don't look so good."

"Actually, I have a terrible headache, which is really bothering me," I answered.

"You should have told me before. I came prepared for this. Here, swallow these two tablets. It's a strong painkiller and should alleviate your headache."

I took the tablets he proffered and swallowed them with the water from his canteen.

"When we get back to Chivay, I'll have you breathe oxygen at the hotel for a few minutes. It helps a lot in these cases."

I thanked Pedro and made an effort to disguise my discomfort. I had to suck it up and hold on until we finished the visit.

Pedro continued with his explanation. "After killing the native shepherd, the assassin gave up the need for silence. He proceeded directly to the tents and executed the four remaining camp followers with a pump-action shotgun. The gun belonged to the geologist. He used it to kill snakes and for protection. This shows how good the killer was. He had to take the shotgun away without being noticed by the sleeping geologist."

"That's a professional skill. And that pretty much clears Engelhard," I said.

"Sorry, I do not follow you, Alan."

"Engelhard was an executive living in New York. He didn't have the training to accomplish something like this."

"We know very little of Engelhard's past, Alan. He had a false identity. What was he before becoming a successful executive—a soldier, a swat policeman, a terrorist? We don't really know, do we?"

"Truthfully, we do not. However, it's unlikely he has ever been one of those. You indicated professionals that tend to keep a degree of fitness, even after they quit their cloak-and-dagger activities. Engelhard did not have the physique."

"I don't know about that, but I grant you one thing: I'm impressed how he escaped overland, on foot, with just llamas to carry his load. This is perilous territory. There is absolutely nothing between here and Cusco. It takes a special person to live out of the land, even if he has taken some supplies with him."

"Yes, that also."

"In my opinion, this is the only piece of evidence in his favor," Jorge who had been listening to our exchange, contributed.

"Would you like to see the tomb now, Alan?"

Pedro turned to the sergeant following us. "*Sargento necessitamos una lantierna para entrar en la sepultura Inca. Usted podria nos aportar una, por favor?*"

The sergeant left and a few minutes later came back with a large flashlight.

"We must take the jeep to drive to the vicinity of the tomb site," Pedro informed. "Then it's a short walk to the actual site."

We took one of the Land Rovers and drove some distance from camp to a spot where the mountain started rising from the ravine floor. We got off, and after a short walk along a very narrow crevice, we reached a roughly-made wooden door, which had been obviously provided by campsite dwellers to protect the tomb entrance. A place for a padlock was provided, but there was none.

"Nothing of value remains to be stolen," the sergeant justified himself, raising his shoulders. "We keep the door just to stop small rodents and snakes from going in."

As we entered the tomb, I was a little disappointed. I was expecting something more elaborate or grandiose, similar to the Egyptian tombs found in the Valley of the Kings. This was nothing more than a hole in the rock, clearly manmade, and with a few figures and engravings on the rock face.

"The mummy was placed in a fetal position at the end of the tomb. The objects to be used in the afterlife were placed around it. The mummy was covered by a very finely woven white mantle, which, incidentally, was also taken away."

"Viracocha's alb," I said.

"Correctly, that's how the museum guys call it. Only the objects of lesser value, like pots and ceramics, were left behind. All the gold artifacts have been stolen. The other things and the mummy have been taken to the museum in Lima."

I already knew that, of course, but I listened with feigned interest to Pedro's explanation.

"By the way, Pedro, did you check for possible fingerprints on the walls, door, and other parts of the tomb?"

"Oh, yes. Believe me, we did all the forensics required in this case. We were very careful. Unfortunately, it was evident that all camp members had a great curiosity in this discovery. We found fingerprints of every one of them. It was no help in providing a clue on whoever robbed it."

"I see. Let me ask you one thing. A few moments ago, you mentioned Cusco as if you were sure of the place where the killer went. How did you reach your conclusion?"

"Easy. Let me explain. We have defined that the killer would have to smuggle the objects out of Peru by sea. It would be impossible to transport them by plane with all the antiterrorism measures adopted by the airports nowadays."

"Yes, I am of the same opinion."

"That would have left him with two alternatives. He could either go to Arequipa, with the intention of reaching the port of Matarani in the south, or he could go to Cusco and later to Lima and the port of Callao."

"Very well, and?"

"Matarani is essentially a bulk commodity port. It's mainly used to export copper concentrates. It's not so convenient when you are looking for smaller cargo vessels. Furthermore, the route from here to Arequipa passes by a lot of pueblos or small villages. A seemingly foreign person dressed in local clothing and leading a group of llamas would certainly call everyone's attention."

"Yes, I understand."

"On the other hand, there is practically nothing between this place and Cusco. It's mostly mountains. The chance of an encounter with local people is drastically reduced, especially when one purposely avoids such an encounter. Callao is a general cargo port. All sorts of medium and small ships can be found there. Certainly, Cusco and Callao provide a much less direct path. Nevertheless, it makes more sense. In fact, it's the only direction that makes sense."

"I find no fault in your reasoning, Pedro. You have convinced me to make Cusco my next destination."

"Then, after we finish this visit, we should return to Arequipa. The best way to travel to Cusco is by air. There are several daily flights serving Cusco from Arequipa, but are you satisfied by what you saw and with what was explained? Do you have any further questions?"

"Just one. Did you search for any evidence on the way to Cusco?"

"We did a few flights over the land lying between here and Cusco, but without too much hope of finding anything and in fact we didn't. But frankly, you saw the type of terrain we covered today. Imagine it multiplied by ten. It's worse than looking for a needle in a haystack. No, if he dropped something along the way, it will be lost forever."

"I see. It was very important for me to visit this place, get a feel of the layout of the area and the method used by the killer. I now have a much better appreciation of his capabilities and a glimpse at the type of individual he is. It will help to orient my investigation."

"Then, I'm glad we have been of help," Pedro told me.

CHAPTER 9

A Night in the Colca Valley

We thanked the hospitality of the campsite PNP personnel, and we embarked on our long voyage back to Chivay. It was close to two thirty in the afternoon when we left. There was no way we could drive down the ravine to the Colca in the dark. We had to hurry over the first and flat portion of the return trip. Luckily, all went well, and a little after six, we were back at Las Casitas del Colca with its civilized comforts—hot water and a cozy cabin with a fireplace, among other amenities. I couldn't see much of the place in the dark, noticing only that the hotel was comprised of several individual lodges interspersed on a eucalyptus tree grove. The buildings had been erected on a sloping plateau on the side of the canyon, probably a former agricultural terrace, suspended between the high road on the canyon's southern rim and the chasm dropping all the way to the river at the bottom. The one they assigned to us had a hipped and steep roof and a front door sided by two shuttered windows, nearly long enough to reach the floor. The interior was spacious, the main room divided into two spaces by a log sofa. One of those spaces comprised the sleeping quarters with a king-size canopy bed. The other formed the living area facing a fireplace. The floor was of ceramic tile and dotted with rag rugs. A large wrought iron chandelier hung from a chain attached to the high ceiling. I went exploring: the spacious bathroom had all amenities. A set of wide doors to one side of the cabin opened on an outside deck, which was provided with sun umbrellas and reclining chairs. The deck, I noticed, had a small heated pool occupying one of its corners. Livy was enchanted with the place.

"This is so, so nice, Alan. I would love to come back some other time, just the two of us. Maybe we could spend a few days and have a second honeymoon." Her eyes sparkled with the notion.

"I would love that, honey, especially if I have the opportunity to get used to high altitude, first. I have an awful headache."

"Take a warm shower, Alan, and let's go eat something. You'll feel better after."

I wasn't in the mood to eat, but Livy forced me to have something. I decided to try the local trout. It was excellent, and to my surprise, I discovered I was famished. This had been my only serious meal during the day. After a warm bath and a decent meal, I was almost feeling human again. The only thing lacking was a soft bed and some much-needed rest. We left the restaurant and walked back to our cabin. In the absence of lights from a city, at this altitude and dry air, the sky was something to watch. The number of stars and the clearly visible Milky Way extending like a band across the sky astonished me. I stopped walking to embrace Livy and gaze at the spectacle before us.

A nice fire had been lit in our cabin fireplace, and I practically collapsed on the bed, but Livy had other ideas.

"Ah, honey, I'm totally bushed," I complained.

"You just relax, Alan. Leave everything to me, love."

"Huh … Livy."

"What? Should I stop?"

"Well … No."

"I thought so." Livy giggled.

"What's funny?"

"Do you remember my friend Angela?"

"Sure. How could I forget her?"

"After the first time we made love, we had a girl talk and she wanted to know if you were, you know … big?"

"Jesus. Really Livy? You two were naughtier than I thought. What did you answer her? I'm curious."

"I said the truth, that I had no basis for comparison, but I was extremely happy with what I had."

"I see."

"But I do think you are big, you know?"

"What? Did you somehow acquire a basis for comparison?" I quipped.

"Don't be silly, Alan."

"Being silly with you is part of my job description."

"Alan …"

"What now?"

"I stopped taking the pill."

"Ah, woman, I see that you are not going to let me sleep. So be it. Come here, now." I bent down and grabbed Livy's arms to pull her to me.

A few moments later …

"Why did you stop me, Alan? Didn't you like it?"

"Oh, I did it. I loved it." I took her hand and led it to my penis. "Do it with your hand, please. Rub the tip with your thumb." I placed my hands on her cheeks and raised Livy's face to me to kiss her lips. I lowered my hands to pull Livy's nightgown over her head. Then, I burrowed my face on the hollow of her neck, kissing and sliding my lips down to her breasts, finding one of her nipples and caching it with my lips, teasing with teeth and tongue while playing the other with my fingers. Livy inhaled and caught her breath when I lowered my hand to the space between her thighs. She was wet and ready. She moaned when I fingered her. I could wait no longer. I helped her to remove her panties and made her straddle me, holding her hips. Livy let herself down, slowly. The feeling as I entered her was so fantastic; it took all my concentration not to come right then. I asked Livy to stop, and somehow, I managed to control myself. After a brief moment, Livy resumed moving. I followed, thrusting my hips up as she lowered herself, meeting her moves, alternating fast and slow until we came together explosively.

"Jesus, that was something," I said. "You know what?"

"What?"

"My headache is gone."

Livy smiled mischievously. "I told you when we met, remember? Nobody has ever taken care of you like I do. It's a fact; I knew exactly the cure for your headache."

"Yeah, sure. You only fucked me for altruistic reasons," I jested.

Livy giggled. "That's exactly right, but you know what?"

"What?"

"We must do it again, several times, to avoid a recurring problem. We must make sure your headache doesn't come back," she teased.

"You are impossible," I laughed.

"Yes, I am, but you like it."

"Wrong. I don't like it. I totally love it."

CHAPTER 10

Cusco

You lose too much time with comings and goings in this type of investigation, checking in and out of hotels, going to and from airports, traveling. It's all a bit frustrating, but you can do nothing other than try to use your time efficiently. It's also hard to use her time efficiently when your investigation companion is your young and gorgeous wife. We woke up late, almost lost our chance at breakfast, and left Chivay close to noontime, much to the impatience of our friends, which they didn't say but we could see it on their faces. Oh well, I could have said a *See, what I told you?* to my wife, but I wasn't complaining. I did enjoy it too, didn't I? Anyway, we took it easy on our return and arrived in Arequipa after three in the afternoon.

After checking in, I had only time to make reservations to fly to Cusco the following morning and call my partner, Tony, in New York. Jorge Vilar was returning to Lima, but Pedro would accompany us to Cusco. He had made an appointment for me with his colleague Eduardo Martinez at PNP's DININCRI in Cusco. Livy and I had decided to go for another stroll in the city before going for dinner. I was hoping my wife wouldn't be as well intentioned as last night. I was still recovering from the previous night's bout of high-altitude adventure. Surprisingly, Livy had fared much better. She told me she had felt a little lightheaded and tired. Really? Judging from the previous night's antics I never would have guessed it. Livy is much younger than I am. Before marrying her and after we became lovers, I used to joke saying that her energy would be the end of me and that I would have to take lots of vitamins to keep up with her. Prophetic words! I would seriously consider starting to take a vitamin complex after going home.

Our flight was short, and by lunchtime, we were settled in Hotel Monasterio, two blocks away from the Plaza d'Armas, in downtown Cusco. Since I had my afternoon meeting at PNP, I suggested to Livy that she should engage the concierge services and try to see the main tourist attractions in the city center. I would be back sometime around six. We would go for drinks, and I was also curious to see a little of Cusco. The city was so well known abroad as a cultural and historic center. It had been declared a world heritage site by UNESCO. Cusco had been the capital of the Inca Empire and was invaded by the Spanish conqueror Francisco Pizarro in the sixteenth century. It had then become the center for the Spanish colonization and spread of Christianity in the Andean world. I had always been fascinated by the Cusqueña paintings, a form of religious art with a lack of perspective and warm colors. I wanted to see some of those paintings. Perhaps I'd find some of the churches still open in the late afternoon.

We were received by inspector Eduardo Martinez, a short and stocky fellow with strong local ethnic traces. He had black hair, dark eyes, and an engaging simile. He seemed agreeable and polite. After the introductions, Pedro explained the purpose of our visit.

"So you are convinced that this killer came to Cusco?" Eduardo asked.

"We analyzed other possibilities of course, but this is the only one that makes sense."

"Quite a fellow this killer was! Even for a local native, traveling on foot from the Colca region to Cusco, would be a difficult and tiring experience."

"Indeed, this case has been baffling us at PNP Arequipa. It has so many contradictory aspects. The killer has shown great skill in committing the murders. He seems to be an extremely dangerous and trained professional. Hardly the traits one would expect to find in a habitant of the region. On the other hand, he has demonstrated a survival capacity and local terrain knowledge unreasonable to attribute to a foreigner."

"He could be a foreigner with a local accomplice."

"Unlikely. All evidence indicates a single individual committing the crime."

"I see. And what would he do in Cusco?"

"He cannot travel by air due to the gold pieces he's carrying. Thus, he must be using Cusco as a relay point en route to Callao."

"In this case, he could have taken the bus or rented a car."

"Or stolen one," I said.

"I'll check that also," Eduardo responded, "but there is a more important aspect to consider."

"Which is?"

"Where are you staying in Cusco, Mr. Leary?"

"In Hotel Monasterio," I answered.

"Imagine arriving at the Monasterio, dirty and tired, after a long and strenuous overland trek, pulling a couple of loaded llamas. Impossible and hilarious, isn't it? Imagine how he would be treated, there or at any other regular hotel, if he tried to check in."

"I see your point, but what do you have in mind?"

"Cusco is a small town. Still, we receive almost 2 million tourists each year. Additionally, we have a large floating native population. Cusco is the place they come to sell their wares, to trade, to buy essential things. We must have lodging catering for both types of visitors. Upon arriving in Cusco, your man needed to clean up, obtain a new set of clothing, get rid of the llamas, and buy a set of suitcases to store the gold pieces. In essence, he needed to metamorphose back into a tourist to emerge in the world."

"Brilliant."

"Thank you. He could do those things at a hostel used by the local population. So I think our search should start there. We must determine his adopted identity before starting to check with buses and car rental places. Obviously, in parallel, I'll look for cars reported stolen."

"When could you start the search?" I asked.

"Immediately, I think. I'll talk about things internally and assign a few of my men to conduct the search."

"May I take part, together with one of your inspectors?"

"I prefer not, Mr. Leary. You see, these are local people. They look different, speak a dialect, and have different habits. I'm going to assign men of the same racial ethnicity, people they can relate to. Excuse me, but you would look so out of place, they would just clam up. Then, it would become impossible to extract any information."

"I understand. When do you expect to conclude the search?"

"I should get results in two or three days."

"That long?"

"You cannot put pressure on these people, and there are many places to check. I'm afraid it can't be done faster."

"Here, I have a photo of John Engelhard. It may be useful in your search. You can make copies of it, if you wish."

"Yes, that will be helpful," Eduardo said, taking the photo I had offered.

"In the meantime, I think I'll visit the car rental places," I said.

"It could be a waste of your time, Mr. Leary. I wouldn't recommend it."

"But why? I have a photo. I can help."

"Mr. Leary, there are dozens of car rental companies in Cusco. All the international names like Hertz and Avis are represented, but there are also several Peruvian and small Cusco companies. Besides, all the hotels also rent cars. Without his identity, you would have to find someone who remembers him. But you must take in account that he might have changed his looks—put on a wig or grown a mustache. It will be a shot in the dark. Please wait until I have found something and informed you."

This was very frustrating. I felt my investigation is stalling. I could see no progress.

"As you know, Mr. Leary, sometimes, police work can be too slow. But do not despair. We will find out what your man did, where he went. Have faith and, please, be patient."

"What should I do in the meantime? I hate to be idle."

"You can profit from our hospitality and our city. Two days can pass very quickly in Cusco. You could go to Machu Picchu. It's an experience you shall never forget."

"Well, my wife will certainly love your suggestion."

"Ah, you have your wife with you here? That's perfect. You should enjoy the opportunity. Do you have a cell phone?"

I gave my New York cell phone number to inspector Eduardo Martinez.

"I'll call you or your hotel, as soon as I find anything. And these are my phone numbers. If you have any doubts or the need to check on the progress of our work, please do not hesitate to call me."

I thanked inspector Eduardo and said my goodbyes. I would get back to my hotel sooner than I had expected. I was looking forward to breaking the news to Livy. She would have my undivided attention for the next two days, at least. It would be fun to watch her reaction.

Two days later, I finally heard from Inspector Eduardo. He was still in the hunt but expected to have news in another day or two. In the meantime, I had to occupy my time somehow. I decided to visit Machu Picchu. Livy would love that. She and I were becoming bored to death of Cuzco, having visited all its churches and historical sites. I went to tell her my decision.

"Livy, we are going to Machu Picchu tomorrow, you and I."

"What? You are kidding, right?"

"Nope, it's the pure truth. I have already bought the tickets. I got them right here, at the hotel. We are leaving in the morning and coming back tomorrow. We will spend one night there."

Livy jumped and threw her arms around my neck. "I can't believe it, love. I'm so, so happy. But what happened? Is the investigation in trouble?"

"No honey, it's not. I must wait until the local police checks to see if our killer used the local hostels. Meanwhile, there is nothing I can do. I have to wait for their results before doing anything else. So I decided to use these two days to do some sightseeing together."

"This is wonderful. We must celebrate the occasion."

"Please don't start, Livy. You'll be the—"

"The end of you, I know. I have heard that before. But I guarantee, your end will be a very pleasant one."

The two days visiting Cusco and surroundings with my wife passed in a rush. I forgot everything else and enjoyed the unplanned holiday with her. It was fantastic. I was awakened from my reverie in the afternoon of the second day by a phone call from Eduardo Martinez.

"Mr. Leary, we have results for you. Would you, please, come to my office tomorrow morning? Ten o'clock would be fine."

"Thank you, Inspector. I'll be there."

Next morning, at ten sharp, I was sitting with inspectors Eduardo and Pedro at the PNP office. Eduardo's team had managed to unveil an identity for the killer and had determined what took place, after he arrived in Cusco. They had faced a lot of reluctance and mistrust from the local native population in revealing what they knew. Luckily, one of Eduardo's men was born and raised in one of the nearby pueblos. They trust him as one of their own and finally consented to tell what had passed.

The suspected killer arrived in Cusco four days after the murders in Colca. He appeared at a local hostel and asked for lodging. Initially, the family who owns the place had misgivings accepting him. They mistrusted an obviously foreign looking person, dressed in typical local garb and leading two loaded llamas on top. Besides, he looked dirty and very tired. But the man offered to pay them double the asked price, and they relented to accept him. He remained with them for approximately forty-eight hours. He asked them to sell his llamas and to buy him two large suitcases and some clothing. He told them his name was Homero. However, he had wanted to change some money and asked them to indicate a currency exchange bureau. They sent their eldest boy with him to show the exchange place where a friend of his worked. The boy was clever and paid attention. The stranger was asked to present an ID, and after he left, the boy went back to ask his friend. The stranger's passport identified him as Feliciano Silva, a Brazilian citizen. In this case, the locals' mistrust and the boy's cunningness worked in our favor. PNP had come up with a treasure trove of important information.

"That's fantastic news," I said. "Did you find out if the stranger was in fact Engelhard or someone else?"

"We showed the photo to the hostel family and to the exchange bureau boy. They did not unequivocally identify the stranger as the man on the photo. All were in doubt. They said the photo looked like the stranger, but they could not confirm. I'm afraid it wasn't conclusive."

"That gives me hope that Engelhard didn't do it," I said.

"You may be right. However, you cannot say that wasn't him. It goes either way."

"Yes, I know."

"You and Pedro were wrong in one point," Eduardo mentioned.

"Which point was that?"

"He didn't go to Callao. He went to Porto Velho, Brazil"

"Really? I'm surprised."

"I am surprised too," Pedro concurred.

"I'm not," Eduardo told us. "From what you said, it makes sense. Surely, the road distance from Cusco to Porto Velho is almost twice that of the one to Lima. But the road isn't bad and the car voyage can be easily made in three days, two if you push it. Customs at the Peru-Brazil border are very easy and tolerant. They are only looking for drugs, and if their dog doesn't smell you, you get through without problems. That's not a normal smuggling route for electronic equipment or other consumer goods in demand. Once you are in Brazil, there are riverboats leaving from Porto Velho, on the Madeira River, to Manaus or Belem. Both of those cities are on the Amazon River, and their fluvial ports have seagoing vessels that sail to different destinations in Europe and Asia, and Manaus is a Brazilian free port. There are no customs to ship cargo from Manaus. Again, the authorities are only concerned with drugs."

"I follow your reasoning. Still, gold pieces are bound to raise eyebrows to say the least."

"Absolutely, but they can be hidden in false bottoms, disguised by a fake paint layer, whatever. In any case, control should be a lot less rigorous than in major ports like Callao or Santos in Brazil, for instance."

"It made a lot of sense. How did you find that he had gone to Porto Velho?"

"Once I had the identity he was using, it was surprisingly simple to discover his destination. We started checking with the car rental companies, and bang! We found one that had rented a car to a Brazilian client. A week later, they got a phone call from the Porto Velho police. The car with a Cusco license plate had been abandoned on a curb parking in a relatively busy street in that city. The police went to investigate and found the car documentation with the Peruvian rental company data. They phoned the company, and a driver was sent to collect the car and bring it back to Peru. It was a big expense for the car rental company, but as the renter had provided a valid credit card, they charged the extra cost to his account."

"And you had no previous knowledge of that?" I asked.

"None, and for a simple reason. The car hadn't been damaged and they recovered the extra costs. They didn't think it was important to tell us."

"A mistake, I would say."

"A big one and I let them have it, for their error. But there you are. You now have a better idea of your criminal's plans."

"And I have you to thank for it, Eduardo. And you also, Pedro, because without the help and kind support of everyone in PNP, this investigation would have never reached the point where it is now. When you see your colleague, Jorge Vilar, please send him my regards and deepest gratitude."

"Don't mention it, Alan. It has been a pleasure to meet you and Mrs. Leary. The important thing now is getting hold of the murderer and making him pay for his crimes."

"I'll do my best to achieve that."

"What will be your next step, Alan?"

"I'll be going to Porto Velho at the earliest possible opportunity."

"You will need a visa to enter Brazil, you know?"

"I already have one."

"In that case you are set. I recommend you take a plane. Certainly, you shouldn't consider driving, especially, if you plan on taking your wife along."

"Okay, I'll fly. I'll try to go tomorrow, if I can find seats."

"You should have no problems with that. There are several flights daily."

"In that case, I would like to excuse myself. I have to return to my hotel and tell my wife of my plans. It has been a pleasure working with you, gentlemen."

"Likewise, Alan. We wish you success in your endeavor.."

CHAPTER 11

Porto Velho

I had tried to convince my wife to return to New York from Cusco, a plan bound to fail. She wouldn't hear of it. Livy can be exasperatingly stubborn on occasions. So she came with me on the uncomfortable two-hour flight from Cusco to Porto Velho. The plane was full, and the seats were narrow and crammed. Going east from Cusco, we rapidly left the Andes behind and passed over the vast and boringly flat Amazon jungle, first the Peruvian portion and then the Brazilian. There is no clear separation, but we can distinguish the Brazilian side when we begin noticing the large areas of deforestation, making space for cattle ranches and timber exploration, a clear proof of human greed and negligent government control.

As we come into Porto Velho, the most significant sight is the wide Madeira River. Porto Velho, the capital city of the state of Rondonia, is built on the river's eastern bank. On the opposite margin is the Amazon state. The Madeira is a tributary of the Amazon, and it is navigable by barges and shallow boats all the way from Porto Velho to Manaus, the capital city of the state of Amazon and farther. In fact, that was the main reason for selecting such a location for Porto Velho. When there were no roads or airports, the river provided the only means of access to the region, which was developed initially by rubber collectors and later by gold and tin prospectors.

When I stepped off the plane, I was immediately assaulted by the heat and humidity. Coming from the mountains with its cool and dry climate, the contrast was a shock. I looked at Livy, who, born and raised in a tropical city, handled these conditions better than I did. She seemed unaffected. Before leaving Cusco, I had done two things: I phoned my friend and former assistant in Rio, Fernando Pinheiro, and I asked our concierge to recommend and reserve for us the best hotel they could find in Porto Velho. Fernando is a retired former federal police chief investigator who had provided invaluable help during my previous investigation in Brazil. I asked Fernando to set meetings for me at the Porto Velho Federal Police and to contact me as soon as he had done so.

The hotel they got us was the Golden Plaza, a new establishment located in a main artery of the city. It was nothing to praise and a far cry from our previous lodgings in Lima and Cusco. However, what could one expect in a city like Porto Velho? Our room was spacious, air-conditioned, and clean, with one double bed, which was okay for Livy and me. We tended not to waste too much bed space between us.

The Golden Plaza was a good distance from the downtown area, which was a plus, in my opinion. I cannot think of a more uninteresting place than Porto Velho. The city has grown as result of the discovery of cassiterite, a tin ore, in nearby areas, and of gold on the Madeira River. In addition, the Brazilian government decided to allow large cattle farms in the territory, the cause for the large deforestation we had spotted from the plane. The town grew with the intense migration of people trying to get rich with gold and tin. This caused much trouble for the city, which quickly reached a population of more than four hundred thousand. As a result of the rapid expansion, its suburban boroughs are nothing but shanty settlements. There are no interesting monuments or parks, the style of constructions is generally in terrible taste, and there is practically nothing in terms of culture. It's a violent and crime-ridden community plagued with drug traffickers. Did I forget anything? Ah yes, there are no restaurants offering a remotely decent meal. This is where I dropped in with my wife to chase a multiple-murder assassin? I had to be mad.

"Livy, Livy …"

Livy was distracted during unpacking. "Did you say something, honey?"

"Nothing important. I was thinking on how imprudent I have been in bringing you to a place such as this. It's unforgivable."

"But I wanted to come with you, Alan."

"I know, but I should have refused to bring you along. This is not like

Lima or Cusco, where I could go to work and leave you by yourself to chase after the things tourists do. There is nothing to see or do here. I cannot leave you alone in the hotel. You'll have to come with me when I go out to continue the investigation. It's an impossible situation."

"You shouldn't worry so much about me. I'll be perfectly fine staying in the hotel."

"I would gladly leave you in a decent hotel with a swimming pool or other attractions to help you pass the time. But this place sucks. Porto Velho is depressing."

"There is you, and that is more important than anything else. So don't fret. I'm very happy to be with you. There is no other place where I would prefer to be now."

How can you argue with that, really? How can you say no to someone like Livy?

"Besides," she continued, "it's not true that there is nothing to do. We can do a lot of things," she told me with twinkling eyes, full of mischief.

"Yes, there is that, isn't it? But first, I need to do a few things. I have to call their state police, or *policia militar,* as they call it here, and try to get hold of Lieutenant Moreno. He's the guy the Cusco police got in touch with regarding the suspect's rented car. The local police had found the car with Cuzco license plates abandoned on a curb in Porto Velho. Then I have to ask the hotel to provide us a reliable car and driver."

"Do we need one?"

"Absolutely, I have no intention of driving, and we need someone who knows the area."

I talked to the hotel reception about the car, and they were solicitous in accommodating my requirements. I was told they knew a nice person who worked driving the hotel guests. They would tell him to get in contact with me. I thanked them and explained I should like to use the car to take us for dinner later today. Next, I asked the operator to dial the *policia militar* headquarters. After a few minutes, after getting switched through a few extensions, I finally got connected with the sector where Lieutenant Moreno was stationed. I was told that he was on leave that day but would be back tomorrow. If I came by any time in the morning, I would be able to talk to him. That wrapped things up for the day. I had to wait for feedback from Fernando, and Moreno wasn't available until next morning. The next step was waiting for the driver.

The driver came to the hotel the next day. He turned out to be a middle-age man called Sergio. He had a small four-door sedan, reasonably comfortable and with air conditioning, an indispensable item in this place. I negotiated his services for the full period of our stay in Porto Velho, which I expected wouldn't be longer than three or four days. Sergio would remain available for us even if we didn't need him, from nine in the morning to nine in the evening. I would pay double-time if I needed him beyond that period. He seemed pleased with the arrangement, and so we shook hands on it.

"When do you wish me to start?" he asked.

"You can start today. Right now, actually. I'm going to need you to drive us to the best restaurant in town, at seven."

"Very well, Mr. Leary. I'll wait for you downstairs. Call the lobby when you need me to go out."

"Will do, Sergio."

Fernando called me in the morning, giving the name of the person I should call on at the Federal Police.

"I don't know him, Alan, but a friend of mine recommended him. He's supposed to be a nice person and a good policeman. His name is Marcio Andrade and my friend has called him up already. Marcio is waiting for you to contact him."

"Great, Fernando. I owe you one. I'm going to call him right away."

"Any chance of you and Olivia coming this way? I would love to see you guys again."

"I don't think so, Fernando. This time, we won't. However, I might need your help. What do you think of working a stretch for Leary & Galliazzi? Could you find the time if I needed you to?"

"The answer is yes. When do you want me to go?"

"Hold your horses, Fernando. I'll advise you when to come. I'll most likely need your help in Manaus. I have to check a few things first."

At that time, I was unable to tell what my next move would be. It was too soon to ask Fernando to travel to Manaus. If my hunch was right, I expected the man I was chasing to have traveled to Manaus or to any other port city along the Amazon harboring seagoing vessels. If this was confirmed, I would ask Fernando to meet me in the city the man went to.

"Please wait, Fernando, but be prepared if I call you, okay?"

"I'm going to pack a suitcase, feed the dog, warn the missus, and wait for your green light."

"Good man." I laughed. "And thanks again for the FP contact."

"Don't mention it."

"Are you ready, Livy? When you are, let's go and have breakfast."

"In a minute, Alan."

"Fine. I need to ask something at the reception. Do you mind if I go first and you meet me there?"

"No, go. I'll be down in a second."

I went to collect information on boat trips from Porto Velho to Manaus and Belem from the fellow at the reception desk.

"Sure, it's possible Mr. Leary, but I'm afraid I don't know much about that." He was clearly shocked by my question. "Please, don't be annoyed if I ask, but you are not considering taking such a trip with your wife, are you, Mr. Leary?"

"I don't know yet. For the moment, it's simple curiosity."

"Because if you are, permit me to strongly advise against it."

"Really, and why is that?"

"Accommodations are precarious at best. The voyage is long and boring, four to five days to Manaus, a lot longer to Belem, and it's not free from risks. There are frequent accidents. The people taking the trip are low class, and there could be thieves among them, individuals who think nothing of killing a person to rob her."

I smiled confidently. "Oh, I'm not really thinking of traveling that way. The truth is I'm writing a book, and I need to get details for the story."

The receptionist seemed relieved. "Ah, in that case, it's different. I'll try to find the information you seek. I know that the boats sail from the old port Cai n'Água, which literally means Fall in the Water. As I said, I'll get better information. Are you going out now?"

"After breakfast," I answered.

"When you come back in the afternoon, I'll have something for you."

"You are very kind. I appreciate it."

By then, Olivia had come down, and we went for breakfast.

My first instruction to Sergio was to take us to the headquarters of the *polícia militar,* which he accepted with no hesitation about address or route. Apparently, it was a well-known location. I asked him to wait for us, and we walked to the building's entrance. A door guard directed Livy and me to the reception desk, where Lieutenant Moreno was promptly located. We received instructions on how to reach the sector where he worked. It was a big building, which forced us to inquire a few times along our way, to confirm our direction, before reaching Moreno's place of work. We were conducted to a small room and asked to wait. A few minutes later, Moreno came to meet us.

"I was told you wished to see me. How can I help you?"

"Lieutenant Moreno, my name is Alan Leary, and this is my wife, Olivia. I'm a detective from New York. Presently, I am investigating the murders of American and Peruvian citizens near Arequipa, Peru."

"Okay, I remember. This has to do with the car with Cuzco license plates found abandoned in the city. I was warned by Inspector Eduardo from PNP Cusco that you would be coming to Porto Velho."

"Well, here I am, Lieutenant. I would be grateful if you would tell me all you found on the case and the person driving the car."

"I regret there isn't much to say, Mr. Leary. The car in question was left in a busy street curb, parked for several days. The owner of the shop in front of which the car had been left called us, and we went to investigate. The car was locked, and we had to break in. Later, we found the keys in the glove compartment. We read its registration and called the rental company in Cusco. They sent a driver to collect the car, paid the fine, and took it back to Peru. We got the name, passport number, and description of the person who had rented the car, a fellow named Feliciano Silva. We discovered that it was a faked identity. The address he provided doesn't exist, and the passport is false."

"Did you collect fingerprints from the car, Lieutenant?"

"Yes, we did. We got some good ones, actually."

"Could you give me those fingerprints? It would be very useful for my investigation."

"Sure, give me your address and I'll send them to you."

"Thank you. And did you find how he left town, where he went from here? I'm certain he didn't remain in Porto Velho."

"Now this is the problem, Mr. Leary. *Polícia militar's* charter is restricted to local law enforcement, traffic control, and similar activities. We cannot and do not have the means to investigate an interstate national crime. This task falls to the federal police. We gave them all the information we were able to unearth. For us, the case has been closed."

"Actually, I plan to pay a visit to the federal police also."

"Do you have the name of someone to look for at FP, Mr. Leary?"

"Yes, I have. I've been referred to Inspector Marcio Andrade."

"Ah, Marcio, I know him well. You'll be in good hands. Have you talked to him, yet?"

"Not yet. I was planning to go and see him after this meeting."

"I'll call to let him know you are coming."

"Very kind of you, Lieutenant."

"There is one thing I could do for you, Mr. Leary. The hotels have to send us the forms, which must be filled by every guest who checks in. Frankly, we never pay much attention to those. In this case, however, I'll ask one of our staff to look them up a few days before and after the date the car was found. I will check if a Feliciano Silva was a guest in one of our hotels."

"That would be great, Lieutenant."

"I'll leave a message of what we find, at your hotel, Mr. Leary."

We thanked Lieutenant Moreno and left. Our next destination was the federal police. This time, Sergio didn't know the address, but Fernando had provided it. Avenida Lauro Sodré, I told Sergio, and he took us there. We went in the building to look for Marcio Andrade. He didn't make us wait.

"Good morning, Mr. and Mrs. Leary. I was waiting for you. I received a phone call from our office in Rio, explaining the reason of your visit, and I have just got a call from my friend Lieutenant Moreno."

"He graciously conceded us some of his time, updating me on the information he had on the case," I said.

"Yes, he mentioned it to me. Unfortunately, I don't have much to add beyond what he told you. But I can contribute the following: the suspect didn't leave town by plane or by bus, and he didn't try to rent another car. We checked those possibilities. We have not received a request from the Peruvian police or by the Interpol to investigate this case, at least not yet. However, false identity is a federal crime, which we must investigate. We would like to collaborate with you. In exchange, we would like you to share all you have on this person with us."

I had told this to so many people so many times already. I was becoming impatient with the repetition. "That's perfect with me, Inspector. It's a long story. If you have the time, I'll be glad to tell it to you."

"Definitely, Mr. Leary. Please take your time. Before we start, can I offer you some refreshments—coffee, water?"

"Water would be fine."

"For me too," Olivia said.

I started reporting the case, from the visit of Anton Deville to our office, revealing everything I knew and the Peruvian police's near conclusion that Engelhard was the murderer."

"It's a fantastic story, Mr. Leary. It would be very exciting to contribute to solve a crime like that. We here are essentially devoted to preventing drug traffic and its associated crimes in the state."

"I see."

Marcio went on. "As I was saying, in this specific case, we are left with three possibilities. One, the suspect changed identity again. We could not discover how he left town because he was using a different ID. Two, he left by boat. Three, he stole a car."

We were interrupted by a lady entering our room carrying a tray with the water we had requested. After a brief interval, Marcio continued his explanation.

"If he stole a car, it will be difficult to find where he went. You see, stolen cars are practically never found in this area. Most end up in Bolivia and Peru, in exchange for drugs. After hearing your story, I am betting he didn't do it—use a car, I mean. In my opinion, he must have traveled by boat."

"I agree with you, Inspector, but I would like to learn the reasons for your opinion."

"The boats are the means of transportation for low income inhabitants. A good portion of those fellows does not have IDs. They have lived all their lives in the outback and never felt the need for one. The boat operators never ask for IDs. Tickets are paid in cash. It's the ideal means of transportation if you wish to remain unnoticed."

"Clearly. Could you do something to confirm this assumption? If he indeed left by boat, it still remains to elicit his final destination—Manaus, Belem, or elsewhere."

"I'll work on that, Mr. Leary. I don't think I can get quick results for you, though. I regret to say, we are very understaffed. This is a new and violent territory. There is a lot of illicit activity to keep us very busy. Nevertheless, rest assured, I will try to do my best. I'll see to whom I can assign this task. I'll get in touch as soon as there are new developments. I assume you won't be leaving us before we get a conclusive result."

This was not the answer I was expecting. I would have liked to see a more proactive reaction, but there was little else I could do at this moment. Perhaps, my continued stay in this city and repeated visits to the police would compel them to take more positive action. For now, I just answered his question.

"You assume correctly, Inspector. I'm prepared to stay as long as necessary."

I left inspector Marcio somewhat disappointed with our meeting. I was hoping for more positive support. From what he told me, I couldn't expect he would move very fast. We had nothing else to do now. I asked Sergio to take us for lunch.

"Would you like to eat fish?" he asked. We have delicious freshwater fish, and I know a very good place where it's served."

"Not for me, thanks. I prefer meat."

"Why?" Livy asked? "You always liked fish."

"Are you aware, Livy, of the large number of placer gold extraction in this river?"

"Not really, but what's the problem?"

"They use mercury to extract the gold, and I'm just imagining a waiter telling me: 'How would you like your fish cooked sir, medium or high mercury?' Not for me, thanks."

"I understand your concern. We'll have meat, please, Sergio."

After lunch, I had to decide what to do. Remaining idle while expecting the federal police to act didn't please me. I decided to pay a visit to the riverboats. First, I should drop Livy at the hotel, but her reaction was predictable: where you go, I go. Ah well, patience is my middle name.

"If you wish to come with me, we have to go to the hotel first. You have to change."

"Why? What would you rather have me wear?"

"There is nothing wrong with your dress, love. Since you are determined to come along, you should look as inconspicuous and less feminine as possible—a hard proposition, I understand, but try anyway. We are visiting a potentially dangerous area. I suggest you put on loose jeans and a plain blouse. We can buy a baseball cap at the hotel souvenir shop. Use that to hold your hair—and, please, no makeup."

"Yes, master. Any other commands?"

"No, that's all," I said, not taking her bait.

I surprised Sergio by asking him to drive us to the Cai n'Água port. I wished to try to confirm that the person I was tracking had left Porto Velho by riverboat. Sergio looked at me with concern, waiting for me to confirm the request.

"There is nothing there, Mr. Leary, nothing to see or admire. It's just an ugly part of the river with boats tied to the margin. It's not even a true port, and it's not a nice place."

"No matter, Sergio. I want to go there."

He shook his head in disapproval and started the car. "Very well, sir, if that's what you wish." His expression conveyed a clear message: *You'll regret it.*

CHAPTER 12

The River Queen

The Cai n'Água port was in fact a crummy place, a shanty community with ugly houses and wooden sheds. Truly, it was no port, just a spot with a collection of boats tied to the margin, a mud bank with a steep slope all the way to the water, several meters below. The whole area looked dirty and unpleasant.

"Where do you want me to stop, Mr. Leary?"

I saw a derelict low construction with a sign announcing MV Navegação Fluvial. I pointed it to Sergio. "Stop there, please."

I got out and went to the building, entering a room separated from the access door by a long counter. An older man and a younger girl were sitting behind it. The man got up when he saw me approaching the counter.

"Good afternoon," I greeted him. "I wonder if you could help me?"

"Would you like to travel in one of our boats to Manaus?" the man asked.

I took Engelhard's photo from my pocket and placed it on top of the counter. "I'm trying to find this friend. I understand he went to Manaus in one of your boats. I would like to know when he left, exactly."

He looked me over. "I don't know. We have many passengers in our boats. I cannot remember everyone. Besides, we are here to sell tickets, not to provide information."

I placed a fifty-reais bill, roughly twenty-five dollars, on top of the photo. "Perhaps, this will help you to recall."

He took a second, more careful look. "What's the name of your friend?"

"Feliciano Silva," I told him.

"Do you have an idea of when he traveled?"

I gave him the approximate dates, based on the discovery of the abandoned car. He went to a shelf with what seemed to be record books and picked one. After a brief consultation, he told me. "No one with that name took passage with us in the period you mentioned. I cannot find his name in our records. However, this doesn't mean anything. Sometimes, they lie about their true name." He called the girl sitting behind the counter. "Come here, Maria. Look at this photo. Can you recognize the man?"

The girl approached us and picked the photo. "No, I have never seen him before."

"Tough luck. I can't help you."

I gave him the money. "Are there other companies where I could go ask?"

"We are the only one with an office. The other companies sell tickets on the boats themselves. And, incidentally, a new one has just docked this morning, the *Rainha do Madeira*, or *Madeira Queen*. They will start selling tickets tomorrow morning. You might go there and see if anyone can help you."

The *Madeira Queen* was a sixty-foot-long boat with three decks, each a mixture of open spaces for cargo, for people in hammocks and cabins for the more fortunate. A single narrow board, bridging the gap between the margin bank and the lowest deck, provided access to the boat. I started descending the bank, with Olivia following me.

"You might wish to stay behind, Livy. This slope looks slippery."

"I want to go near the water, Alan."

"Okay, grab my arm then, and take care not to fall."

Near the water, two men were crouched around a deck of cards on an improvised table, with a bottle of rum between them. They raised their heads and looked at us as we got near the access plank.

"Livy, you better let me go first. This looks precarious." I stepped on the board with the intention of embarking when one of the nearby men started shouting.

"You there, gringo, what do you think you are doing? Stop! You cannot go into the boat if we don't give you permission."

I turned around. Both men had stood and were walking in my

direction. I stepped back on land to face them. "No need to get excited, fellows. I only want to talk to the ship's master or his deputy."

"Isn't he cute?" the bigger one said. "He wants to talk to the ship's master," he mocked me. Both laughed. "What's that with him, eh? What are you, a boy, a girl, or a faggot?"

This thing was getting ugly. I tried to ignore the offense. I had no wish to get involved in a fistfight in this place, especially with my wife watching. "Look, I do not wish any trouble," I told them. "If you don't want me to go on board, I'll leave peacefully."

"You cannot run away, gringo. You think you can come here and treat us like garbage. You are wrong, and we are going to show it to you."

Okay, I wasn't getting away free. "Livy, go to the car."

"I can't leave you alone, Alan."

"Livy, go now!"

Surprisingly, my wife obeyed me, and I got ready to face the two guys. The bigger one had a fat, thick waist but looked very strong. He had the type of muscles you develop when your job is hauling cargo every day. The second fellow was shorter but equally strong looking. I was evaluating my possibilities and studying my next moves. The big one came straight at me with the clear intention of assaulting me. They seemed overconfident, ready to teach me a lesson. They were strong, and there were two of them. Instead of assaulting me simultaneously, the big one came first, the smaller guy lagging a little behind. This was a big mistake. The big guy jumped me. I moved out of his way. He was fast, however, and landed a punch to the side of my head. It was a glancing blow, but it hurt like hell. I was shaking my head. The second man tried to grab me. I kicked his knee, and he went down. My biggest worry was still the big one. I turned to face him. He punched me again. I ducked avoiding most of his blows. He hit me again. This time with a solid punch to the side of my head. I went down on one knee. He tried to kick me, but I was able to deviate his leg with my arm. I got up. The man rushed me again. I pushed my right shoulder against his chest. At the same time I grabbed and pulled his arm, throwing him over my back into the water. The second man was getting up. I punched him hard. He fell down again and passed out. He was going to stay out for a while. In the meantime, the big one was coming out of the river. He was climbing the riverbank slope on all fours. I kicked his head before he could recover, and he dropped unconscious. Had he been a weaker person, I think I could have killed him.

These things happened so fast, in a blur of action, and I needed a few seconds to get my bearings. With my two assailants down I began recovering my breath and raised my head. Two other fellows were running in my direction, holding clubs. I might not get out of this fight in one piece after all. So be it. I was firming my resolve, preparing for the worse when two things happened in quick succession. A middle-aged man showed up at the top of the riverbank and started shouting. My wife came back with two policemen in uniform.

The newcomer was directing his attention to the fight and shouting at the two men about to attack me.

"What the hell is happening here? You two get rid of those clubs and stop immediately. If you don't have anything better to do, I'll find work to keep you busy."

The situation was becoming very confusing. Olivia was running to me, followed by the two policemen.

"Are you okay, love? I was so afraid they would hurt you, that I wouldn't reach you with help in time to prevent something bad." Olivia squeezed me in her arms.

"Ouch, honey," I moaned. You don't feel the blows in the heat of a fight. It's after you stop and cool down that you begin experiencing pains. I had won, but my opponents had worked me over pretty good. I was going to be sore for a few days. I might even have a broken rib.

Olivia let go of me, alarmed. "Where does it hurt, honey?"

She started crying. I took her back in my arms, carefully this time. "I'm fine, really."

The two policemen were attending to my two aggressors. The big guy was still out, but the other was recovering, and the police were questioning him. By that time, the middle-aged man had joined us.

"Allow me to introduce myself. I am captain and part owner of the *Rainha do Madeira*, and those men work for me. I'm called Chico Pereira, and I would like to beg your forgiveness for their stupidity."

"Would you like to press charges against these two?" a policeman asked me.

"It was all a misunderstanding, Officer. I'll take care of them," Chico Pereira intervened.

"No thanks, Officer," I said. "Nobody got hurt. It was, as the gentleman here says, a misunderstanding, but it's over."

"Thank you, sir. I'm grateful for your tolerance with my men after their inexcusable behavior. If I could do something to compensate your trouble, I will do that," Chico told me.

"That's all right. There's no need for anything. I appreciate your concern, anyway." I was actually very happy that this guy had showed up when he did. His arrival had been providential. Tired as I was from the fight with the first two, if the guys with clubs had reached me, I would have fared a lot worse. "I would like to ask you something, if you don't mind. This was actually my reason to come here and what started this whole mess. My name is Alan, by the way."

"I'll be glad to tell you what I know, Alan. Let's go aboard. I would like to offer you something to drink, a cold beer and a soft drink for the girl, perhaps."

Before Livy got mad, I corrected Chico. "Her name is Olivia. She's my wife."

"I'm sorry, *Dona* Olivia. As I was saying, I'll be honored if I could offer you something aboard my boat."

"A cold Coke would be nice," Livy told him.

"Absolutely, you can choose. I have also a local soft drink, *guaraná*."

I went ahead traversing the narrow plank, which did the job of embarkation board, extending my hand to help Livy negotiate the precarious access. Once onboard, Chico led us to a mess room on the top deck. He excused himself and came back a few minutes later with cold drinks—a beer for me and a Coke for Livy.

"You wished to ask me something, Alan."

I placed Engelhard's photo on the table in front of him. "I'm looking for this person. He's traveling under the name of Feliciano Silva, and he may look different from the photo. I believe he has taken passage in one of the boats leaving from Porto Velho to Manaus or Belem, probably the former. He is using a Brazilian ID, but I don't know how good his Portuguese is. I don't think he is really Brazilian."

Chico took a good look at the photo. "May I ask what's your interest in this man?"

"He's a thief and a murderer—if he is who I believe him to be. I am a detective from New York, and I have been hired to investigate this case. I'm trying to confirm that he left Porto Velho by boat to determine his destination. I inquired at the boating company office on land, but he didn't travel with them. I saw your boat, and I was coming to ask when the trouble with your men started."

"I'm afraid he didn't travel with us. I would have remembered, especially if he claimed to be Brazilian and didn't speak the language well. Incidentally, your Portuguese is remarkably good, *Dona* Olivia."

"That's because I'm Brazilian, Chico. My husband is American. We met and were married in this country. He does speak Portuguese, but not so well, as you can notice. He learned the language when he worked at the US consulate in Rio de Janeiro years ago, before we met. I am still trying to teach him more."

"That explains it. I was surprised that a foreigner could speak Portuguese so well. You speak it well too, Alan. Obviously, your wife's is much better."

"I realize that, Chico. Actually, she does everything better than I do," I quipped.

"Hum … very funny," Livy mumbled.

"I will help you find your man, Alan. I am sorry you were mistreated by my men. I would like to make up for it."

"It would be a great help, Chico. I don't know how I could repay your favor."

"Nonsense. It's the least I could do after the earlier treatment by my men. Anyway, you cannot remain for over thirty years on this river, like me, without getting to know every person who works on it. It's a close-knit community. I'll send a message to the masters of every boat—all of them long acquaintances of mine—to ask about this Feliciano. Rest assured, if he has traveled using this name, we will find him."

"That's fantastic, Chico. If you can unveil this, I'll be in your debt forever. It would really make my work easier."

"Fine, Alan, but before you start thanking me, let me see what I can get. Give me your address and a phone where you could be reached. We are leaving to Manaus the day after tomorrow, early in the morning. It may take longer than that to get you an answer, but I'll get in touch as soon as I have results."

This had gone better than my expectations. What had started bad, with that unprovoked fight, had turned out extremely well. Chico's help in finding my suspect could provide a faster response than any action by the FP. I wasn't looking forward to spending an extra day or two in Porto Velho, but it was a small price to pay to get the information I wanted. There was nothing else to do here. We left the *Madeira Queen* and went back to our hotel. I had a few bruises to attend to and a gorgeous wife to nurse me. Indeed, life had its compensations.

CHAPTER 13

Following the Trail

It took less than twenty-four hours for Chico to return with an answer. One of the boat captains had responded to his query. A passenger called Feliciano Silva had sailed with him to Manaus. The boat captain remembered him for several reasons. First, he had occupied his cabin three days before departure. He had paid extra for that and to have his meals brought to his cabin during the trip to Manaus. He never left the cabin for the duration of the four days it took to reach their destination. The captain had seen him only on the day he occupied his cabin and when he disembarked in Manaus. He was carrying three large suitcases, and they looked heavy. The captain thought he was moving and bringing his household items with him. He had claimed to be Brazilian, but his Portuguese was poor and heavily accented, like a Spanish-speaking person trying to talk in Portuguese. He had seen the photo I had provided but could not confirm if it belonged to the same man. He looked a little different on the photo. However, Chico said that the facsimile type machine used to send the photo did not render a good image quality.

I was surprised that my suspect was still moving with his Brazilian ID, but when I pondered on the matter, it made a lot of sense. Obviously, the fellow expected to disappear in Manaus. Probably, he already had an escape scheme outlined for him. He might have been counting on assistance for that. He would have to transport the gold pieces and sell them to a crooked art dealer abroad. He could have contacted that party and engaged their assistance. To travel abroad, he would have needed a different ID. He wasn't going to use it to leave Porto Velho. It was better to risk the Feliciano alias. It didn't matter, in the unlikely event of being discovered. He was planning to vanish from sight the moment after setting foot in Manaus. Yes, it made a lot of sense.

Last night I had phoned my partner Tony, to report on the latest developments. In turn, he told me that a Peruvian court had issued an arrest order for Engelhard. This changed things. Engelhard had been officially charged with the murders. If I found him, I would be under the obligation to deliver him to the law. Otherwise, if I let him go, I would be committing a crime. Tony contacted Anton Deville to confirm his wish to proceed with the investigation. Anton told him that nothing had changed. He wished us to continue more than ever. He was adamant that Engelhard was innocent. The court order legalized actions by the police in other countries and by the Interpol. From now on, we could formally request their support. After Chico's news, I intended to fly to Manaus as soon as possible. I wouldn't go before paying a second visit to both Lieutenant Moreno of *policia militar* and Inspector Marcio of the federal police. They hadn't been useful. Moreno's hotel search had produced nothing. No Feliciano had been registered as guest during the period in case, by no means a surprising result considering the information provided by Chico. The suspect had not used a hotel. He had gone directly to his boat cabin and stayed there until departure. Also, I didn't think the federal police had started to work on the case. I gathered from my interview that my problem was not one of their priorities. However, I did not know if and when I would need them again. It didn't cost to be diplomatic. I was going to need a lot of help to catch the trail of my suspect in Manaus.

Livy was still sleeping. She had opened her eyes when the bedside phone rang with Chico's call and went right back to sleep. I had a few things to take care of, like getting plane tickets for us, making a hotel reservation in Manaus, and phoning Fernando to ask him to join us. First, I had to wake my wife.

"Livy, we have to pack, honey."

Livy moaned, turning on the bed, and slowly opening her eyes. She stretched her arms. "Are we going somewhere else?" she asked, still dizzy from waking up.

"Yep, we have to go to Manaus."

"Hum …"

"Hum what, Livy?"

"What time is it?

"Nine. You slept well."

"I was tired, Alan. What about you? How are you feeling? I was worried about you. You have a few serious bruises where those idiots hit you."

"That's nothing, honey. I don't even feel them any longer. They are a lot less blue this morning."

"I was amazed how you were able to fight and prevail on those two brutes. One of them was a monster. How did you do it, honey?"

"We trained in hand-to-hand combat in the special forces, and I have always been good at it. Besides, I've continued my training. I have a martial arts instructor at my athletic club who coaches me twice a week." I was showing off to my wife, of course. But I was enjoying her expression of awe with her husband, the hero.

"I'm still impressed."

"You are biased," I said, taking her face in my hands and kissing her nose, her lips, ear, neck. It really wouldn't be polite to go on describing what I did. Suffice it to say, my plans to get things moving quickly had been severely impaired.

CHAPTER 14

Manaus

Thanks to the boat captain report, I knew the exact day of my suspect's arrival in Manaus. I guessed he wouldn't remain there any longer than was necessary to arrange shipment of the gold pieces. I was assuming he didn't have to search for the means of accomplishing the transport. All his previous decisions indicated a preordained action line, an absence of hesitation. Thus, his actual permanence would depend on the frequency of shipping from Manaus, of which I knew nothing. Additionally, I had a photo and general information on Engelhard—his age, height, color of hair and eyes, and weight. I was counting on those to pick the trail interrupted in Porto Velho and hoped to wrap up my investigation in Brazil.

The flight to Manaus was shorter and a lot more agreeable than our previous one from Cusco to Porto Velho. We couldn't catch an earlier flight. Things moved a bit slower traveling with my wife, but that was all right by me. Actually, concerning Livy, everything was fine with me, and there lay the problem. She knew she had me wrapped me around her little finger. As she looks at me pleadingly with those green eyes, I melt, all resistance forgotten. Otherwise, how could I have consented to the notion of conducting an investigation with a wife in toll? I still had one trick in the bag to convince Livy to go away. I had suggested she take the chance while in Brazil to visit her brothers and sister-in-law. It was still a long way from Manaus to Rio, but less than half the distance from New York. She was tempted and said she would think about it, a small victory. Not that I enjoyed the notion of parting her company, but the incident at Porto Velho was a reminder of the dangers lurking in an investigation like this.

Manaus is an incongruous pocket of civilization in the middle of the Amazon jungle. Located almost one thousand miles from the sea, at the confluence of the Amazon and Negro rivers, it's a major port for ocean-going vessels. Due to its isolated position, accessed only by boat or by plane, the government set it up as a tax-free zone. With more than 2.2 million inhabitants, it was the most populous city in northern Brazil.

When we arrived at the hotel, Fernando was waiting for us. He had not joked when he told me he would leave a packed bag waiting for my call. I invited him to dine with us to discuss our agenda for the morrow. The FP in Manaus is run by a superintendent whom Fernando didn't know. He had been given the name of one of their *delegados,* Inspector Antonio Carvalho, who would see us the next day. "I have never met him either, but being an ex-FP cop and colleague, I'm sure he will help us," Fernando had said. As for Livy's activities, I suggested she visit the Manaus opera house, famous for its opulence and beautiful neoclassical design. It was erected during the region's first rubber boom, when Manaus became one of the richest cities in the country. She could also go on a boat trip to witness the encounter of the waters of the Amazon with the Rio Negro. The two rivers have waters with different amounts of solids in suspension and temperatures. They didn't mix for a very long distance, forming a clearly distinguished line of separation observable from the air or by boat. Manaus is a big city and a free-trade zone. I reminded Livy of the fact. She might be interested in checking what was available for shopping. I didn't think there would be anything that couldn't be found in Manhattan. She approved the idea. Knowing Livy, she would come up with some unique and indispensable object or piece of clothing. That would keep her busy, however.

On the next morning, Olivia left us to go sightseeing. Fernando and I went to the Federal Police headquarters to meet Antonio Carvalho. Fernando made the introductions and I explained our case and the purpose of our visit.

"I know the exact day in which the suspect arrived in Manaus. I also believe he must have counted on assistance to send the gold pieces abroad. They must have been shipped in the days following his arrival in Manaus. Probably, within a maximum period of ten days."

"I see Mr. Leary. What help can we provide to you?"

"I must tell you that an arrest order has been issued by a Peruvian court against an American citizen, Mr. John Engelhard, who the Peruvian police consider to be the murderer. There is strong evidence against him, but I'm not totally convinced of his culpability. Until I find the man who took the gold and I have unequivocal proof, I'll keep referring to the person I am following as the suspect."

"I understand," Inspector Carvalho said. "The Peruvian court order changes things. It gives us the right to act officially. We have yet to receive official communication, but I trust your word. You are an ex-FP agent, Fernando. What do you think of all this?"

"I trust Alan's judgment. If we fail to find where the suspect went, if we lose his trail in Manaus, we might never catch this man. If he's not the murderer, he took part as an accomplice. He has stolen the gold. That's unquestionable."

"Yes, I agree, and this is what I'll do. I'll place my best agent on the case. He will start consulting the hotels with the photo and data you provided."

"Allow me to give another suggestion, Inspector. I don't deny the importance of checking the hotels, but I have a hunch that he may not have used one. In Porto Velho, he avoided hotels and went directly to the boat. He remained for three days in its cabin before departure. He may have done the same here. I think your inspector's time would be better employed checking the shipping lines and freight forwarders. He should limit his search to the ten days following the arrival date I gave you."

"Fine, Mr. Leary. I'll follow your suggestion."

"Would it be asking you too much if I request to work together with your agent, Inspector?"

"I see no problem with that, Mr. Leary. I'll ask him to come to this office, so that you two can meet."

A few minutes later, we were joined by a young man who appeared to be in his early thirties. Carvalho introduced him to us as Agent Felipe. After Carvalho explained our problem and outlined the assistance he should provide, Felipe invited us to his room—his office, if you could call that the cubicle he occupied one floor below—which had one desk with piles of documents on top and a large computer screen.

"Make yourselves comfortable," he told us, gesturing to the two chairs, which had seen better times.

"Let's see now. I'll consult an Internet site giving information on vessel movement in the port of Manaus. We see which ones departed within your timeframe. Then we ask the corresponding shipping line/agent to provide us with the vessel's cargo manifest, and we analyze those. What do you think?"

"It seems practical. Let's do it," I said.

Felipe faced the computer and started typing commands. A few minutes later, he had a list of eighty-four ships sailing from Manaus during the period in question."

"That many?" I was impressed.

"Manaus is a busy port."

"Can you filter those results?"

"Certainly. Which constraints do you wish me to apply?"

"Consider only the ones whose final destination was an European, Middle Eastern, or North African port."

"Will do."

Felipe played with the computer some more and came up with twelve ships, a much more manageable number.

"That's much better. Can you ask for the manifests of these twelve?"

"Certainly, and I note that two of those ships have the same agent, which narrows down our search even more. I only have to ask eleven different agents. I'm going to phone each one of them and send an official request by email."

In the next hour, Felipe was busy making phone calls and forwarding emails. Then we went out for lunch.

When we returned, five cargo manifests had arrived.

"What are we looking for?" Felipe asked.

"Anything unusual; it's difficult to say, really. We just have to examine the cargo of the twelve ships and see what we find."

Four of the five vessels were discarded. All left Manaus to load cargo in other ports. The fifth had a cargo of timber and a few containers and was separated for reanalysis. By the end of the day, two other manifests arrived, also judged without interest. We would have to wait for the next day to check the five still remaining manifests.

"How was your day, honey?"

"It was very nice. It's a pity you couldn't come with me. The opera house is spectacular. It's bigger and nicer than the ones in Rio or São Paulo. You should have seen it."

"Next time, perhaps, when I'm not working."

"I bought this cute dress for Larissa. Isn't it nice? What, why are you smiling?"

"It's nothing, Livy. I'm just enjoying the way you are, baby."

"Alan, you are teasing me."

"Never, how could I? I love you. I find you beautiful and clever—and thrifty." I put my arms around her and started sliding my lips along her chin."

"Stop Alan. Fernando is waiting downstairs to have dinner with us."

"Since when do you pay attention to these things, Livy? Usually, I am the one who must be sensible and moderate things."

"Later," Livy looked at me with sparkling eyes. "You'll be rewarded for your patience," she said, smiling.

The next morning, the remaining five manifests arrived in Felipe's office. Olivia was still using her free time in Manaus to explore the place. We sat to review those, and after a while, we came up with two possibilities. Both transported cargo of mostly timber or raw rubber and a few containers with different declared contents. One vessel was sailing directly to Bremen, Germany, the other to Genoa, Italy. The latter, however, was stopping at Curacao to disembark one twenty-foot container loaded with Brazil nuts packed in boxes. Felipe told me that he found that peculiar, because the nuts are normally packed in bags, and Curacao is an unusual destination for this commodity. He decided to have a word with Antonio Carvalho on the matter.

"This shipment is odd, boss. Look, the consignee/notify party is a freight agent in Willemstad, but the buyer is a company registered in the Bahamas, obviously a paper company."

"Who is the seller?"

"A local firm called AR Comércio Ltda."

Carvalho whistled. "That must be it, then."

"What?" I asked. "Why are you surprised?"

"This is confidential, but we have been discretely investigating AR Comércio on suspicion of smuggling and drug traffic."

"Let's go and pay a visit and talk to them," I said.

"I cannot do that, Alan."

"Why not?"

"I do not wish to warn them of our suspicions before our investigation is concluded, and I cannot show up at their office without an acceptable reason."

"But how are we going to get further details? For sure, the gold didn't stay in Curacao. We need to find out where it went from that port, or we'll lose the trail."

"I'll contact the Willemstad police and ask them to check what happened with the container, where it was shipped to from Curacao."

"It's not going to work. They will have changed documents and sent the container to a different destination. Do you know how difficult it is to identify a single container in a large port like Rotterdam, for instance? It's practically impossible. We'll lose track, and with that, my suspect will vanish from the face of earth." This investigation was proving much harder than I had expected. Every time some progress was achieved, another huge difficulty appeared. I felt like moving from frustration to frustration.

"Don't be so pessimistic, Alan. The Willemstad police are very good. They can place pressure on their freight agent."

"The same way you are putting pressure on AR Comércio?"

"I'm doing all I can, Alan. We'll find your man—have no fears."

For the time being, I had to be satisfied with the help Carvalho was providing. We went out after lunch, and I decided to rent a car and go pay a visit to AR Comércio myself.

Fernando wanted to know if he should come along.

"No, I have another errand for you. Please go to the port where the boats from the Madeira River arrive. I learned it is near the municipal market Adolpho Lisboa, on avenue Manaus Moderna. Check with the taxis serving that area to see if any of the drivers can remember a man carrying three large suitcases on the day of the suspect's arrival in Manaus. He must have used a cab. If we are lucky, you may find the driver who had taken him and learn where to."

"Fine. I'll do that and see what I can get. I'll see you later, at the hotel."

The office of AR Comércio was on the outskirts of Manaus. Without the GPS, I never would have found it. It was really a storage shed with a single floor office on its front. The whole thing was surrounded by a wire mesh fence with barbed wire on top. I proceeded to the gate and identified myself as a potential client with a freight-forwarding requirement. I was directed to the office where I explained the purpose of my visit, and after a brief wait, I was conducted to the office of Mr. Alfredo Rocha, owner and general manager of the company.

"How can I help you Mr. …"

"My name is Alan Leary, Mr. Rocha. Coming here, today, I was thinking how to breach this matter to you. I concluded that directness was the best strategy. I am partner in a detective company in New York. Our company has been hired by the Peruvian Museo de la Nacion to investigate the theft of some valuable archeological objects."

"And what has this has to do with me?"

Rocha's expression was changing from one of surprise to anger. His stance was of open animosity.

I continued, "Let me tell you, Mr. Rocha, before discussing anyone's involvement, that the museum is offering a handsome reward on information leading to the recovery of the items in question. They have been conservatively evaluated at seven-and-a-half million dollars. The reward we are discussing is of twenty percent, or a cool one and a half million dollars."

"It's a lot of money, but why do you think I can help you?"

"We followed the objects all the way to Manaus, Mr. Rocha and discovered that they had been shipped abroad from this city. Presently, we do not know their final destination, but we will shortly. The opportunity I'm offering is one million and a half dollars in exchange for the information on the destination and name of the persons who received the items just that—no questions asked, no action whatsoever taken against the party providing the information." I was paying close attention to Rocha's body language and the look in his eyes as we talked. He was trying to show the exterior appearance of calm, but his discomfort was on clear display, quickly turning to anger. He was obviously shocked and internally debating the action he should take.

"I do not have the slightest idea, and I have nothing to tell you. In fact, I find your insinuations offensive."

"I regret you feel this way. The intention of my visit is not to offend anyone; rather, it is to present an advantageous alternative. There is strong evidence that the shipping originated from this company. I am convinced that the gold pieces have been shipped by your firm. We will find exactly how it was done. If you refuse our offer now, you'll suffer the legal consequences when your involvement is proved, but we would like to save time and cost with the investigation. Recovering the articles quickly is more important. Thus, the alternative to being prosecuted and eventually going to prison is to tell us what you know, collect the reward, and free yourself any harmful consequences."

"That's it. This interview is over. I have nothing else to tell. You should leave now."

"Very well. If this is how you wish to play, so be it. Don't bother to accompany me to the door. I know my way out." I got up and, without saying goodbye, left his office and walked back to my car.

I was one hundred percent certain that the container supposedly carrying Brazil nuts had transported the gold pieces. Rocha's reaction had convinced me of his culpability beyond any doubt. I still had no clues on the final destination of the items, but if necessary, I had plans to remedy that situation.

CHAPTER 15

An Evening by the River

I returned to our hotel. Fernando, who was coming from his taxi drivers' errand, joined me a few minutes later. He had been lucky and found a driver who recalled having transported a man with three large suitcases, on the day of the suspect's boat arrival in Manaus. They went to a warehouse on the periphery of the city and his description perfectly matched the place and facilities of AR Comércio. He left him there. The man did not return to the city with him. This was excellent news, providing a direct link between the person I was chasing and AR. The driver was willing to testify, and Fernando got his phone and the taxi license plate number. I had to take this information to Antonio Carvalho immediately. With this new evidence, he would have to take a more positive action. Before going to the police, however, I wanted to make absolutely sure we were talking of the right location. We left to find Fernando's driver and asked him to take us to the same spot we were discussing. It was. We turned around, and I instructed him to the hotel. I wanted to collect my rental car and go visit Inspector Carvalho.

Carvalho wasn't thrilled to see us back so soon. Nevertheless, he went through the formalities of receiving us, bidding us to sit and stoically preparing himself to endure us one more time.

"How can I help you today, Mr. Leary?"

I went on to explain the new development. "You see, Inspector Carvalho, earlier, we received some promising clues that the gold pieces had been smuggled by or with the help of AR Comércio, but this is proof of their engagement with our man. There is no doubt now. The gold pieces were shipped in those nut boxes. You have to arrest them and force them to reveal where and to whom they sent the artifacts."

"I wish it were that simple, Mr. Leary. The information you brought is very important, but we are dealing with dangerous and clever criminals. The testimony of the driver shows that they knew your man. But it would be stretching the evidence too far to assume that knowledge of the person in case proves the items were shipped by AR. It would never stand in court. We need stronger evidence. Otherwise, we risk losing the whole investigation. It would be a disaster, and I wouldn't like that to happen. Not at all."

"But what are we going to do, then? We cannot just do nothing and let them go free, not to speak of losing the gold pieces for good, never knowing what happened to John Engelhard. It would be inadmissible."

"I quite agree with you. Mr. Leary and I have no intention of doing nothing. First thing I'll do is to get a search warrant to comb their office thoroughly. Don't expect this to happen too quickly. I don't think it will take long, either. We have already tapped their phones. Still, judges have their own agendas and schedules. I figure a day or two to obtain a warrant."

"I wasn't aware you were tapping their phones."

"That's because it has nothing to do with your investigation. After I heard your story, I asked Felipe to recheck the recordings and see if he could find anything having a connection with your case. There was nothing, believe me. We are talking of professional criminals. They are too cunning to discuss their activities openly over a landline. They use prepaid mobile phones, and even those can be protected."

"Will you let me know when you get the warrant?"

"Sure, I'll call you."

"Can I participate in the search?"

"Definitely not. If you, a stranger, are involved in the search, any evidence I find won't be accepted in court. No, I'm afraid you shall have to wait. Please, Mr. Leary, be patient. I understand you have your wife with you here in Manaus. There lots of things to do in this area. Two days can pass very fast. Enjoy your time with us."

There was nothing else to do other than thank Inspector Carvalho for his help and return to my hotel.

"Are you hungry, Fernando?"

"I could eat something, why?"

"I heard of a nice steak place. It's not so close, but its location is supposed to be very nice with a good view of the river. I'm going to call Livy to see if she would like to come with us. I still have the car and nothing else to do for the time being."

"Super. I would like to go, certainly."

The restaurant, in a neighborhood called Ponta Negra on the margin of Rio Negro, had indeed a very nice view of the river, which was wide and flowed majestically in front of us. The sun was beginning to set, painting the sky in vivid yellow and orange tints and outlining in crimson the tall trees of the forest on the opposite banks. A cool breeze came from the river, helping to alleviate the oppressing humidity and warmth of the day. The restaurant was obviously popular. At this time, and on a working day, it was well attended. We couldn't get one of the tables with the best view but secured another almost as well placed. We had barely sat when we were presented with the most beautiful sunset, providing an incredible spectacle of red, yellow, and orange colors typical in this region. I'm told the spectacular sunsets are due to the high-water vapor content in the atmosphere. It never fails to enchant whoever is fortunate in watching its full grandiosity, and we, visitors from other lands, were no exception. We were absorbed by it before thinking about food of our preference. It definitely wasn't to be enjoyed every day or even frequently. Today, however, was special. I was feeling a little like a bum, without anything serious to do, but at least I was profiting from my wife's companion, a luxury I cannot afford as often as I would like. It was an agreeable reunion, and I was trying to put aside my worries and thoughts of work.

We took some time to order our food and then drinks in our hands we relaxed and prepared ourselves to enjoy a carefree evening by the riverside, in agreeable company.

"So are you enjoying your voyage, Olivia?" Fernando asked my wife.

"It has been truly fantastic. I loved it in Peru. Everything was so beautiful, but I think the high point was our tour of the Colca. I was amazed by the beauty and grandiosity of the mountains. It was so incredible. We crossed this high plateau, a vast patch of green among the browns and grays of the surrounding elevations, with no tracks and not a sign of people or habitation for as far as you could see. You really felt alone in the middle of nowhere."

"It does sound like you had a very good time."

"Indeed, I had. Furthermore, I had never been in the Amazon in spite of being Brazilian, I'm ashamed to say. There are so many nice things to see in your own country, and you end up traveling abroad rather than trying to know the place where you live."

"Well then, I'm glad that you could accompany Alan in this investigation."

"Can you imagine that he gave me a hard time agreeing to bring me along?"

"I did not," I protested. "I was just being cautious. You are too precious to me," I said, grabbing Livy's hand and inclining to kiss her cheek.

"You are sweet, and I love you, but sometimes you exaggerate a little. Apart from that nasty affair by the river, in Porto Velho, we have never had any serious problem, and I was never even remotely in danger. We have been safe the whole time."

"We were lucky," I assented.

While we talked, my eyes wandered to the restaurant entrance. The odd man entering didn't fit with the place. He looked like most of the population: he was thin, of average height, with dark hair. But it was the folded newspaper under his left arm and the way he dressed that set him apart. He seemed not to be looking at us, but I felt it was a guise, and he was getting closer to us. All my training told me, when in doubt, act. I might be proven wrong, but it's better to make a mistake and stay alive. Excuses can always be offered up later. I reacted on reflex. Standing up, I pushed Livy from the table and threw a heavy glass ashtray, as hard as I could, at the oncoming stranger. He drew a gun that had been concealed in the folded newspaper. He brought the gun up and shot me. My ashtray hit him on the shoulder, spoiling his aim. It was just enough to make him miss me. I felt his bullet passing very close to my head. It missed me by a fraction of an inch. I didn't stop to think. I used the same momentum to grab a steak knife and throw it at him. He jumped to avoid it. By then I was on him, too close for him to shoot me again. He was no match for me physically. I had him disarmed and pinned on the floor in a second. The whole restaurant had exploded in a big commotion of shouts, overturned tables, and panicked patrons. Fernando had picked the gun our assailant had dropped and was calling the police.

I was worried about my wife, whom I had roughly pushed from the table to get her out of harm's way. "How's Livy, Fernando?" I asked, still holding our attacker.

"I'm fine, Alan," my wife answered, getting up from the floor.

"Fernando, could you get me something to tie this piece of shit?"

"Here sir, a waiter had materialized with a length of rope and, with Fernando's help, I tied the guy's legs and arms behind his back. I left the man lying on the ground and we sat to calmly wait for the authorities to arrive.

We didn't have to wait long. In a short time, we had two patrol cars from the *polícia militar* as well as Antonio Carvalho and Felipe from the federal police. Fernando had warned them also.

"Well, well, what do we have here? Our old friend Tonico. He's a known hitman and escaped convict. Thanks for catching him for us, Mr. Leary. Do you care to tell me what happened?" Carvalho asked.

I tried to summarize what we had done since leaving his office and the sudden appearance of the hitman in the middle of our dinner. I said I had overcome him, preventing the man from shooting us.

"I'm impressed Mr. Leary. You have qualities that are not apparent. This scum Tonico has become a hit man in demand. He is known never to miss his target or to fail in his missions. Frankly speaking—and this is no contempt for your abilities—I am surprised you got the better of him. I am curious. Did you have any warning? How could you guess with sufficient lead time that he was going to shoot you?"

"Frankly, Inspector Carvalho, I had a hunch. Call it professional intuition."

"Amazing." Carvalho turned to one of the policemen and pointed to the shooter. "Take this garbage away and deliver him to the federal police detention, please. I want to question him. He must sing to us the name of the party who hired him."

Tonico was carried away in cuffs by two policemen.

Carvalho turned to me. "This attempt on your life concerns me. I told you, we are dealing with very dangerous criminals. You must have done something that made them nervous and they felt threatened. Beware, Mr. Leary, these people won't stop. They will try again."

"I'll be ready if they do."

"I know you are good, Mr. Leary. I have no doubts regarding your ability to defend yourself. The problem is, no person can win every time, and in this game, one failure is all it takes."

"I'll be extra careful, from now on. Besides, I'm expecting you'll get a search warrant and come up with the answers I need. The quicker that happens, the sooner I can leave Manaus."

"We'll see about that. How are you feeling? Would you like me to drive you and your wife to your hotel? I can send someone to take your car back if you wish."

"We are fine, really," I answered for the others and myself. "Nobody got hurt, and if you don't mind, we would like to finish our dinner." The area around our table had been trashed by the commotion, with overturned tables and shards of glass and of broken plates littering the floor.

Carvalho laughed. "That's the spirit, Mr. Leary. Anyway, please come to our office tomorrow morning. I must take an official testimony of what happened here, tonight."

"I'll be there, Inspector."

"In that case, good night to you. I hope you can enjoy the rest of your meal."

Slowly, the atmosphere in the restaurant was returning to normal. Tables were turned back, waiters were again setting the places, and debris was swept away. It was still early, and I was beginning to feel the end of an adrenaline rush. I needed a drink badly. During my fight, I had kind of forgotten Livy, occupied as I was with subduing our assailant and saving our lives. To get her out of the way, I had pushed her too brusquely to the floor. She had gotten up and was sitting at one of the chairs left standing. I noticed Livy affected by a bout of shaking, and I moved closer to embrace her. I took off my jacket and placed it around her shoulders.

"Shush, it's over, honey. You can relax, you are safe now."

"Fernando, please, get me something with lots of sugar. Ask the waiter to bring an orange juice and have him put sugar in it. I think Livy is going into shock."

The waiter brought us the juice and I made Livy drink it. Slowly, the shaking began to subside and finally stopped.

"Are you hurt, Livy? I'm terribly sorry I had to push you out of the way so hard."

"I'm fine, Alan, and no, I'm not hurt, only my pride."

"Oh, how did you hurt your pride, baby?"

"When I fell, my skirt went up. I must have provided quite an spectacle to the men on the next table, who must have thought we were having a violent matrimonial fight, by the way."

"Poor baby. You want me to go there and kick their asses too?" I joked.

"Certainly not. How did you know, Alan? How could you guess that horrible man was going to try to kill you? I saw him too. He did look peculiar, but a lot of people do. He wasn't even looking at us."

"Livy, I was taught to act instinctively in battle conditions. If you see something fishy that you think may be wrong, don't stop to confirm it. Shoot first, confirm later. It's a cynical attitude, I recognize, but one that saves lives. Take the case in question. Had he been an innocent person, looking for a place to sit and eat his meal, I would have been terribly embarrassed about throwing an ashtray at him. I would have felt ashamed and forced to beg his pardon, but I would be alive. But, if I had hesitated trying to identify his intentions, I would be quite dead."

"I see your point. You realize I am being confronted by another side of you. Earlier, I only knew the loving husband, the amorous father, the gentle and kind Alan. Now, I am being presented to the fighter, the warrior. I knew you were a soldier. Still, it's a little unsettling to see you under a different light."

"I hope you don't love me less for that, Livy."

"That's utterly impossible. Nobody loves you the way I do, Alan. I'm proud of you, actually, and feeling quite protected."

"Hmm, you too doves want me to leave, to be more private?"

We had become absorbed in each other and completely forgotten poor Fernando.

"Absolutely not, Fernando. Please, give us the pleasure of your company for the rest of the evening. Let me see if they have bourbon in this place. Would you like a caipirinha, Livy?"

"No, I think I'll taste your bourbon this time."

"Good girl. I'll make you a true New Yorker still. Well, let's put the excitement of this event behind us and try to enjoy the remaining evening. Tomorrow, the investigation continues, and we must visit Inspector Carvalho in the morning."

CHAPTER 16

A Night Adventure

In the following morning, as requested, I presented myself in the office of Inspector Carvalho at the federal police.

"Would you care to repeat last night's story for me, Mr. Leary? I'm curious about how you were able to escape alive, unarmed, from one of the most vicious killers in the territory. On top of that, you disarmed and subdued him. I'm amazed."

"There's nothing more to say besides what I have already told you, Inspector." I tried to recap the events of the previous evening.

"I'm glad you and your wife escaped unscathed last night, Mr. Leary. As you had the unfortunate opportunity to experience, these fellows, when threatened, will stop at nothing to defend themselves. Killing is nothing to them. Incidentally, how is your wife today? Has she recovered?"

"She's much better, thanks. Olivia stayed at the hotel. She had been thinking of taking a tour this afternoon to go visit the encounter of the waters of the Amazon with the Rio Negro."

"Ah, good. She'll love that. It's quite a sight. The waters are very distinct in color and remain unmixed for miles. Coming back to our story, I think you did amazingly well. By the way, the man has a nasty bruise on his shoulder. You must have thrown the ashtray very hard."

"Yeah, lucky thing is that none of my beer-drinking baseball buddies were around to watch. I would have become the target of their unending jokes."

"I don't think I understand you, Mr. Leary."

"Are you aware of the game of baseball, Inspector?"

"Sure, I've seen it played. I don't know the rules, but yes, I'm familiar with the game."

"I aimed at his head but missed. In the commotion, I failed to throw it right."

"Had you hit him on the head, you might have killed him."

"Possibly."

"Hmm, good thing you didn't. It would have meant additional complications."

"Did he tell you who hired him, inspector?"

"Yes, he did. He was a little reluctant, at first, but your ashtray produced several other bruises, and he wasn't feeling so well. You follow me?""

"Absolutely. These ashtrays are very treacherous. Sometimes they fragment in the air, hitting the targeted body in several parts, just like multiple warheads," I joked.

"Quite. You catch on quickly. Anyway, this fellow in Belem, who acts as a kind of agent, hired him. I have already requested our colleagues in that city to pay him a visit and put on the squeeze to discover who originally ordered the crime. What I find curious is the why. Did you get in contact with AR Comércio Alan?"

"Yes, I did," I confessed. "I had to do something, Inspector. Those guys had to be made aware that we suspect their involvement with the shipment of the gold pieces. It worked. It got them worried to the point of making an attempt against my life. Hopefully, they continue making mistakes, which may play in our favor."

"I regret to say, this disturbs me, Alan. I clearly remember telling you to keep away from those guys. Your contact with them can harm our investigation, and this I cannot tolerate. I must tell you again to refrain from doing anything independent of our knowledge and approval. Otherwise, I shall have to take more severe measures, and I wouldn't like that."

"Understood, Inspector. I'll behave from now on."

"I hope you do."

"Do you have news on the AR Comércio search warrant, Inspector?"

"Not yet, I'm afraid. The court is still analyzing my request."

"When do you expect to have it?"

"Hopefully, in another day or two, but I cannot guarantee it."

"Okay. In this case, if you don't have any other questions, I would like to leave."

"Certainly, Mr. Leary. Please, keep in touch. I'll let you know the instant the warrant is granted."

I left Inspector Carvalho to find Fernando. He had decided to go to Felipe and to make acquaintances with other policemen in the house. He had elected not to partake in my conversation with Carvalho, preferring to become more familiarized with FP Manaus. I found him back in Felipe's office.

"I finished my meeting, and I need to go. Would you like to leave with me, or would you rather stay longer?"

"I'll come with you, Alan."

We excused ourselves and left Felipe.

Back in the car, I exposed to Fernando my concerns with the progress of the federal police's investigation, which presently seemed to hang on securing an elusive search warrant. As far as I knew, it could take weeks until a local court judge, with better things to do, went through the trouble of considering the reasons behind the warrant's request and took some action. I couldn't wait that long. I was contemplating taking matters into my own hands, irrespective of Inspector's Caravalho's warnings. I was planning an unauthorized entry of AR Comércio's premises to search for evidence. Fernando strongly opposed my idea.

"Please, don't do it, Alan. It's very risky, in addition to being totally illegal. Do you know that you could be killed if caught? Under Brazilian law, they wouldn't even go to jail for killing you. You would be the invading party, and they would be defending themselves."

Oh man. This meant, if I proceeded, paying attention to risk and to all the fine details of the law, this investigation might never come to an end. I understood the police imposing limitations. It was their job. Fernando, however, was on my side. He should have known better. But I knew my lack of patience. After all, he had been a policeman himself. He couldn't escape his legal training. "No matter. I still have to do it, unless I would become reconciled with the idea of spending weeks in this city, which would be impossible for me, for my wife, and for the investigation. I'm not asking you to help me, Fernando. I do not wish to implicate you if something goes wrong."

"Bullshit, Alan. I'm just giving my advice, but if you must do it, of course, I'll help. We are together in this."

"Fine then. In this case, I have to get a couple of things. I must find a hardware store to buy some tools and a computer shop. I need a backup hard drive. Let's go search for those items."

The rest of the day went by quickly. I used my newly acquired tools to produce a few articles which I would later need. It involved cutting, bending, and filing, and I used Fernando's room to do it, away from Livy's attention. By early afternoon, everything was ready for my impending adventure. I returned to my room to rest and eventually invite my wife for dinner. I knew I would have a problem convincing her to let me leave in the evening without bringing her along. I wasn't looking forward to it.

"Why can't I go with you?"

"Because it will be too dangerous. I would have to worry about you the whole time, and it would put us both in danger. I'm sure you wouldn't want that."

"You are not contemplating going to a strip club or a pick-up bar like that disgusting hovel you went to just after we met, are you?"

My wife was recalling a girlie bar in the vicinity of a murder I had been in Brazil. I had just met Livy, but she didn't want me to go and was mad that I went to the place.

"No, I'm not, and if you recall, that was work. I didn't go there for fun. I do not go to places like that, Livy. Don't you trust me?"

"Oh, I trust you, I do. It's the others I don't."

"Who are the others, honey?"

"The other girls. You are too desirable."

"Ah, Livy, this is absurd. You know I love you and have no eyes for any other woman."

"That may well be, but if I smell the faintest whiff of a different perfume when you return, you'll be in trouble, big trouble. You'll prefer contending with a hungry Amazon jaguar next to dealing with me."

"Come, Livy. Don't be jealous. There's no reason for it. It's just work, and I'm not going to any disreputable hovel, as you put it. Really, I don't take you with me because it would be dangerous to you."

"Fine, be very careful, and come back soon. I will not sleep until you return."

"We have time for dinner before I leave. Let's go down and join Fernando."

We took it easy at dinner. I didn't wish to be too early at AR Comércio, before its night routine was in full play. The security staff had to be allowed to settle into their customary tasks before attempting our surreptitious entry. I told Fernando to drive slowly and park the car far from the entry gate, among the trees and hidden from view. We left it and walked the rest of the way, until we arrive at the fence enclosing the building. I parted from Fernando with my bag of tools and surveyed the place, walking stealthily around the fence. Luckily, there were no dogs. I spotted a side entrance, which appeared to be an easy break-in. There were two guards who took turns going around the building. Unfortunately, there wasn't a pattern to their movement that I could discern. Occasionally, one of the guards would leave the entrance box and go on his inspection stroll. I noticed, however, that the tour never lasted more than fifteen minutes. I went back to the place where Fernando was.

"I found a possible way to enter the building. It's on the other side. Let's go there."

He got up and followed me, bringing the tools to a spot in front of the door I had seen.

"This is how we are going to do. First, let's synchronize our watches and place our cell phones vibrate only. Please move to the front and hide where you can see the entrance gate and access road. Call me once every thirty minutes and whenever you see the guard leave the gate to tour the perimeter. When you call, I'll pick up the phone, but don't say anything unless it's the guard going by. In that case, say just one word: guard. This will help me keep track of time and of the guard's position. Obviously, call me also if you see something unusual or unexpected."

"Understood, Alan. Leave it to me."

Fernando went to take his watch at the front. I gave him a few minutes to reach his position and opened the bag to remove a large wire-cutter. Carefully, I cut an L-shaped opening in the wire mesh. Then, I put on gloves and a hood I had fashioned from one of my wife's nylon stockings. I didn't have the time to be on the lookout for security cameras, and I didn't wish to be identified. I squeezed myself through the fence, pulling the bag after me. I bent back the flap of wire mesh trying to disguise the gap in the fence as well as I could. It wasn't a perfect job, but it was one that would remain unnoticed safe in the case of a close inspection. There was no moon, which worked in my favor. I crossed the space between the fence and the side door, running half crouched.

The door was kept closed by a simple padlock. I used the wire-cutter to snap it open and carefully went inside, turning on a flashlight I had brought along, paying attention to point down its beam, so its light could not be detected from the outside. I was inside a high ceiling warehouse full of boxes, bags, and other diverse merchandise. This was not what I was searching for. I decided to take a look around nevertheless but encountered nothing of interest. I was about to turn around and go to the office when I spotted a box with the letters painted on its side: *Castanhas do Pará* (Brazil Nuts). This deserved a closer inspection. I used a crowbar I found lying nearby to open its top cover. The box was empty, but there was something peculiar, which I couldn't quite put my finger on. Then I saw it. The box inside was too shallow. I turned it upside down and used the crowbar again to pry open its bottom. There was a hidden space, disguised under a false bottom. This was important, so I used my cell phone to take a few pictures, knowing Carvalho would love to see this. I didn't know how I could bring this information to him without jeopardizing my position. I had committed a forced entry, a crime under Brazilian law. I would have to think of something, perhaps an anonymous message.

At the front left portion of the warehouse a door provided a connection to the office, which faced the main access to the facility. The door had a Yale-type lock. I had fashioned improvised lock picking tools, using pliers to bend pieces of a strong wire and filing their points. I used those to open the lock. The phone vibrated once. No word. Thirty minutes had passed. I proceeded straight to Rocha's office and found its door closed by another Yale lock.

The phone vibrated again. I heard one word: guard. I entered the office and moved straight to Rocha's desk and to his computer, which I turned on. It required a password, but I was expecting that. I plugged my pen drive in one of the USB sockets and the backup drive in the other. I turned the computer off and on again, booting it first in the safe mode. Then, I rebooted from the pen drive, using the software developed by Judith, our computer expert. I began to back up Rocha's hard drive. Its data was encrypted, but I was hoping Judith would be able to break its code. The phone vibrated a third time: one hour had passed. The back-up operation would take thirty minutes or more, depending on the amount of data and the speed of the computer's processor. In the meantime, I decided to take a look into Rocha's files. I wasn't expecting to find any important information. They were too clever to leave something in writing. Still, since I had to wait for the hard drive to finish copying, I decided to investigate.

The phone rang a fourth time: guard.

As expected, I couldn't find much in Rocha's files. I looked at the documents in the folders, but they all gave the impression of innocent business material. I noticed that a few folders had identifying tabs with unusual proper names such as Efruz, Burak, Kartal, Rizzo … I didn't know their meaning. They sounded like Turkish and Italian names, probably clients of AR Comércio. They had no immediate significance, but I decided to make a note of the names I found.

The phone vibrated once again. "Alan, you have to come out. Someone has arrived, and they are going into the building. You'll be found."

I hung up and turned to the computer. Still two minutes to finish the backup. I had to wait. Felipe phoned me again.

"Alan, what's wrong with you, man? Get the hell out of there. They drove past the gate and are parking their car. They'll be inside in a minute."

I looked at the computer screen. The process was finishing. I waited until it did, yanked my pen drive, and disconnected the hard drive. I didn't bother to shut down the computer, just pulled the power cable from the wall socket and ran back to the door I had used to enter the building. I could hear the front office door being opened. When I came out of the building, one of the guards was passing on his regular tour. He hadn't seen me yet, but he would in seconds, and I would be cornered between him and the party entering by the front door. I took off the hood and gloves, sticking them in a pocket.

"Hey, you there, what do you think you are doing? Come here immediately," I said, speaking loud and imparting the most convincing note of authority I could muster. The guard stopped walking, perplexed by the sudden appearance of a person giving him orders. He hesitated, not quite sure what to do. I quickly walked to him, and before he came to his senses and tried to enact a reaction, I punched him. He fell half-conscious, and I removed the gun from his holster.

"Stay down. Don't shout, or I'll shoot you," I said and ran to the opening in the fence. I heard a shout behind me, but I didn't turn back to look. I passed through and started running. I got my phone out and called Fernando.

"Run to the car. We have to get away in a hurry. We have people after us."

I had dropped the tools, but the hard drive and the pen drive were safe with me. I arrived at our car almost simultaneously with Fernando.

"Let me have the keys, please. I'll drive, Fernando."

I started the car and floored it, watching the rearview mirror to see if we were being followed. I couldn't see the headlights of a car coming after us, and after a while, I began to breathe easier. They didn't pursue us, and we were able to return to our hotel without incident.

CHAPTER 17

A Farewell to Manaus

Tonight's action had almost backfired, but I wasn't putting my faith in results from the federal police search. I was counting on the information Judith could extract from the data copied on the hard drive after I returned to our office in New York. When I left the car to enter the hotel, Fernando stopped me.

"Are you going to walk in with that revolver on your back, Alan?"

Darn, I had forgotten all about it. I should have tossed it on our way back.

"I forgot to throw it away. I'll leave it in the glove compartment, and I'll think of disposing of it tomorrow."

I turned the key to my hotel apartment door and entered as quietly as possible so I wouldn't disturb Livy, but she wasn't sleeping. She was in bed, still awake.

"Alan, is that you?"

"Yes, baby, I'm back."

I went to sit on her side of the bed. "What do you think of going home tomorrow, honey?"

Livy was fully awake now. "Really, Alan? It would be wonderful to go back to see Larissa."

"You can start packing tomorrow morning. I'll see to the available flights." Livy was sitting on the bed, and I put my arms around her. See," I told her, "no perfume."

"True, no perfume, but you smell sweaty. Go take a shower, please."

"Yes, ma'am. Don't go away. I'll be right back."

It was the fastest shower I took in my life.

"How do I smell now, madam, more to your taste?"

"Hmm … yes, you smell very, very good," Livy murmured with her nose buried in my neck. "And I missed you a lot. I'm sorry I've been nasty and gave you a hard time earlier tonight."

"Oh, I think of a way you could redeem yourself."

"What would I have to do for that?"

"Here, let me show you."

"Alan, that tickles."

The next morning found us in a flurry of excited action. We were going home. After breakfast, Olivia was busy packing, and I was tied up on the phone checking for flights, calling my office and my sister, Jessica. I wanted her to beg our brother to send his car to get us at the airport. Jessica was happy to learn of our return but a bit sad she would have to send her niece back to her parents.

"Larissa is such a joy, Alan. She enchants me. I think I'm going to steal her from you."

"Well, sis, you will have to negotiate that with her mother. However, I wouldn't recommend you try. Livy can be a lioness when it comes to her daughter."

"What? What's wrong with Larissa?" Livy wanted to know, having heard the mention of our daughter's name.

"Relax, Livy. Larissa is just fine. I was joking with Jessica—that's all."

"Let me talk to her." She extended her hand to collect the phone from me. "Jessica, hi. Where is Larissa. Is she well? Has she been eating well? How is she feeling? Please, let me talk to her."

Mothers …

Satisfied that our daughter was well and after exchanging a couple of inane words with Larissa, my wife returned the phone to me and continued with her packing. Interesting—I didn't recall her bringing so much luggage when we left New York.

"That's strange."

"What's strange, Livy?"

"I cannot find one of my stockings. I see only one pair. The other is missing."

"Perhaps you had packed just one pair when you left home."

"No, I used them in Colca. It was cold, and I put them on. I can't believe a hotel maid has taken just one pair. If someone wanted them, they would have taken both. It doesn't make sense. What a nuisance. I'll have to recheck among the things I've packed. Perhaps the missing pair went unnoticed with something else."

"Don't bother, Livy. Forget it. We'll buy new stockings when we get home."

My wife was still shaking her head, puzzled by the mystery of her vanishing stockings. Should I tell her what I had done? Best not; I didn't think she would take it lightly, and I would have to provide too many explanations. If Livy learned of my exploits the previous night, I would have received a long lecture about how foolhardy I had been and reminding me I had a daughter and a family to care for. No, definitely not. I was finally able to secure two business seats for us on a late evening flight. We would have to stop and change flights in Miami, which was not convenient but better than staying another day in Manaus. Besides, I was eager to bring the hard drive to Judith's expert care.

"Livy, I have to go meet Fernando. Then I must go and say goodbye to inspectors Carvalho and Felipe and thank them for their help. Also, I have to return my rental car. I'll order a hotel limo to take us to the airport. I should be back around two."

"I'll wait for you, honey. I'll keep busy with the packing, and I might go out to get a few things I have forgotten to buy."

I rolled my eyes. Buy more stuff, honestly?

I met Fernando in the lobby, and we left the hotel to go to the federal police. I told him of our impending departure plans, and we discussed his disengagement from the job. I still needed him to keep a connection with the Manaus Federal Police and to warn me of any development concerning our case. Carvalho had promised to contact me as soon as he had news, but I felt the professional relationship between former colleagues would make it easier for Fernando to keep track of things. I suggested that Fernando stay a day or two more in Manaus before returning to Rio, if possible, until the warrant was granted and the police had the search results. I would leave instructions at our hotel to charge his expenses to my credit card. I offered to leave some cash with him to cover his needs during the extra days, but he declined, saying he would charge our office after returning to Rio.

Our meeting at the federal police was short. Apart from the usual pleasantries—"Please, look us up if ever in New York." "We remain at your disposal and are happy we could assist you")—it was just a question of thanking them and saying our goodbyes. I had taken care of all my obligations. I was looking forward to enjoying a peaceful time with Livy before the hassle of the airport and our voyage.

I stopped the car in a traffic light. I had been having an idle talk with Fernando, reminiscing of events from this and the previous case we had worked together. Casually, I looked out of the window to my left. A motorbike with two riders was pulling by. The rear man was taking a long object from under his coat. My reaction was instinctive. I stepped down hard on the throttle, and we shot through the red light. Cars screeched as they tried to avoid a collision. Horns blared, followed by curses from angry drivers. I didn't care. The biker caught up and fired at us. I felt the impact of bullets on the car's body: *thwack, thwack, thunk*. The bullets hit the rear window, and the glass shattered. Strangely, the firing was not accompanied by a loud noise. It was more like violent and very rapid coughing. They must be using an automatic gun with a silencer.

We had gained a small distance from the bike, which apparently had some trouble negotiating the traffic light. They were still coming after us, and I had no illusions. It would be impossible to shake a motorbike with the small, underpowered car I was driving, especially in an urban environment. Then, I remembered the gun I had forgotten to dispose of.

"Fernando, get the gun in the glove compartment and shoot back at them."

Fernando leaned out his window and shot twice at our assailants. This did not dissuade them, but it did slow them down, gaining us a few precious seconds. I turned into the oncoming traffic of an intersecting street, still hoping to lose the bike, swerving to avoid a few near head-on collisions. It was a mistake. In my rearview mirror, I saw the bike using the sidewalk to gain on us. They shot at us again. I felt a bullet whistling by my head. It wouldn't take long for either Fernando or me to get hit and probably killed by one of those bullets. Fernando kept shooting back, but we were clearly under-gunned. Besides, his gun would soon be empty. If we wished to escape, I had to do something desperate. I did a Scandinavian flick to turn into a side street, without losing too much of our short lead on the bike. Immediately after taking the corner, I applied a hand-break-turn maneuver, which sent the car spinning in the opposite direction of its original trajectory. When the bike came barging through the corner, I was facing in their direction. I floored the throttle to ram them.

The bike's driver was startled by my unexpected action. He did a high-speed turn to avoid me, practically spinning in place. The shooter in the back of the bike was caught unaware by the sudden turn. He lost his grip and was tossed from the bike. It was too late to stop. I ran him over. I felt the awful bump as I passed over the body. The motorcyclist didn't stop and gave up chasing us, running away. I drove on a few meters. I could see in my rearview mirror the bloodied, broken body of the man I had just run down. It was over. I lowered my head and remained still for a few seconds to control my nerves. This time, we had escaped by a hair's breadth.

I could hear the sirens of police cars approaching, and I got out of the car. Fernando was cleaning the gun he had used. He went to the fallen shooter and stuck the gun in his belt—a clever way to dispose of it. With luck, the gun could be registered as the property of AR Comércio. I hadn't thought of it. I went to take a closer look. The weapon used by the shooter was lying a few feet away from him. It was a .45 caliber AR automatic gun with a suppressor, not very accurate but deadly at close range.

"Give me the keys, Alan."

"Why, Fernando? Why do you need them?"

"Look, if they ask, I was the one driving, and I ran over that man."

"I can't let you take the rap. It wouldn't be fair."

"Alan, if you are identified as the responsible person, you'll be forced to remain in Manaus for weeks until all formalities are cleared. With me, it will be different. I'm a policeman who killed a murderer in self-defense. That's what we are supposed to do, kill bad guys. The formalities will be much reduced in my case. Besides, I'm Brazilian, and I'm not leaving the country, as you are about to do. Believe me, it's the best thing to do. Don't worry. I won't have to face any rap, as you were saying."

I could see the logic in Fernando's decision, and I had no intention of being detained in this city.

"Thank you very much, Fernando. I'll owe you this one."

A patrol car had arrived, and the officers were coming in our direction, guns drawn.

"Calm down, officers. Federal police," Fernando, said showing his badge. The two officers holstered their guns and came to talk to us.

"What happened here?"

"Two men on a motorbike tried to kill us. We ran away trying to escape, but they gave chase. I managed to surprise them around this corner. The bike driver escaped, but the shooter, who is lying dead, fell from the bike, and I accidentally ran him over."

Our car was in a horrible state, full or bullet perforations, broken windows, and at least one flat tire. It was going to be hell to explain this when I returned it. I hope they had insurance to cover that sort of damage. Would they believe if I claimed an attack of vicious Amazon termites? I didn't think they would buy it.

"Why were they trying to kill you?" one of the officers asked.

"I'm afraid I can't tell you the reason," Fernando answered, Federal Police business. Please call Inspector Antonio Carvalho at FP. Here is his phone number."

"I'll do it, but you should come with us to the police station. This car is evidence. It can't be moved before forensics arrive and clear it. I'll ask this Antonio Carvalho to meet you at the station."

We accompanied the officers to the police precinct, where we had to repeat our story—or, rather, Fernando had to repeat it. Half an hour later, Carvalho joined us.

"Mr. Leary, it appears you have an ability to attract people trying to kill you. How did you escape this attempt?"

"Actually, Fernando is responsible for that. He managed to neutralize the killers all by himself."

Carvalho looked at me and at Fernando. "Why don't I believe that? No offense meant, Fernando."

"None taken." Fernando smiled.

"Hmm, I'm becoming an admirer of your abilities, Mr. Leary. One day, you shall have to tell me how you *did not* defeat the bad guys this time."

It was my turn to smile. "I'll be glad to, Inspector. One day."

"Well, let's clear this mess to free you both. You have a plane to catch later tonight. I fear you will have a little more bureaucracy to contend with, Fernando. I'll try to keep that at a minimum. Let's go back to my office. Incidentally, I have good news. The search warrant was conceded. I received it only minutes after you left my office. We'll be paying a visit to AR Comércio later today."

"That's indeed good news, Inspector."

At least one good news, although of limited practical value at this point.

"I'll inform Fernando all the results we get from the search. I hope we can find something useful to your case, Mr. Leary."

One can never be too hopeful. Let's see what the police came up with.

Carvalho did not keep us too long in his office. We had just to clear a few formalities. He even helped me with my car. He phoned the rental company to inform of the incident and to tell them that the car would have to be retained as evidence. We said goodbye again, after which I could go back to my hotel, where, as I feared, Livy wasn't happy with my tardiness.

"What took you so long, Alan? I'm famished. You said two, and it's already past four in the afternoon."

"I'm sorry, baby. I had car problems. I'll make it up for you. You can have two caipirinhas."

"It's not funny, Alan. Let's go eat. I have packed everything, and I'm ready."

"Great, let's go."

Fernando came to the airport to wish us a safe return and to say farewell. After a quick pass through immigration, customs, and security checks, we boarded our plane. We were finally going home. I could hardly believe it. I settled myself in my seat, prepared to rest during the six-hour flight ahead of us.

"Olivia, no mile-high monkey business tonight, please! I really do need to rest."

"Hmm, fine. Spoilsport."

PART 2

Intermezzo

While he spoke we scoured along the dazzling
plain, now nearly bare of trees,
and turning softly under foot. Then the sand
increased and the stones grew rarer, till we
could distinguish the colour of separate
flakes, porphyry, green schist, basalt. At last
it was nearly pure white sand, under which
lay a harder spectrum

— T. E. Lawrence, "The Seven Pillars of Wisdom"

CHAPTER 18

The Trek

The first two days of his long trek from Colca to Cusco passed without problems. The land was mostly flat, with lots of grass for the llamas and small creeks to replenish his water supply. His only misgiving was the possibility of being detected by other travelers—you could see things a long distance away in this landscape of unimpaired vision—or by air, which was his biggest fear. He didn't expect a fast reaction from the authorities, but he knew nevertheless that an overland flight would spot him easily. He debated resting by day and traveling by night but gave up the idea. He couldn't risk even a small fall or stepping into a ditch or hole. A broken leg or a strained ankle would seriously impair or force him to abort his trip. No, he would have to move by daylight. Fortunately, his fears of detection did not materialize; he saw no other traveler, and there were no overflights. His only serious problems in those two days were the altitude, to which he had yet fully adjusted, and the cold during the night. He had brought along a supply of green coca leaves and some altitude tablets. Still, he had felt the effects and had to cope with them in the initial days. During the night, he had to prepare a roofless shelter with stones, open on one side, to protect him from the wind. The stones reflected the heat from the small fire he was forced to make. Without it, he would have certainly died. The fire also kept away the undesirable snakes and scorpions. The cold was difficult to support. He was wearing the killed Indian's garb, which was warm but did not compare with a good down coat.

On the evening of the second day, he arrived at his first serious land obstacle, the Garganta de Supay. This was a deep, narrow chasm at the limit of the plateau he had been crossing and the foothills of the mountains barring his way to Cusco with their formidable height. The Garganta stretched for miles along an almost straight line in front of the mountains. It would take days to go around it, and it was too deep and its walls too steep to negotiate without climbing equipment. Besides, he could never go down one wall and climb back the other pulling two llamas. The other llamas, the ones not carrying his load, he intended to let loose on this side. They were stupid animals and did not return to their original place. With the grass and water available, they would probably just stay in the area at least until a mountain lion caught them.

He knew there was a pass over the chasm, a natural stone bridge straddling the two sides of the precipice. Once, in the time of the Sendero Luminoso, they had used it to evade pursuit by the Peruvian Guardia Nacional. But, he had only a vague recollection of its exact location, which he thought to be near the middle of the chasm length. The problem was, he didn't know where it was relative to his position. He had a compass and a small GPS to guide him. They were useless in this case. He had no idea of the bridge coordinates.

He tossed a coin. If heads, he would walk north. If tails, he would go south. Heads. He went north. His luck held. He found the bridge after a few kilometers. It was a ways across, but it was no easy pass for the faint-hearted or the unsure of foot. The bridge couldn't have been more than twenty inches wide, and its surface was irregular with, differently shaped stones. It extended for a good thirty yards, and on both sides, there was nothing but a precipitous drop. Llamas are surefooted beasts, as their natural habitats are the crags and mountain trails. He tied his leading llama to the one trailing and pushed it to the bridge. He went after them, holding to the tail of the animal in front of him. He didn't look to the sides but kept his eyes on the rear legs of the llama, carefully watching where they stepped. He lowered his head and breathed deeply a couple of times after they got through. Yes, it was quite an experience. It had been terrible the first time he did it years ago, and it was as bad or worse now. He had no intention of doing it a third time.

For the next three days, he wandered in the mountains, following trails, climbing, sometimes being forced to double back when progress became impossible due to an insurmountable peak or impassable gorge, but always moving toward his final destination. He should have remembered to add sunblock to the items he was carrying. The unrelenting radiation, free from clouds under a bright blue sky and not abated by a thick atmosphere, was exerting a terrible effect. He had covered his face, leaving only a narrow slit for his eyes, and he wrapped his hands with rags torn from his shirt, trying to protect himself as much as possible. Nevertheless, he had developed severe and painful sunburns, which he tried to treat by applying cooking fat to no great avail.

There wasn't much for the llamas to eat, and whenever he found a patch of hardy high-altitude grass that had resisted the inclement weather by taking advantage of a protected gulch, he had to stop to allow the two llamas to graze on the non-nourishing vegetation. Water was also rare, and he had to share the little he had with the llamas. There were no creeks or fountains, only snow that had to be heated to produce a few cups of water.

Three days after having crossed La Garganta de Supay and five from leaving the Colca campsite, he emerged from the mountains and was presented with the view of Cusco and of the lower hills before it. He was exhausted and several pounds thinner, with blisters on his feet, but he was alive, and his llamas had also survived with their precious loads. He had covered more than 250 miles over one of the most rugged terrains on this earth. He decided to camp and rest before his final walk to Cusco.

The next morning, he started his descent and soon was joined by an increasing human procession of local inhabitants, taking their wares to Cusco for sale and trade. His skin had become so dark from exposure to the sun that only his height denounced him as a stranger to this group, which he tried to disguise by walking slightly curved. He arrived at the city's outskirts in the early afternoon. He had to find a place to rest and to clean himself. He couldn't go to a regular hotel. He would never be accepted as a guest under these conditions. He had to find a hostel catering to the local natives. He followed the people entering the city and soon spied a prospective place, a house bearing a sign saying, "Posada Puno." When he arrived, he found a young boy sitting by the door.

"*Joven, llama a tus padres. Quiero permanecer en tu albergue.* (Boy, go call your parents. I wish to be a guest of your hostel.)"

The boy went inside, and a couple came out in a short while to talk to him. After some haggling, which resulted in having to pay double the usual price, he managed to secure a room. He said he would stay with them for at least two days, and after hauling his luggage into the room, he asked if they could sell his llamas, which they agreed to do. He gave them additional money to buy three suitcases, some clothing, and basic toilet items, such as a shaving razor and cream, soap, a new comb, and a toothbrush.

The room they gave him was very small, with a window opening to an interior patio. The bathroom was outside, at the end of a corridor. The first thing he did after receiving the items he had asked for was to shower and shave. Then he asked for something to eat and drink, told them to dispose of his old clothing, and collapsed on the narrow bed provided in the room. He slept for more than sixteen hours, woke up, ate some more, and went right back to sleep. The next day, he had to exchange the dollars and soles he had with him into Brazilian reais. He used one of his fake IDs, establishing him as a Brazilian citizen, Feliciano Silva. After his second night at the hostel, he felt sufficiently rested to continue his journey. He rented an economy car for a whole week and left Cusco for good. His next destination would be Porto Velho on the Madeira River, in Brazil.

CHAPTER 19

From the Mountains to the Jungle

Before leaving Cusco, he still had to take care of a few things: first, he had to buy clothing, enough to fill his three suitcases. Second, he had to procure a thin metal handsaw. Lastly, he needed a few cans of spray paint—dull gray. These tasks consumed a good portion of the morning, and it was close to eleven before he finally drove out of the city. As usual, the weather was fine, but at this season and hour, he couldn't count too much daylight time. He had to find a place to stay for the night. He stopped at a *gasolinera,* not because he needed fuel for the car but to inquire about possible lodging. He needed to find an overnight location with a closed parking space for the car, a space secluded from curious eyes where he could work on the gold artifacts. He was directed to a family who used to have a truck and still had an empty garage for it, with rooms on the second floor. It was perfect, and after some negotiation, he rented the place with all the rooms. He didn't want to share it in the unlikely event another voyager showed up looking for shelter. He drove his car in the garage and shut its doors. The upstairs rooms were modest but would do for the night. The car space, however, was perfect for his needs. He unwrapped the gold staff from its bindings and used the metal saw he had procured in Cusco to cut it into three pieces of approximately the same length. He was disgusted by the damage he was causing, a true sacrilege, but there was no other way he would be able to place its original long shape hidden among the clothing in the suitcases. After he delivered the pieces to his dealer, it would have to be professionally restored.

Next, he used the spray cans to apply a coat of grey paint over each one of the gold pieces he had brought along. It was a fast-drying paint, and he let it set for some time. After he finished, he observed the overall result and was satisfied with his work. He tested for the adherence of the coating layer. It wouldn't peel off easily. It would need to be removed with a paint solvent. He got the clothes he had bought to accommodate the pieces in the suitcases, making sure they were well packed and wouldn't shift. Having completed his work, he still had a few hours to rest until morning.

He woke up early to continue his trip before daybreak. He had roughly four hundred miles to reach the Brazilian border. Nearly a third of this distance would be going down from the Cusco height, almost eleven thousand feet, to the average Amazon basin level of less than three hundred feet. The mountain road was narrow and full of sharp curves where the safe driving speeds could rarely be kept above forty miles per hour. If he didn't stop, except for refueling, he expected to arrive at the Brazilian border city of Assis Brasil during the late afternoon or early evening. He wanted to cross the border during usual working hours. Those would be his best chances of avoiding problems, especially if there were other cars going across, besides his own.

The mountain portion of the road required his driving attention as he drove, but the scenery was beautiful, with the majestic Andes' snow-covered peaks and craggy mountains. This scenery passed quickly, seeming to last shorter than expected. The flat portion of the trip was another story. It was dull and demanded a great effort from him not to fall asleep. At the town of Puerto Maldonado, he reached the Madeira River, which, at that point, is called Madre de Dios. A new bridge was being constructed, but crossing the river was still done by an old barge. This gave him the opportunity to rest from driving, and while waiting for his turn to board the barge, he drank strong unsugared coffee to keep him awake, which was sold by street vendors out of large thermoses carried by handcarts. He had made good time until that point, and only one hundred and forty miles separated him from the border—another three and a half hours of driving. He should arrive at Assis Brasil around five in the afternoon, just as he had planned.

He reached Inapari on the Peruvian side of the Acre River, which marked the border between the two countries, at twenty past five in the afternoon. First, he had to register the departure of his car from the

Peruvian side, a procedure that was handled by a few lady attendants in the customs office of that country. There, he experienced his first problem.

"I see that your car was rented in Cusco, Mr. Silva."

"Correct. I'm going to meet my wife, who is in the Brazilian town Epitaciolandia with her very sick mother. I'm bringing her some clothes and personal belongings. Her mother is terminally ill, and my wife will have to stay with her longer than she expected. I'll have to return to Cusco on the day after tomorrow. I cannot stay away from my job too long."

"What do you do for a living, Mr. Silva?"

"I am a mining engineer. I work for an American company in Peru, Horizon Mining."

"I see. But you need a special permit from the rental car company to cross the border with their car."

"Oh! They didn't tell me anything. How could they be so irresponsible? I'm going to give them hell after I go back."

"I'm afraid you won't be able to cross the border with your car, Mr. Silva."

"What? That can't be. My wife needs the items I'm bringing. It will be terrible if I'm forced to return without giving the things to her. They are also for her mother. Those stupid car rental people. I don't believe you will let my wife and me suffer the consequences of their mistake. Please, don't do it."

"Well, I could phone them and ask if they authorize you to drive their car to Brazil."

"Please do that. I would be very grateful if you did."

She told him to wait and left to call the company in Cusco. She returned after a few minutes.

"Unfortunately, nobody answers the phone in Cusco. I wasn't able to reach anyone. You shall have to come back tomorrow for us to try again."

"Ah, miss, please, don't ask me to do that. I have been driving for more than twelve hours without rest. I want to get home and to my wife. You know this is just a formality. Don't let me lose another eight or ten hours before I get home."

While he talked, he placed two fifty-soles bills inside the folded car release document and pushed it in her direction. She looked at him for a few seconds, debating how to respond, and finally decided to accept his bribe. She took the form, removed the money, stamped the document, and returned it to him without saying a word. He thanked her and left to return to his car.

The next test was at the Brazilian customs. He stopped the car, turned the ignition off, and gave the car release form and his Brazilian ID to the customs officer.

"Welcome home, Mr. Feliciano. Do you have any items to declare?"

"No officer, I have nothing to declare. I only have personal belongings."

"Very well, please, open your hood and trunk, Mr. Silva."

A uniformed guard approached his car. He had a dog on a leash to sniff the car and its luggage for drugs. He was asked to step out and was also submitted to the dog's scent.

"Could you open your suitcases, Mr. Silva?"

He complied and the customs officer searched the top suitcase. He removed one of the gold pieces, a cup covered by the grey metallic paint.

"What is this?" he inquired.

"It's a metal cup, a reproduction on an Inca artifact," he said innocently.

"It's heavy."

"Yes, it is. It's a pewter alloy with tin and lead. I collect these items."

"I see. Anyway, I must check these pieces. It's unusual to see artifacts like these coming through customs."

"How are you going to do that, Inspector? It's late. You will have to wait until tomorrow to find someone able to do the checking. Please, don't keep me here for nothing. I must meet my wife at Epitaciolandia tonight. My mother-in-law is terminally ill. I must be there if she passes away."

"I sympathize with your plight, Mr. Silva, but there is little I can do. Even if I accepted your claim that the objects are made of a pewter alloy, the problem of applying and collecting the appropriate custom taxes would remain."

"It is important to me to reach my wife as soon as possible. I would be willing to risk overpaying the due taxes. I could leave money with you, begging for your understanding and generosity. Could you, please, pay the taxes, tomorrow, when the customs office opens?" He extended to the policeman a wad of bills totaling two thousand reais. He could see his initial reluctance being overcome by greed.

He picked the money and closed the suitcase. "You may go, Mr. Silva. I wish you a good remaining portion of your voyage."

He thanked him, closed the trunk, went back to the driver's seat, turned the car motor on, and left customs. He breathed a sigh of relief. He had made it up to now. The total road distance from Assis Brasil to Porto Velho is 486 miles. After crossing the border, it was still early, not quite yet seven in the evening. He decided to push until Epitaciolandia, seventy miles away, to stop for the night.

He proceeded early the next day to Porto Velho. He was told to take extra fuel gallon with him as he could find the few gas stations on his way inoperative. It was wise advice. There was practically nothing between the two towns. If the route from the foot of the Peruvian mountains to the border had been dull, the road from Epitaciolandia to Porto Velho was indescribably boring. Where previously there had been forests, now there was nothing but devastated land, cleared of its original vegetation to open space for extensive cattle rising. Luckily, he had found a reasonable hotel and had been able to rest the previous evening. He covered the remaining four hundred miles in roughly eight hours, and by three in the afternoon, he sighted the Madeira River. He had arrived in Porto Velho.

He drove into the downtown area of the city and waved to the first taxi that he saw in the traffic. He asked him by signs to pull over and stop. He parked his car behind the taxi and went talk to the driver.

"Hi, do you know where the riverboats depart to Manaus?"

"Yes, friend," he answered. "That would be the Cai n'Água port."

"Can you take me there?"

"Certainly. Hop in."

"Just a minute. I have to bring over my luggage."

"I'll wait, but you shouldn't leave your car there. You'll be fined."

"Oh, I'll come back to move it later."

The driver raised his shoulders to demonstrate his lack of concern, and he went to get his suitcases. He placed his car keys inside the glove compartment and shut the car doors.

"Okay, I'm ready. Let's go."

The port didn't deserve to be called as such. Its colorful name, which, in Portuguese, means "Fall in the water," is indicative of its true nature. It's just a high and steeply-graded margin to which the boats are tied. He could imagine that, when wet, it would be easy to slip trying to descend it and actually falling into the water. He told the driver to stop at a spot near, where he could see two boats tied below.

"Do you know where one can get tickets for those boats?" he asked.

"I believe you have to inquire in the boats."

"Wait for me here, then. I am going down to ask. I'll pay you when I come back." He left before the driver could protest and went to the boat nearest to him. Embarkation was made possible by a long, flat piece of timber placed from the margin to the boat, doing the job of a gangplank. A man was on the boat near the embarkation door.

"I'm looking for transportation to Manaus," he shouted.

"This boat is stopping in Santarem," he answered me. "The boat docked ahead is traveling to Manaus."

He thanked him and moved on to repeat the procedure with the next boat.

"Hey, there. I wish to take passage to Manaus."

"Right, we are sailing there," he was answered. "How do you wish to travel, on the common deck or in a cabin?"

"A cabin, please."

"It costs three hundred reais for double occupancy and four hundred for single."

"I'll take the single, please."

"Fine, but the boat is undergoing minor repairs, and we won't sail before two days. You can pay now, but you shall have to come back in forty-eight hours to embark."

"Couldn't I just wait for departure on board?" he asked.

"It would cost you another hundred."

"That's perfectly fine with me."

"Well then, you can bring your things and move in. Payment is in advance, in cash."

"That's fine also. I'll return with my luggage."

He went back to his taxi and, with the driver's help, brought his suitcases to the boat. He paid his boat fare to the person who had negotiated with him and who happened to be the boat's master. He showed him to his cabin, a tiny room with two bunks, a toilet, and a shower. After bringing in the suitcases, there was practically no space left. The cabin was kept from being intolerably claustrophobic by a small window to the outside. This would be his home for the next week, at least. But he was on his way to what would be, hopefully, his last leg in Brazil.

CHAPTER 20

The Boat Voyage

The boat started sailing from Porto Velho after a delay of three days. He was already becoming very impatient, having to remain restricted to his minuscule cabin to keep a permanent eye on the gold. Finally, on the morning of the third day, they cast off, sailing to Manaus. The number of passengers had multiplied during the last days. He was impressed and a little alarmed to see how many people were aboard. The majority of passengers were accommodated on the open deck, where they strung their hammocks and had their meals. Surprisingly, they were not a noisy bunch. In the evenings, there was always some music provided by a lone guitar or mouth organ.

He kept to himself and refrained from mingling with the others, taking his meals in the cabin. He had befriended a cabin boy, João. He always tipped him to serve him, and he was always solicitous in bringing him the best dishes and saving him a cold beer and hot coffee. He usually left the cabin for a few minutes in the morning and in the afternoon. There were a few old books found in the mess room, which had belonged to former passengers. João brought him a few, and he used his moments outside to exercise and to read, sitting in a portion of the open deck, which faced the access corridor to the cabins. This assured him that no one tried to enter his cabin. Sometimes, he asked João to serve him a gin and tonic or a whiskey. The alcoholic beverages had to be paid separately, obviously, and he always paid João, adding a generous tip to the check. The voyage became more endurable, and for the first time in weeks, he was able to unwind and put behind him the physical and emotional stress of the last few days. After his grueling crossing of the Andes, the tension at the border, and the uncertainty of being discovered before the boat's departure, he could finally give himself the pleasure of relaxing a bit. He was especially fond of watching the sunsets, which were beautiful in this region. Also, from time to time, he could see flocks of birds flying over the boat—noisy parrots, colorful macaws, strange massive-beaked toucans, and long-necked flamingos. This was the extent of the wildlife that could be observed. He saw no alligators or four-legged beasts such as tapirs and capybaras. Usually, they sailed too far away from the forest covering the river margins, which spoiled any chance of spotting monkeys. It was curious that wildlife could be seen a lot easier in temperate forests and fields rather than in a tropical jungle, where they remained hidden from the eyes. But calm and peace were conditions he could never take for granted.

The boat made two short stops on its way, to load and unload cargo and people, first at the port of Humaita and then at Manicore, both small villages along the Madeira River.

On the eve of their arrival in Manaus, João came looking for him.

"I overheard these two guys discussing their intention to rob and kill you. They must have seen, or someone told them, that you embarked with three suitcases. They must think you are bringing lots of things, valuable stuff. Those guys are very mean. They voyage in the boats only to rob the women, the old, and the weak. Nobody complains because all are afraid of them. They have killed other people before. I came to warn you."

"Thanks, João. I owe you this one, and I won't forget."

That was indeed very bad news. Obviously, he had to defend himself, but if he killed those two, this will create complications. He would have to give explanations to the Manaus police, and he neither wished for nor could afford that. He still had his knife and an old rusty revolver he had found in the Colca campsite. But the gun would make too much noise, and the knife would leave a lot of blood.

"I need to ask you another favor, João. Do you know these meat skewers the cooks use to make barbecue?"

João nodded.

"I need you to steal one of those from the kitchen and bring it to me. Do you think you could do that for me?"

"Yes, I'll do it, Mr. Silva."

"You are a good boy, João. Like I said, I'll owe you big."

João left and returned a few minutes later with a tool used to pierce meat, to insert stuffing and seasoning. It was in the shape of a pointed rod, maybe fifteen inches long and with a handle at one end.

"This is perfect, João. It's even better than what I had in mind. Do you think you'll get in trouble if you do not return it?"

"I don't recon I will, Mr. Silva. I don't expect they will notice if it goes missing."

"Anyway, João, here, take this money. You can buy a new one if they complain."

"Thank you, Mr. Silva."

"Ah, João, this is between you and me. Don't mention it to anybody else. Okay?"

"I won't tell anyone else. I don't like those guys. I hope you take care of them."

He prepared himself for the undesired visit during the night. He sat on his bunk and set his weapons at hand. He knew they would wait to make sure all passengers and most of the crew were sleeping before making their move. He had to stay awake.

He turned the lights of his cabin off. Sitting in the dark, he waited for the sounds and noises of the boat to subside. After a time, the music and voices coming from the deck below ceased. Complete silence was broken only by the water passing under the hull and the occasional cry of a nocturnal bird. They came around eleven. He heard their muffled steps approaching his door. They were not too careful. There was the low tinkle of small metal parts. Then, he heard the noise of his door lock being tampered with. He got up silently. Went to the door. The intruder would use a tool to force the door bolt. That was the jingle he had caught seconds before. They would put pressure on the door to make it give in. He sensed for the exact moment the lock would break, and then, suddenly, he opened the door. The thief lost his balance, stumbling into the cabin. He hit him on the side of the head with the revolver. The man dropped inside, unconscious. He slipped sideways past him and went for his companion, standing on the corridor, a few steps away. The second man had a knife, which he tried to use. He parried his thrust, then stuck the meat-piercing tool under the man's ribs, forcing it upwards into his lungs. The assailant let his knife drop from the shock and the pain. He used his weight to push and pin his attacker against the wall. He placed a hand over the fellow's mouth, the palm pressing firmly on his lips and using two fingers to pinch his nose. The thief was mortally wounded and quickly losing strength. His lungs were being inundated by his own blood; he would drown in it in less than a minute. He held him for an instant longer and then allowed his body to slide gently to the floor. He left the meat-piercing rod in his chest. There was very little external bleeding and spillage. The hemorrhage was internal. He went back to the other fellow lying on the floor of his cabin. He had hit his head very hard, but he was still breathing. He grabbed the man from the back, his legs wrapped around the man's waist and his arm around his neck in a stranglehold. He held him like that for a few minutes. The man trashed near the end, but he held firmly and killed him. It was finished. The whole action had not lasted more than five minutes and in almost total silence. He waited a few minutes longer to regain his strength and dragged the bodies, one at a time, and tossed them overboard. He waited to see if the splashes of the bodies hitting the water had been noticed over the boat's engine noise. He heard nothing. The bodies would eventually come up if they didn't get snagged in the river bottom, but even if they surfaced, they would be rendered unrecognizable after being dealt with by piranhas and alligators. Besides, by then, he expected to be very far away.

CHAPTER 21

Shipping Out

He had made it to Manaus. He had a local contact provided by the art dealer, who would arrange for the archeological pieces to be shipped to Europe without calling the attention of the authorities. He had his address and phone number. Immediately after disembarking, he decided to pay him a visit. He got one of the taxis waiting by the port, and after loading his luggage, he gave the driver the AR Comércio address and told him to take him there. He was expected. As soon as he arrived, his luggage was unloaded, and he was conducted to Mr. Antonio Rocha owner and general manager of AR Comércio.

"Mr. Feliciano Silva—I believe this is the alias you are presently using—you are welcome. I have taken the required measures to ship your goods to our mutual friend in Europe. May I see the pieces?"

"No problem. They are in my suitcases."

"Just a minute." Rocha proceeded to call his secretary. "Please, have Mr. Silva's luggage brought to the back room."

He followed Rocha to a room in the back of the office. His three suitcases had been placed on the ground. He opened them and carefully started removing the items.

"A very clever idea to have them painted," Rocha said. "I suppose the paint can be easily removed."

"Definitely. Any paint solvent will do the job."

"In this case, let me show you how they will be shipped."

He followed Rocha again to a warehouse adjacent to the office building.

We stopped in front of some wood boxes marked on the sides with the words "*Castanhas do Pará* (Brazil Nuts)."

"The pieces will go in the bottom of the boxes, held in place by wire mesh and covered by the nuts. Initially, I had thought of a false bottom, but I abandoned that idea. It's too easy to detect the double bottom. I still have one or two of those boxes lying around, but I'll not use them. The wire mesh is a simpler and more elegant solution. And it's harder to detect. If someone starts probing for the bottom with a testing rod, he would have to hit exactly on top of one of the pieces to notice anything. Even in that case, a detected lump could be attributed to a bunch of nuts sticking together due to humidity."

"Yes, it is clever," he conceded.

"I'll have them embarked tomorrow. Today is too late." AR had the required contacts at the port. They would turn a blind eye on the loading thanks to a customary small monetary contribution.

"We must wait for the right work shift tomorrow. We will be embarking twice as many boxes as declared in the bill of lading. Half the boxes will leave Manaus to be unloaded at Curacao. At that port, the captain will receive a new set of documents for the remaining boxes, still on board, listing Genoa as their final destination."

"I see. So, for all purposes, the vessel will appear to be transporting a certain number of Brazil nut boxes to Curacao. Here in Manaus, there will be no indication of another destination. But, for the Italian port authorities, the new set of documents, switched at Curacao, will show boxes loaded in Manaus and shipped to Genoa."

"Precisely. We control things here in Manaus. They will test the cargo with dogs to make sure we are not shipping drugs. That's really the only crime not allowed by customs. They don't care about the rest. It is a free port, after all."

"How will the matter be handled in Genoa? What happens there?"

"That's under the responsibility of our Italian friends. It's their job to see that the cargo clears customs without any problems."

"How am I traveling? I'm supposed to accompany the artifacts."

"And you will. I have a new set of documents identifying you as one of the ship's crew."

"Can I embark tomorrow, as well?"

"If you wish. The ship is taking other cargo. It may take an extra day or two before it sails. You would be more comfortable in a hotel. Don't you need anything—a girl, perhaps?"

"No thanks. I'll embark tomorrow."

"Suit yourself. Would you like to go to a hotel tonight?"

"Could I sleep here somewhere?"

"That can be arranged."

The next day, with the gold pieces safely stored aboard and with him comfortably installed in the ship owner's cabin, the final leg of his adventure was about to commence. He would sail to Italy, where a new life was waiting for him. He could hardly believe that his adventure was coming to a conclusion.

PART 3

CONCLUSION

What had that flower to do with being white,
The wayside blue and innocent heal-all?
What brought the kindred spider to that height,
Then steered the white moth thither in the night?
What but design of darkness to appal?
If design govern in a thing so small.

—Robert Frost, "Design"

CHAPTER 22

Back in Manhattan

I was home, finally. It had been a very tiring trip, hopping from place to place and almost never staying longer than a day or two at any location, being exposed to high altitude, attacked by thugs, and shot at twice. All this would have been acceptable if not for the failure in achieving the purpose of my quest. We had been hired to elucidate the disappearance of John Engelhard and to prove his innocence. The evidence collected seemed to point just the opposite—that John had committed murders and robbed the Inca gold artifacts. I had a meeting in my office this morning, with my partner, Tony, and our client, Anton Deville. I wasn't hoping for a warm reaction from the latter. Most probably, he would sever our contract.

My wife was coming with me. After the meeting, we were taking the train to White Plains. We had been invited to a barbecue at the home of one of my former SEAL comrades. Ian McDowell had been wounded in action during the first Gulf War and was confined to a wheelchair. This had not abated his spirits, however. He had remade his life and now worked from home as an artwork restorer. He was inviting other friends from the service and their wives. I had some doubts to bring Livy. This crowd was so different from her. Livy had been living in New York for the last two years, and she had adapted extremely well. Still, my friends were a boisterous and irreverent bunch, from a culture so different from hers. I mentioned this to her.

"So what's the problem, Alan? I understand. It's a boys' get together. Go. I'll stay with Larissa. I might visit your sister."

"Well, Livy, in fact, I would like you to come."

"I don't follow you, Alan. You wish me to go to your barbecue, but you give me arguments against it."

"No, no, it's not like that. It's more complicated."

"Kindly explain. I'll make an effort to keep up," Livy said sarcastically.

"This is really embarrassing. I would love to show you off, you know? Kill those guys of envy with my beautiful, gorgeous, and sophisticated wife."

"Well, I'm game for that, and thanks for the praise. You are biased, of course, but it still feels good to have your husband think that of you."

"They may joke with you. As I said, they are irreverent but not unkind. They won't treat you badly or give you a tough time."

I expected that my friends would definitely try to tease Olivia. I would make certain they wouldn't push too hard.

"Oh, I can cope with that," Olivia said.

"Another thing, honey—the wives."

"What about the wives, Alan?"

"These are typical middle-class American wives living on Navy wages. They are nice, unsophisticated people."

"I get the message, Alan—no overdressing."

"You got it. We are taking the train to White Plains and a taxi from there to Ian's home. I don't wish to drive. There's always too much to drink at these get-togethers. And you are coming with me to the office. I have a meeting with my client before we go."

"Sorry I'm a little late, Tony."

"That's all right, Alan. Deville hasn't arrived yet. You have a message—two, actually. A lady called Anna Maria from Arequipa said something about jeeps. I didn't understand it, but it may make sense to you, and an Inspector Moreno from Porto Velho sent you some fingerprints."

"Those must be the fingerprints from the assassin, taken from his abandoned car. He was using the name of Feliciano Silva, which the police have determined to be a fake ID. You could ask your friends at NYPD and at FBI to run the prints in their database."

"I'll do it, Alan, and tell you if they come up with a match."

I turned to my partner. "Do you have Anna Maria's message?"

"I believe I have." Tony sat in front of his computer and came back with a printout. I read it briefly.

"That's interesting."

"What?"

"She tells me that three Land Rovers were found on the burned-down site, but there should have been only two. Two of the guards returned to Arequipa on the eve of the murders, driving one of the jeeps. She's still checking this information, which indicates the existence of an unaccounted-for element in our puzzle."

"That's important, indeed," Tony agreed. "If correct, someone other than Engelhard could have committed the murders."

"Or he could be an accomplice, or some person who was assassinated and buried by Engelhard, away from the camp."

"Or the other way around—Engelhard is the one dead and buried," Tony contributed.

"Precisely. We have to wait for the conclusion of Anna Maria's inquiry. If the information is correct, we shall have to ask the Peruvian police to conduct a search, outside the camping area, using dogs, to see if they can find another buried body."

"Did she tell how long it would take for her to check?"

"No, she did not. If she doesn't return in the next few days, I'll call her up. In the meantime, let's work with what we have. I brought a hard drive for Judith to work on. It's a mirror copy of the one in AR Comércio's computer. They smuggled the gold pieces from Manaus. The data is encrypted, but I'm hoping she'll be able to break its protection and decipher the code."

We were informed of Deville's arrival in the office.

Deville had the same appearance as I had seen him last, dressed in a very formal black charcoal suit and with the same ivory pommel cane. His dark black eyes possessed the usual unsettling gaze, attentive, not missing anything and seeming to bore into you. After the initial formalities, I went on a long tirade describing my trip, all that I had been able to uncover, the evidence pointing to Engelhard as the probable culprit and of the Peruvian police being convinced of the fact.

"I can appreciate your disappointment with this result, Mr. Deville.

After all, you hired our office to prove the innocence of John Engelhard. We will understand if you decide to sever our contract."

"Just the opposite, Mr. Leary. More than ever, I wish you to continue. I understand that all this evidence weighing against John is circumstantial. I'm still convinced of his innocence."

"Actually, this morning we got new information, which might raise doubts on the culpability of John Engelhard." I explained to Deville the message received from Anna Maria concerning the Land Rovers.

"See what I mean, Mr. Leary? Don't give up hope. Continue digging. You shall have my full support for whatever you need."

"Let me ask you a question Mr. Deville: Were you aware that John was using the identity of a deceased person? That the real John Engelhard had passed away several years ago?"

"No, I did not. I'm very surprised."

Deville was a cold fish type of person. He claimed surprise, but his outside appearance did not betray that. I wondered if he was playing straight with us.

"Do you know if our John Engelhard ever had his fingerprints taken, perhaps for some company record?"

"I don't believe so, but I'll check."

It again sounded false. How could the guy not know a simple thing like this from his boss and so-called friend? "Do you know anyone called Feliciano Silva?"

"No, I do not. Why?"

"This is the alias the assassin was using when I tracked him from Cusco."

"I'm sorry I can't help you. I know no Feliciano Silva."

"I would like to interview the other two vice presidents of Horizon. Could you ask Helen to arrange a meeting for us?"

"I can arrange the meeting. Helen has quit the company."

"Really? When was that?"

"A few days before you returned to New York. I don't think you'll get much from Robert Burn or Eduardo Peña, by the way, especially Eduardo. He was on vacation when the crimes occurred. He returned to the company briefly but quit soon after. Apparently, he got a better position and decided to leave. The first time I came to your office, he was no longer working for Horizon. He must have decided that, without John, the future prospects of the company weren't sufficiently attractive to him."

"I see. I'll settle to talk to Robert and to Eduardo's second in command, then."

"That would be Michael Justin. I'll ask Helen's substitute, Mrs. Ferrer, to arrange a meeting. She will call you."

"I'll wait for her to call."

"I think you should also interview Thomas Lowell. He was John's chief banker with whom he had many business dealings. Certainly, he'll be able to provide useful information."

"That's fine. Would you please set a meeting with him?"

"I shall do it, Mr. Leary. I'll inform you after contacting Thomas and fixing a date. And as I said before, your office continues to get my total support. I wouldn't like to see you abandon this investigation. Please, continue. As for whatever resources you need, you shall have them."

"So what do you think of the meeting?" Tony asked after Deville departed.

"We still have a job, essentially. Let's see what we have to do to continue this investigation."

"It doesn't look as if we can count on much," Tony said.

"We have to wait for news from Anna Maria. If she does confirm the story of the jeep, we would have to admit the existence of an additional person who until now had remained undetected and who could be either a victim or an accomplice or the murderer himself. I'm not admitting the possibility of a live accomplice. Both in Cusco and in Porto Velho just one person was reported."

"They could have gone separate ways."

"In that case, why leave the Land Rover at the site? No. It makes no sense that they went separately overland. I'm betting the police will find a corpse not far from the campsite. I don't think the killer would take the time to dig a deep grave—probably only a small pit, sufficient to keep scavengers away. Dogs will have no problem finding it."

"Okay, that's one point. What else?"

"We know with almost certainty that the killer traveled from Manaus with the gold pieces. I think he would be reluctant to part from his hoard. The ship went to Genoa and the Piraeus. He has landed in one of those ports. Surely, he didn't stay in Curacao. We should alert the Interpol in Italy and Greece. Obviously, he could have gone elsewhere, starting at those two locations, but I have a gut feeling that he stayed in Italy. I recall the Peruvian police and museum guys mentioning art dealers who were known to occasionally transact in stolen goods, in Rome and in the Middle East."

"I'll talk to my friends at NYPD. See if they have an Interpol contact in those places."

"When you do, Tony, tell them that the Peruvian police has already issued an order to detain John Engelhard in connection with this crime."

"Okay, I'll do that."

"Continuing our discussion, I am curious about what Lorna is able to extract from the hard disk I brought back. I hope it will be something useful to the investigation."

"I know she's already working on it, Alan."

"And Tony, please, try your best with the fingerprints. If the guy lived in the US or even visited, his fingerprints must be filed somewhere."

"As I said, I'll ask my NYPD friend to look in their files and with the FBI. Obviously, since no crime has been committed in this country, it can't be officially requested. It has to be handled as a favor, but I'll stress its urgency and ask them to look at other places, if they find nothing in their initial search."

"Excellent. Now, if you will excuse me, I have a barbecue to go to with Livy."

"Ah, that's why your wife came with you to the office this morning. Enjoy it then."

I laughed, picking up my things, and waving Tony goodbye.

CHAPTER 23

With Friends and Comrades

The taxi took us from the train station at White Plains to a middle-class residential neighborhood. Ian's house was a small two-storey off-white house halfway down a street lined by similar residences with common front lawns. I paid the driver and went around the car to open the taxi door for Livy. We walked to the front door of the house and rang the bell. A short blond lady came to open it.

"You must be Ian's wife, Agnes. I'm Alan, one of his service buddies. This is my wife, Olivia. Olivia, Agnes," I made the introductions.

"Ian will be so happy to see you, Alan. He talks a lot about you. Olivia, it's so nice to meet you."

"Nice to meet you too, Agnes."

"Aggie for friends, please. But come inside, please. The barbecue is in the backyard. Everyone is there."

We followed Agnes to their backyard, and I could hear the voices of a group of people and the smell of the barbecue. Ian had set a few tables in the open space behind the house, where a small group of teenage and younger kids ate and talked loudly. The older guests were in a slightly separate group, where, in addition to Ian, I recognized two other chums from my time in active duty. Aggie called Ian, who turned his wheelchair to face us as we approached and greeted us effusively.

"Alan, buddy, how are you, man? Do I have to throw a party every time I want you to visit me?"

"Hi, Ian. Let me introduce my wife, Olivia."

Ian turned to face Livy. "Jesus, Miss, would you like me to call the cops? He must have kidnapped you, right? A beautiful girl like you would never, ever, wed an ugly guy like Alan out of her own free will."

"Very funny, Ian."

Livy smiled. "We'll thank you, Ian, but he didn't kidnap me. I found him kind of lost, in Brazil. It touched my good feelings. But don't worry. I'm trying to improve him."

"I didn't know that Brazil had such gorgeous ladies. Maybe I should move there," Ian jested.

"Oh yeah, and what should I do then?" Agnes protested with feigned annoyance.

"You'll come along, obviously. How could I live without you, honey? But come, let me introduce you to the others. You must have already seen Paul and Hendricks. They are commissioned officers now, both commanders. Let's got and talk to them."

Hendricks and Paul stood up when they saw us coming to their table.

"Why Paul, doesn't that fellow look like our former buddy Alan Leary?" Hendricks mocked.

"It's kind of hard to say. He does resemble that guy. Nah, I don't think so. This one is fatter and much softer. No respectable former SEAL would look like that."

"Have you two ladies finished having fun at my expense? This is my wife, Olivia."

"Poor lady," Paul jested. "So beautiful and mentally deficient. She has to be, right? Otherwise, how could she marry him?"

They came to embrace me, and Paul talked to my wife.

"Please, excuse our manners, Olivia. We were joking. We like your husband a lot. I do think that he came out the winning party in your union, but you didn't do so badly. Alan is a decent and reliable guy. I think he'll be a good husband. If he fails, let us know, and we'll shoot him."

"Please, don't. I don't want to lose this one."

"Gents, this is my wife, Mary," Hendricks said, pointing to the lady joining us."

"Hi, Olivia. Hi, Alan," she said.

"Hi, Mary," we greeted in response.

"My wife is somewhere inside the house with my kids," Paul told us.

"Olivia let me take you away from your husband," Agnes said. "I want to introduce you to the other wives. They are all interested in meeting you and Alan. They are dying to quiz you. It's so romantic. You too, Mary. Come along. Let's leave the gentlemen to their silly boyish talk."

Paul went to get us some beers, and we all sat at their table to update our recent experiences and recall the old ones, the easy occasions and the times of trouble, the dangers we had faced together, our successes and failures. We went on to discuss what each of us was doing presently. It was an agreeable meeting among friends who had spent a long time away from each other. We were all married now. We had become serious family men. The wild adventures, now a fact of the past, were recalled with some melancholy, not because we wished to relive them but because they brought the awareness of the inexorable passage of time. We weren't getting any younger, the bane of men who had been always fit and undergone exciting and dangerous experiences, well above what any normal person could expect. The other three had kept in contact more, and they wanted to know what I had been doing. I told them of my detective firm and also about some of the cases I had worked on. I told the story of how I had met my wife while investigating a case in Brazil, and I mentioned my current job. They wanted to know more about the latter, and I was forced to provide a detailed report of our voyage to Peru and Brazil. Their curiosity wouldn't be satisfied with less than the full details.

"You didn't break the neck of that prick who tried to kill you in the restaurant," Paul asked? "You must be getting soft, man."

"Yeah, a good thing you redeemed yourself by killing that scum who machine-gunned your car. Too bad the other escaped," Hendricks contributed.

"I think your man went to Italy," Ian told me. "In the restoration business, you get to hear a lot of stories about crooked dealers. Sure, Europe doesn't lack those. I've been told of this type of criminal exists in several countries. However, listening to your story, I must conclude that fellow obtained professional help to smuggle the gold artifacts from Brazil. This had to be arranged well in advance, probably by the fence himself. If this buyer of stolen goods was located in a country other than Italy, why use a ship sailing to Genoa? Certainly, he could have used a different vessel, one that could have led to his closest port as a destination."

"What if he had a special arrangement with a crooked customs agent in Genoa?" Paul contributed.

"No, a receiver of stolen goods capable of arranging such a complex operation would have developed the necessary connections at his nearest port of call," Ian retorted.

"I think exactly like you, Ian," I said. "It's comforting, nevertheless, to learn that someone else can come to the same conclusions independently."

"What will you do now, Alan?"

"I have a few leads to follow, and I am alerting the Interpol to be on the lookout for any development in Europe—Italy, in particular."

"Do you remember the SAS chap we met during the Iran-Iraq War? What was his name?" Paul asked Hendricks.

"I believe it was Emmet," Hendricks answered. "He's a bloke."

"What?"

"That's the word they use over there—bloke, not chap."

"Ah, thanks. I was saying, the last I heard of Emmet was that he was working for the Interpol. He's a decent bloke, as Hendricks corrected me. I'll track him down and talk to him. I believe I still have his phone number."

"That would be super, Paul. Do you think he will help us?"

"Absolutely. We are former comrades-at-arms, after all. This is what we do: cover each other's backs. What do you wish me to tell him?"

"You could say I'm going to call him to explain my problem. I would be grateful if he kept discreet attention on the known buyers of stolen art and archeological objects. There shouldn't be many in Italy. He must be looking already for Engelhard, as requested by the Peruvians. It would be great if he could get permission to tap their phones, although I understand it may be difficult to secure it without a serious reason."

"Okay, I'll tell him that, Alan."

Our conversation drifted into other more mundane and lighter subjects—how the Yankees were doing, who was going to play in the coming July All-Star Game, and so on. I saw Livy on the other side of the patio, talking animatedly to a group of wives. They seemed to be quizzing her, each one taking turns to pose questions. I debated for a second if I should excuse myself and go save her, but she gave the impression that she was doing well, smiling once in a while. The contrast of Livy from the other ladies was shocking. She was so much more beautiful—tall and slim but with a shapely body, black hair, and emerald eyes made more striking by the judicious application of light makeup. Simply but elegantly dressed. She was something to watch, clearly at ease under a visible bombardment of questions. I was so mesmerized by my young and gorgeous wife that I tended to forget what was happening around me when I started watching her like this.

"Hello, are you still there?"

I reluctantly turned my head. Ian was talking to me and the other two were watching me, amused. "Yes," I answered.

"Who were you spying so intensely?" Hendricks quipped.

"I hope it was not my wife," Ian joked. The others chuckled.

I was a little discomfited. It was embarrassing to be caught by this bunch, ogling my wife. So I just smiled in response.

"Oh, don't mind us," Paul said, punching my shoulder playfully. "We are just teasing you and a little envious. This girl has really set her hooks into you, and to all outward appearances, you love it. It's nice to watch."

I wanted to find out what had transpired during the conversation Livy had with the other wives. We caught a full train on our way back, and I had to curb my curiosity during the half hour it took for the express train to cover the distance between White Plains and Grand Central Station in the city. Finding a taxi to drive home was going to be a hassle. We decided to take the subway, which was also crowded but mercifully fast to reach our Upper East Side stop. Naturally, Livy's first interest upon entering our apartment was our daughter. She went inside, calling her name, and Larissa showed up running to greet us in the wobbly gait of toddlers who have just recently learned to walk. An attentive Claudia, ready to catch Larissa in the event of a stumble, followed her. Livy opened her arms to embrace Larissa and pick her up, playfully kissing our giggling daughter. I came closer to them, also to greet Larissa and to participate in my share of the fun. I kissed them both and played with both for a while before leaving to shower and change for a quiet, peaceful evening at home.

"So are you going to tell me what you have discussed with the other ladies at the barbecue? You gave the impression of being very … animated."

"You can't imagine their curiosity. They wanted to know about Rio and the place where I lived, Macaé, and obviously everything about us."

"Everything?" I asked, alarmed.

Livy laughed. "Almost everything. I wasn't going to tell them the more piquant details."

"I certainly hope not."

"They asked how we met, how we dated, what I had felt when I met you. It was a bit disconcerting. On a few occasions, I just pretended I hadn't heard the question."

"Poor love. You did admiringly well. I almost went there to save you, thinking you wouldn't cope with the barrage of questions. But then I reasoned, no, Livy can fend by herself. I am proud of you." I embraced my wife and kissed her head.

"They were particularly interested in the beaches. They had all heard of the scanty bikinis the girls wear. They wanted to know if I wore those in Brazil."

"What did you say?"

"The truth, of course. I did wear them, as all the other girls do. One of them inquired if we also went topless."

"No, really. That's beyond curiosity. That's nasty."

"I didn't mind. I told her we would never go topless. The idea was to show as much as we could without showing all. We left something for the imagination, enticing the boys to devote themselves to finding what was hidden."

"Good for you. That will teach them."

"They weren't abashed in the least. One demanded if you had devoted yourself to the task, and I answered, but of course, and I rewarded you for the effort."

"Livy, you are impossible, but totally delightful. You probably left the poor ladies very agitated. I'm sure their husbands won't have it easy after they get home and try to put into practice what you have told them."

Livy giggled. "Do you think I was too nasty?"

"No, honey. You were perfect. I'm proud of you."

CHAPTER 24

The Interview

"What? Wait, no, don't get up, please. Let's stay longer in bed."

I realized it wasn't a weekend or holiday. Still, it felt so nice to linger in bed.

"Don't you have to go to work today, Alan?"

"Yeah, later. I only have to pay a visit to Horizon's office, after lunch."

"Well, I have things to do." Livy stretched her arms. "What do you want, Alan?"

"Guess."

Livy smiled. "Oh … well, let me help you, then."

"Hmm, that's so good, honey."

"Shss … don't make so much noise. You're going to wake Larissa. Claudia will hear us."

"No, they cannot. Thick walls," I mumbled.

Livy giggled. "You'll be responsible for providing the explanations later."

"My turn now," I said. I kissed Livy's lips, the line of her jaw, the hollow of her neck, and continued exploring downward.

"Lower, Alan," Livy murmured. "A little bit lower. There! Shoot … ow, that hurt."

"Sorry, honey. Here let me kiss it. Hum, you smell good."

"Ridiculous, nobody smells good there."

"You do."

"Yeah? Oh, don't stop. Don't dare to stop."

"Jesus, talk about making noise."

Livy laughed. “And whose blame is it?”

I had been under such tension with this difficult investigation. It was nice to break the stress once in a while. I was the only way to keep going, to persevere in the search of an explanation.

I made it to the office a little before noon, and there was news. Judith had made progress in deciphering the files in the hard drive. She had decided to engage the help of a hacker of her acquaintance, who assisted her occasionally on similar jobs. She was hoping the job of breaking the code protecting the files in the drive could be completed in a short while. The second important new information was the positive identification of the fingerprints taken from the Porto Velho car. According to the FBI, they belonged to a Cuban national, Fernando Peralta, who escaped to Miami in the seventies. He attended college in the US and then left to South America. For a time, he was suspected of involvement with drug trafficking to the US, financing the Sendero Luminoso terrorist activities in Peru and Ecuador. He visited the US a couple of times, but nothing was ever proven against him.

The last piece of news came from Anna Maria. She was confirming that three Land Rovers had been found abandoned at the campsite. Together with the fingerprints identification, this could provide conclusive evidence of Engelhard’s culpability or innocence. But the Peruvian police should first find another body near the camp. I sat down to write a message to Inspector Pedro Nuñes, in Arequipa, detailing these developments and attaching the file with the fingerprints. I explained how important it was to find the body to compare fingerprints. I had a strong feeling that the murderer wasn’t Engelhard. This would please Deville, I thought.

The office of Horizon Mining was close to our own, just a few blocks south on Third Ave. I arrived early for my interview but didn’t have to wait. Mr. Robert Burn, the company’s CFO, came to the reception to greet me.

“Ah, Mr. Leary, I was expecting you,” he said affably. “Let’s go to my office. We shall be more comfortable there.”

I thanked and followed him to a spacious room facing Third Ave. It was occupied by a big working table with a glass top and two black leather chairs placed in front. A larger and more imposing chair, also in black leather and with a high back, sat behind it, for the room’s occupant. An arrangement composed of a small beige sofa and two smaller brown side chairs was placed on one side the room. The set was fronted by a low tea table with a ceramic vase and a small bronze sculpture for decoration. The walls were covered with framed pictures of mines. He pointed me to one of the sofas and sat facing me.

"How can I help you, Mr. Leary?"

"I am investigating the disappearance of the president of your company, Mr. John Engelhard, as I'm sure you know. I need to get a better feeling of the person Mr. Engelhard is—or was. I should have come earlier, but my trip to Peru was urgent and prevented me from coming sooner."

"Yes, a very sad business this affair is. John will be missed by the company and my other colleagues, who have all come to count on his knowledge of the market and his uncanny sense of opportunity. It's a big loss."

"Mr. Anton Deville believes John is still alive," I said.

"Oh, well, he is an optimist."

"Did you know that he's being considered by the Peruvian police as the perpetrator of the murders that took place in that country?"

"I did not, but I can tell you it's a ridiculous notion. John would never kill anyone. I've never met a nicer person than him. He was a very humane individual, always looking for the welfare of his employees and coworkers. You can't imagine the prevailing labor conditions in some of the countries where we operate. John never took advantage of that. He was adamant on demanding that we treat our overseas employees the same as we do the ones in this country, offering them the same conditions and benefits."

"Impressive," I said.

"John's posture was a cause of irritation for our competitors, who were forced to extend to their employees conditions approximate to our own. No, Mr. Leary, believe me, John would never kill another human being."

"I see. Did you know that he lived under a false identity, that the true John Engelhard was deceased a long time ago?"

"No! That can't be. I'm shocked." Robert Burn sat straighter in the sofa, hands spread out against its arms. Apparently, the news had shaken him. "Are you certain of this, Mr. Leary?"

I observed his reaction. If it was faked, he was an excellent actor. "Absolutely. There's no doubt. The only question is who he really was. What type of person he had been, what kind of life he had lived before becoming the billionaire owner of a mining empire. Actually, that's why I'm here today, to see if you knew something of his past, of his life previous to Horizon."

"I'm sorry. I cannot help you there. Socially, John was a very reserved person. He didn't confide; he didn't discuss his personal life. He didn't open up to others. Helen, his secretary, was the one closest to him. She would be the only one in this company who could answer any questions about his personal life. Unfortunately, she no longer works for us."

"Yes, I know. He wasn't married, I understand. Still, someone must have known him more closely. He was very rich. Didn't he employ a governess, a butler even? Where did he live?"

"Right here in town. He had an apartment on Park South, a comfortable place, not too large or ostentatious. He lived quite modestly for a man of his means. He had a cleaning lady who came every day to do the house and prepare something for him to eat in the evenings, although I think he mostly ate out. Whenever he had friends, he would hire outside help, a catering service."

"He seems to be a real enigma, this John Engelhard."

"Quite."

"Did he enjoy feminine company?"

"John was not a homosexual, if that's what you are implying. He had a string of girlfriends and female companions. He was reasonably attractive. He kept himself in good shape, and he had one particularly irresistible feature: a very fat wallet. He took advantage of that—and why not?"

"Why not indeed! So you don't believe he could be the killer?"

"Mr. Leary, whatever other people think or tell you, be absolutely sure that John wouldn't kill a fly. It was not in his nature. I would stick my hand in the fire to vouch for him that he's no killer."

"Thank you for taking the time to talk to me, Mr. Burn. I think I have a better understanding of John's character after our conversation." Burn seemed so confident of Engelhard's innocence. That went a little against my gut instincts. I didn't have enough data to dismiss the guy as a killer.

"Don't mention it. It has been a pleasure."

"Could you please ask someone to announce me to Mr. Michael Justin, your interim mining vice president? I would like to have a word with him as well."

"Certainly. Just a second, please." He picked his phone and made a couple of calls to warn Michael Justin and to ask someone to take me to him.

"This is Alicia, Mr. Leary. She'll take you to see Michael. Goodbye and, please call me if I can be of further help."

I followed Alicia to my next meeting. She took me to a considerably smaller room with a simpler decoration. Michael Justin stood up from his table and came forward to meet me.

"Mr. Alan Leary, I presume."

Great, a joker, I thought. "The one and truly," I confirmed. "I left my hunting rifle with your secretary, if that's acceptable to you."

He laughed. "Come. Take a seat, please, Mr. Leary."

"I understand you are substituting for Eduardo Peña, Mr. Justin."

"That's correct. Peña left us a month ago, roughly."

"I would like to ask you a few questions."

"I'll be glad to answer them, but you must understand that I wasn't close to Mr. Engelhard. Peña, my boss at the time, was. I was only a manager. On the few occasions when I talked or had contact with Mr. Engelhard, he gave the impression of being a nice person. He was always polite, quiet, and a little aloof, but that must be standard behavior for an person of Olympian stature talking to a mere mortal. He had a good reputation among the staff, of treating well his employees and of being very fair."

"I realize this is an unfair question, but do you think of Engelhard as being able to kill anyone?"

"Judging by his public persona I would have to say no, definitely no. However, you never know what goes inside a human being. Maybe the image he projected was a false one, a veneer covering a deeper, more violent nature."

"Interesting analysis. What is your impression of Anton Deville?"

"Between the two of us, I think he's the weirdest guy I ever met. Engelhard and he formed a strange pair, the mysterious and the sinister."

"I see what you mean."

"I think this summarizes what I could tell you about John Engelhard."

"Very well. What can you tell me of your former boss, Eduardo Peña?"

"He was alright, I guess, undoubtedly a competent and experienced mining engineer. His American citizenship was acquired. He wasn't born in the US. I don't know where he came from, probably from somewhere in South America. He went to college in this country, nevertheless. He has BS in mining engineering from the Colorado School of Mines."

"Interesting. How was he as a person?"

"Severe, very rigid in his actions, not unfair but not a likable individual, either. If you did your job and were dedicated, you had no problem with him."

"Was he married? Did he have a family?"

"He was not married, and I don't know of a family. He didn't talk much with his subordinates, just what was the necessary to convey his instructions on how to do your job."

"You are describing a very difficult person to work for."

"As I told you, if you did your job correctly and in the time required, you had no problems with him."

"Do you know why he left?"

"Apparently, he got a better offer, and maybe he had misgivings about the company's future without Engelhard. I forgot to mention that Engelhard and Peña were close. Engelhard was probably the only friend he had in Horizon. Actually, he was brought to the company by Engelhard himself."

"Do you know who he went to work for?"

"No, he was very secretive about it. I don't believe he told anyone, not to me, at least."

I talked to Michael Justin a little longer before leaving Horizon. It was late to return to my office, so I decided to go directly home.

Livy welcomed me home with a hug and a kiss.

"Hey, love, how was your day today? Did you make any progress with your investigation?"

"Nothing important. We are waiting for new developments. The Peruvians have to find an additional corpse. Judith has made some progress but still has to decipher my hard disk. In the meantime, it's dull work—talking to people, that kind of thing. But let's forget all this drudgery and discuss lighter subjects. Would you like to go out for drinks and dinner, go and see a movie, maybe?"

"Not tonight. I'm tired. I was awakened too early this morning," Livy said with eyes full of mischief. If it happens again tomorrow morning, I wish to be well rested."

"I'm sorry, love."

"Don't be. I enjoyed it, but what got into you, Alan? Was that because of what I said to your friends' wives? Did it affect you also, honey?"

I squeezed Livy in my arms and whispered in her ear: "You gorgeous delightful devil, don't tease me too much. One of these days, my heart is going to burst. I love you. You own me totally and you know it." She didn't say anything but the pleasure and passion in her eyes were enough.

CHAPTER 25

Visit with a Banker

Deville had confirmed my meeting with Thomas Lowell and I went to see him, next day, in his posh office in the Wall Street area. It was located on the twenty-third floor of an office building, with a fantastic view of the southern tip of Manhattan. The room was large and tastefully decorated. The wall behind his desk was occupied with shelves filled with books. A few paintings hung on the other walls. A bronze sculpture, illuminated by spotlights from the ceiling sat on a waist-level pedestal, in one of the corners. Everything shouted wealth, undoubtedly to impress any first-time visitor. After the preliminary introductions and I stated the intention of my visit, he began telling me what he knew of John Engelhard.

"John Engelhard started his mining empire with the acquisition of a modest copper deposit in Peru twelve years ago. I only got to know him six years later. In that short time, he had grown from an unimportant regional producer to an international base metal conglomerate."

"What's a base metal? It may sound as a naive question to you, but I have absolutely no knowledge on this subject."

"Excuse me, Mr. Leary. I shall be more careful in my explanation. Anyway, in the mining business, the base metals are copper, zinc, lead, and nickel. Sometimes, these metals occur combined in complex minerals. Horizon is mainly in copper and zinc. Recently, they have started to diversify into iron ore. Our bank has syndicated a large financing package for their new iron ore project in Kazakhstan."

"How did Engelhard's activities grow so fast? Isn't twelve years a short period for the transformation you mentioned?"

"Absolutely, it's surprisingly short."

"How did he achieve it? Was he extremely profitable? Did he buy others?"

"I want you to understand that I had a professional banker's connection with John and his companies. We provided loans and did his hedging. I do not have a complete insight into his growth. During our relationship, he was certainly profitable, and he did, in fact, acquire other properties. I understand, however, he was amazingly lucky and efficient in his mineral exploration work. This was general knowledge in the field and a reason for the envy of his competitors."

"Could you expand on this subject, Mr. Lowell, and provide more details?"

"You see Mr. Leary, mineral exploration is a risky activity. It's usually conducted in two stages, remote exploration first, to define the most attractive target areas, followed by fieldwork. Modern science has provided miners with powerful tools. Nowadays, anyone can acquire satellite images to start defining a macro region for the studies. This may be followed by aerial surveys, using radar of different wavelengths and scanning for magnetic anomalies. Once certain areas have been selected, the field teams take over to conduct sampling, geochemistry and geophysical studies, and other techniques. Am I boring you with all this technical mumbo-jumbo, Mr. Leary?"

"Not at all. It's actually quite interesting and instructive. Please, do continue."

"Very well. In spite of all the techniques I described, mineral exploration is far from an exact science. Combined, the large mining corporations spend billions of dollars per year on exploration. Still, the success average is comparatively low. I think that as many mineral deposits have been found by small prospectors, by word of mouth information, or even by accident, as have been uncovered by million-dollar exploration campaigns."

"Incredible. And the mining groups continue willingly to spend vast sums of money on those exploration drives?"

"Indeed, yes. They consider the expenditure as part of their production cost. You may think of it as the corporate equivalent of looking for the pot of gold at the end of the rainbow. And a few times, they have managed to strike it rich. There are quite a few examples for the latter case."

"Okay, I have a much better understanding now. But how does this correlate with Engelhard's unusually fast expansion?"

"Simple. All the exploration work conducted by John's companies has met with success."

"All of them?" I asked.

"Yes, all without exception. It was almost as if the man could smell the metal in the ground. He was unbelievably lucky. It is a cause for amazement for all in the business. His success is legendary. Apparently, he oriented the work himself. He hinted to his geologists where to look for, and discovery was followed by discovery. That, more than anything else, was the fuel for his rapid growth."

"Please, don't be offended by my question. If he was so successful, why did he need banks?"

"It's a valid question. The answer is simple: to cover time gaps. You may have a fortune in the ground, but to be able to transform it into cash, you need funds to open the mine, build roads, and construct ports. That's where we come in—providing the money for it. Essentially, we sell money, Mr. Leary. The mining company's merchandise is the metals; ours is the money."

"It's clear," I told him. I was learning a lot about the nature of Engelhard's business. Of one thing, I was certain. Money didn't appear to be one of his problems.

"For all that, we didn't lend as much money to John Engelhard's mining enterprises as we would have liked to. He was just too solvent. His cash inventory was quite fat. However, we have been very active hedging for him."

"Ah, yes, you mentioned hedging. Could you explain it to me, please?"

"Ever the curious detective, eh? Fine, let me try to explain. You can speculate with hedging, but its true purpose is price protection. It ensures that a metal buyer, acquiring the metal today, will not lose money in the eventuality of the price decreasing when he sells it in the future. Actually, hedging is not usual for miners. They consider themselves naturally hedged during the useful life of the mine. For them, hedging only comes into play when they must borrow to open the mine. Even then, they may not use it."

"In this case, why did Engelhard hedge?"

"Because he was a metal trader besides being a miner. He bought and sold metals and he needed to hedge one way or the other, if prices were in contango or in backwardation.

"Hoa! You got me lost there. Again, please, in English this time."

Lowell smiled. "I'm sorry. I keep forgetting that you are not in the trade. We say the situation is in contango when the future price is higher than the current one. As the name implies, backwardation is the reverse situation, when the current price is higher than the future one. You can perform different hedging procedures in one or the other case."

"It sounds awfully complicated," I said.

"Hardly, and this is only a portion of the things you can do. There's also arbitrage, price-fixing, as well as other means you may employ."

"Price fixing seems straightforward, but what is arbitrage?"

"The two most important metal commodity exchanges are the London Metal Exchange, LME, and COMEX, in New York. Sometimes metal is bought from a producer in Europe and quoted in LME. Later, it might be sold to a consumer in the US, who wishes to quote the metal in COMEX. At the same date, there might be a difference in prices quoted by each exchange. This difference is usually small but may become significant under certain conditions. One may seek protection against this difference or even to profit by it, increasing his net result. The operation that allows this is called arbitration."

"Interesting."

"I forgot to tell you how impressively accurate John was on his market predictions. He must have had a fantastic team of analysts behind him. He was never wrong. After a while, we began to trust him so much that we started to follow his moves. We made quite a profit for the bank like that."

"Sorry to ask, but are you allowed to do that?"

"It's not unethical if you inform the client and ask his permission, which we did."

It had been an educational meeting. I was getting a better idea about the person I had been following. Also, it was interesting to learn the kind of incestuous relationship these money power players kept. Engelhard needed the liquidity, which Lowell was glad to provide, at the right interest rate. At the same time, Lowell was making a fortune, probably on a personal basis, from the stock market tips he got from the operations with Engelhard. I wondered if SEC would regard that kindly despite Lowell's assurances that everything was legal. Nevertheless, Lowell's report contributed to firm my belief in Engelhard's innocence. It was difficult to imagine someone as rich and successful as he was committing a murder to steal gold objects. As valuable as they could be, they were a pittance in the face of his wealth. Lowell seemed convinced that John Engelhard could not be a murderer, an opinion shared by Robert Burn and several others. There was nothing else to do today. I thanked Lowell for receiving me and left his office.

CHAPTER 26

The Hard Drive

I woke up with the phone ringing and turned over in bed, gently removing Livy's arm, which was stretched over my chest, to answer it.

"Hello," I said in a low voice.

"Alan, this is Emmet Colin. I'm friend of Paul and Hendricks. Sorry to call you at this hour. Did I wake you up?"

"Oh yes, you must be the SAS fellow who works for the Interpol in Rome. No problem, I was getting up," I lied. "Paul was going to give me your telephone number, and I was going to call you. It's nice of you to phone me, really."

"My pleasure, Alan. I'm glad to be of help. Those chaps are good friends. They might have told you we had lots of fun together. Paul contacted me and explained your problem. As I told you, he's a good friend, and I consider his friends to be my friends as well."

"That's very kind of you."

"Don't mention it. Besides, this is my job. We got a request from the Peruvian police to arrest John Engelhard as the chief suspect of six counts of murder. I understand you are looking for him as well."

Livy awoke to the noise of the phone conversation. "Who is it, Alan?"

"Suss," I murmured, covering the mouthpiece with my hand. "Go back to sleep honey. I'll explain later."

"Hmm." Livy turned to the other side and went right back to her interrupted sleep.

I started talking to Emmet again. "Sorry for the interruption, Emmet. You are right. I'm looking for Engelhard, but for reasons unrelated to those of the Peruvians. You see, I believe Engelhard is innocent. I have another suspect for the murders, a man called Fernando Peralta." I went on to explain the latest developments.

After my somewhat lengthy explanation, Emmet murmured, "I see. Obviously, we are also looking for the stolen archeological objects. Paul explained how you and he came to the same conclusion—that they have been taken to Italy."

"That's right," I confirmed.

"Well, we have been keeping an eye on a few dealers suspected of receiving stolen art and historical items. With all the archeological sites being discovered in Italy, you can imagine what a problem this is in this country. We have already put a few such miscreants behind bars, but several remain on the loose. One of the most important is a bloke called Giovanni Benedetti, here in Rome. We have clear evidence of his criminal activities but have not been able to prove anything against him, yet. He's definitely a very clever crook."

"Wait a second, Emmet. I'm going to get something to write on. I want to take down your phone, email, and address. I'm going to send you everything I have in this case: a list and photos of the stolen objects, fingerprints, available data on John Engelhard and Fernando Peralta—the whole jazz. I'm also going to write a detailed report to update you on all the details of the investigation conducted by my office and by the Peruvian police. I would like you to be fully informed. I may have to pay you a visit in the near future."

"It will be a pleasure, Alan. Come whenever you deem necessary. I'll wait for your material. In the meantime, I'll keep a close watch on Benedetti and ask my colleagues in the other Italian cities to be on the alert to any development."

"Thanks, Emmet. Now, if you'll excuse me, I'm going to look for a pen and paper." I got up. Livy was fully awake by now, sitting on the bed. I made a sign for her to stay and went searching for the writing materials.

"Okay, Emmet, please, tell me your address and contact data."

We exchanged a few pleasantries, promising to keep in touch, and then I hung up.

"Who was that?" Livy asked.

"A friend of Paul's, a former British soldier now with the Interpol, in Rome. He's going to help me with my case."

"I see." Livy tapped my side of the mattress, signing for me to sit next to her.

I was watching Livy, just awakened but looking fresh, gorgeous without any makeup, smooth black hair falling in gentle waves to her shoulders with that incredible look of youth, which had always amazed and troubled me: on the one side the attraction, the desire to make love to her, on the other side the unjustified feeling of doing something wrong, of loving a girl too young. I had to keep reminding myself of Livy's true age—no longer an immature teenager but a full woman, a mother, my love. She was so beautiful sitting like that in her diaphanous nightdress, revealing the contours of her body, the darkness of her nipples. I was transfixed by her image, like a bird caught in the sight of a serpent. I couldn't move even had I wished to. Livy broke the enchantment.

"What? Why are you looking at me like that? Is something wrong with me?"

"No, honey. Nothing is wrong with you. It's just that I find you so incredibly beautiful. I can't stop looking."

"Alan, please … you are making me blush."

This can't be normal. Livy is not the first woman ever had. I'd been married before, for God's sake. But the way she looked—so soft, so alluring, so delicious, so desirable. I had to be losing my mind, in a good way.

"Come here," I said, pulling out of my reverie to embrace her.

Two days later, when I arrived at the office that morning, Susan, our receptionist, informed me that Judith was waiting to see me. I immediately assumed that she had finally cracked the code protecting the hard drive.

"Please ask Judith to come to my office, Susan."

I proceeded to my room, anxious to learn what had been found in the encrypted files.

"Good morning, Alan."

"Hi, Judith. Come right in and sit down. I am curious about what you have been able to dig out of that hard drive. Please tell."

"In the end, the code was simpler than I had expected. Essentially, it was based on a simple letter permutation, using as key—"

“Spare me the technicalities, Judith. Please go straight to what you found.”

“Obviously, it doesn’t make much sense to me. Perhaps you’ll be able to understand the data better than I can. The material is mostly in Portuguese, or so I assume. I’m really not familiar with that idiom. A smaller portion is in Spanish. What language do they speak there, Alan?”

“Portuguese is the only language spoken in Brazil. I assume some goods come out of Peru and Colombia through Manaus. The rivers are a natural waterway, and depending on where they are produced, it’s cheaper to ship them east rather than to take them to the Pacific. Besides, there’s the drug traffic, and those guys are suspected of involvement with that.”

“I see. Anyway, I made a printout of all the material in the drive for you. I still have it on electronic media, but I thought it would be easier for you to have a hard copy.” Judith took two large folders from her backpack and placed them on my table.

I whistled. “All that? We’re going to need some coffee. It’s going to take a long time to go over all this. I’m afraid I shall have to ask you to stay, Judith. I’ll probably need your help.”

“Fine, Alan. I came prepared to stay.”

I began examining the material. The first file was an agenda with names, telephone numbers, and some email addresses. I noticed phones from Brazil and other countries, some from Europe, Germany, Holland, Italy and Greece.”

“Judith, could you email only the phone records from Europe to a friend of mine?”

“No problem, Alan.”

I scribbled a note to Emmet, asking him the favor of checking the numbers to see if he could find any familiar one. Judith excused herself to go and send the message. I continued my scrutiny. The next file was a series of copies of emails. They made no sense to me. Anyway, I wasn’t expecting to find incriminating references. Those fellows were too clever for that. I hope to detect the name of a person or place that I could identify. After more than two hours of intently looking at the material, my eyes were beginning to smart. After sending my message, I turned to Judith, who had returned.

"I need to stretch my legs, Judith. Let's go out. We can grab something to eat and walk a little. Come. I'm inviting you."

We returned to the office forty minutes later and resumed our analysis. I was now reading a type of ledger. Each file was identified by a name and a product: rubber, timber, Brazil nuts. Each had a series of entries or records and several fields like date, quantity, value, and so on. One of those caught my attention. It was a rather small shipment of Brazil nuts, only ten boxes, not even a full container. The client's name was Rizzo, but there were no entries for value or port of destination. I had something on the name, which I tried to remember. Then I got it. On my hurry to leave the premises of AR Comércio, I had just enough time to write down the name on the tabs of folders in the file cabinet. I went searching for my notes, and sure enough, the name Rizzo was there. It didn't mean much at the moment, but might have significance together with other evidence. I was sorry I had no time to examine the Rizzo folder when I was in AR Comércio.

I looked at my watch. It was almost five. I decided to call it a day. We were dining with Jessica at her place, and I didn't want to be late.

"Let's quit for the day," I told Judith. "Are you going to be in tomorrow?" I asked.

"If you want me to. I'll come, by all means."

"Please do. We still have lots of material to examine."

"See you tomorrow, Alan."

CHAPTER 27

Discovery

Two days had passed since I started examining the hard drive material and sent my email to Emmet Colin. I hadn't been able to find anything more of interest in the files. Anyway, to be sure, I had engaged the help of Susan and Lorna to go over the material once again, more thoroughly. However, I didn't hold much hope of finding more evidence in it. One thing was clear to me. I had noticed lots of clues to support a drug traffic prosecution case. I discussed with Fernando how to send this data to the Manaus Federal Police without implicating myself in a breaking-and-entering crime. He told me to forget it. They had conducted a meticulous search themselves and confiscated their hard drive, among other things. So now I had to wait for developments.

The news arrived in the afternoon. Tony came to give me the message from the Peruvian police. They had found another body near the campsite, buried in a shallow grave, as I had predicted. However, the killer had cut off the fingertips, and those could not be found. We could not discover the identity of the body, unfortunately.

"This is a setback," I said, shaking my head.

"Wait," Tony said. "There is more."

They had found the shovel used to dig the grave. It had been tossed near it. The killer had been careful, wiping all fingerprints. However, he had made a mistake. The police did a thorough job of checking the shovel for prints, and they found one on the metal blade, near the junction with the wooden handle. The killer had missed removing that one. The police compared this print with the ones we had sent them and found a match.

Thus, the murderer was Fernando Peralta, and the body found belonged to John Engelhard. I had to report this to Mr. Deville.

"Well, Tony, I think this fulfills the terms of our contract. Deville won't be happy with the news confirming Engelhard's demise, but at least we were able to clear his name. Obviously, Peralta committed the other murders as well.

"This throws us out of a job," Tony thought aloud. "We have to tell Deville. Will you call him, or shall I do it?"

"Leave it to me. I'll phone him, Tony."

Deville was emotionless with the news. The man was really weird.

"I believe this concludes our work, Mr. Deville. I'm terribly sorry to report Engelhard's death. I know you had hopes of finding him alive. However, I'm glad having been able to prove him innocent. I hope this will be a consolation for you."

"Mr. Leary, I'm reforming the terms of our contract. I wish you to track down his killer and ensure he faces justice. If you accept this new charge, you shall, as before, count on my total support. You can ask for anything you need. If it's in my power to grant, you shall have it. I'll spare no cost to see this criminal behind bars."

"Very well, Mr. Deville. I accept your offer. I'll go after this Fernando Peralta. Incidentally, I have a reasonable notion of who he is. The Horizon person closest to John Engelhard was his vice president for mining, Mr. Eduardo Peña. I understand Mr. Peña was on vacation at the time of the crime. Who else could this Horizon inspector be, aside from Peña, who showed up in Arequipa and drove the third jeep found at the campsite, the killer in effect. Only Eduardo could have Engelhard's trust and get away with some excuse for showing unexpectedly at Colca. I suspect that Eduardo Peña and Fernando Peralta, the killer, are the same person."

"I follow your reasoning, Mr. Leary. It makes sense."

"I need you to collect all the information on Peralta, available in Horizon. Photos, driver license, passport number or photocopy, social security—everything. Fingerprints, if you have those."

"I shall look into this personally. I'll send all I can get hold of to you, Mr. Leary."

"Thanks. I'll try my best to succeed in this new task and catch Peralta."

"I trust you, Mr. Leary. I know you will."

A short while after talking to Deville, I received a phone call from Emmet Colin.

"My dear fellow, sorry I couldn't call you earlier, but you sent me a lot of data to analyze."

"I know. Sorry for abusing your goodwill, Emmet."

"Not at all, not at all. But among the phone numbers, we found two that belong to our friend Benedetti."

"Really? That's good. Does the name Rizzo mean anything to you, Emmet?"

"Yes, indeed. Rizzo Antiquities is the company owned by Benedetti. It's an old traditional Rome antiquary. It belonged to a respectable and honest family. Benedetti acquired it by unknown means two or three years ago. He didn't bother to change the name."

"Bingo!" This was certainly the dealer who had organized smuggling the gold artifacts. If Peralta wasn't still in Italy, this Benedetti should know of his whereabouts. I had to go to Italy. I explained my problem to Emmet.

"It will be a pleasure to meet you, Alan. Do you need anything from me? Should I make a hotel reservation for you?"

"No, thanks, Alan. I'll take care of everything from here. I look forward to meeting you too. Bye."

"Just a second, old chap. Let me know exactly when you arrive and your flight number. I'll come and get you at the airport."

"Don't bother, Emmet. I'll take a cab."

"No bother. I insist."

"In that case, thanks. See you in Rome."

I arrived home, and Larissa came running to meet me, with Claudia close behind.

"Daddy, Daddy!"

I picked her up. "How is my princess, the cutest girl in the world?" I said, tickling her. Larissa giggled happily and turned her face for my kiss.

"Where's Mrs. Leary, Claudia? Isn't she home?"

"No, Mr. Leary. She didn't come back from the university yet."

"Oh well, I hope she arrives soon," I said with some disappointment. I wasn't looking forward to having to tell Livy I was going to Rome. She wouldn't like it, I was sure.

I heard the key turning in the front door and turned, still holding Larissa in my arms, to greet my wife. "Hi, baby."

Livy's eyes lit up when she saw both of us standing in the entrance hall.

"Hey! Enjoying our daughter?" she asked, smiling.

"More now that the mother has arrived. We were missing you. Come join us."

"Hang on to that invitation. I'm going to take a quick shower, and I'll be back."

"Livy, I'm traveling to Italy tomorrow afternoon."

"Oh, Alan, do you have to? I hate it when you are not around. I miss you."

"I miss you too. I miss you both, but I must go. I hope I can finish this job. Perhaps we could take a few days off after I come back, spend a long weekend in Vermont or in Maine, just three of us. What do you think?"

"That would be great. Do you have an idea how long you'll be away this time?"

"It shouldn't be more than a few days, a week at most."

"Too bad I cannot go with you this time."

"Yeah, I know. I'll miss you and your silly mile-high ideas."

CHAPTER 28

In Rome

I got settled in my business-class seat on the flight to Rome, getting ready to face the more than nine-hour flight ahead of me. One of the stewardesses, a nice-looking blonde with great legs, came to offer drinks and ask if I needed anything. She was carrying a tray with small cups of orange juice and champagne.

"Could you bring me a scotch on the rocks, please?" I told her. I needed a stiff drink to help knock me out. Normally, I don't sleep well on flights, and I was missing Livy. If felt funny not having her near me. The stewardess gave me a suggestive smile and said, "Later."

"After takeoff, I'll bring your drink, Mr. Leary." She smiled again.

Tough luck, lady, I'm not buying today, nice legs or not.

The plane taxied to the takeoff position, and after a short delay, waiting for other flights ahead of us, it was finally our turn. The plane accelerated down the runway and started leaving the ground. We were off to Italy. The stewardess returned with my scotch after the fasten seatbelt was turned off.

"Here you are, Mr. Leary. Call me if you need anything else," she said, smiling again.

"Hmm, thanks, miss."

My thoughts wandered back to Livy. Probably due to the flirting stewardess. I recalled her silly Mile-High Club suggestion. I smiled at the recollection. Livy behaves like a much younger girl on occasion. It's definitely one of her cutest charms; it makes me feel as if I'm dealing with a daughter rather than a wife.

Emmet was waiting for me in front of the exit of Terminal C, holding a sign with my name written on. I greeted him. "Hi, Emmet, I'm Alan."

"My dear fellow, it's such a pleasure to meet you. Did you have a good flight? You must be tired."

"I'm okay. Thank you, and the flight was fine. I even managed to sleep a little."

"Great. I have my car outside in the airport parking lot. Let's get you to your hotel. You should freshen up and rest before starting your activities. We have a meeting this afternoon with inspector Carlo Albanese of the Italian Polizia di Stato. Emmet grabbed my suitcase, and we started walking to his car. "Just for your knowledge, the INTERPOL has a National Central Bureau in Italy, which is part of the International Police Cooperation Service. The latter is a branch of the Italian Central Directorate of Criminal Police, which coordinates international investigations. The directorate is headed on a rotation basis by a high-ranking official of either the Polizia di Stato, or the Carabinieri or Guardia di Finanza. This year, the directorate is headed by the Polizia di Stato. Let me not bore you with this now. You'll learn more as you meet Carlo. Where are you staying, Alan?"

"I made a reservation at the Saint Regis," I answered him.

Emmet whistled. "Remind me to apply for a job with your firm, after I retired from Interpol.

"I'll be glad to have you, but why?"

"The Saint Regis Grand is one of the most expensive hotels in Rome, totally out of reach for a policeman."

"My client pays me well," I said, a little embarrassed. I didn't want to project a snobbish image to Emmet.

"I'm sure he does."

It took us an hour to drive from the airport to my hotel. Traffic in Rome is terrifying. Whenever we arrived at a crossing, drivers seemed to play a game of chicken to decide who had the right of the way. When we reached the hotel, I understood Emmet's manifestation of awe. It was a fancy place. I went in to register, and Emmet told me he would wait downstairs in the lobby.

"Take your time, old chap. Don't worry about me. I have a few reports to read. I'll be here when you come down. Perhaps we should eat something before going to see Carlo."

I went to my room to take a shower, shave, and change into a formal suit and tie. I finished unpacking the few items I had brought. It was too early to call home, so I texted a short message to Livy: *Hi, love, had a good flight, arrived well in Rome. Take good care of my heart. I left it with you. Kisses to my girls, Alan*. I went down to meet Emmet.

The office of inspector Carlo Albanese was located at the Questura di Roma in Via di San Vitale. After a second session of Roma traffic, we reached our address. Emmet showed his ID to the guard at the reception counter, and we went inside. Obviously, this was not the first time Emmet had visited Carlo Albanese. We stopped at a door with a frosted panel on its top half, and Emmet knocked before walking in. A short, slim middle-aged gentleman with dark hair and spectacles rose from his desk and came forward to meet us.

"Ah, signore Alan, you were expected," he greeted me in English with a pronounced Italian accent.

"Inspector Carlo, thank you for receiving me."

"Please," he said, stretching the first E and stressing the second, "you don't have to thank me. It's my job. Do sit down. We need to discuss this problem of the murders in Peru and the stolen objects."

Carlo returned to his seat. Emmet and I sat in chairs facing the desk.

"Now, if you wouldn't mind, Alan, I would like to hear the whole story from you. I already know its main points. However, you have been close and even experiencing some of the events for a long time. I'm sure you'll be able to provide us with important details that will help our investigation."

I recounted everything I knew and all I had done from the moment of Deville's first visit to our office onwards, sparing no detail, advancing my conclusions, and explaining how I had reached them. Occasionally, either Carlo or Emmet would interrupt me, asking me to clarify their doubts and explain specific points. I took me almost an hour to report everything I knew. In the end, both Carlo and Emmet seemed satisfied with my account.

"Very impressive, Alan. You did an excellent job."

"Thank you, Carlo."

"Now, I understand perfectly well why John Engelhard would never have committed the crime. He had no motive to steal; besides, how could he have survived the rough mountain crossing? He is a city person. Even with his obscure background and false identity, he didn't fill the pattern. With Peralta, it is a different story. The man had connections with Sendero Luminoso. Perhaps, he had been a terrorist himself and was familiar with the Andean terrain. And you believe Peralta and Eduardo Nuñes to be the same person?"

"I'm almost convinced of it. It's a logical conclusion. Eduardo has disappeared, by the way. He left Horizon with the excuse of having found a better job. However, he told no one the name of the company he was going to work for. Nobody seems to know where he went."

"That's very interesting, Alan."

"I brought to you the evidence that I have," I said. I gave Carlo a CD I had prepared for him. "In it, you'll find photos of Engelhard and Eduardo Nuñes, fingerprints from the car in Porto Velho, and the one print found on the discarded shovel. I also recorded all the data that Horizon Mining provided on Eduardo and the one on Fernando Peralta, taken from the FBI files."

"This will be very helpful, thanks. You believe this Peralta is in Italy?"

"I'm almost one hundred percent certain that he landed in Genoa. I cannot guarantee he stayed in Italy. But we ascertained that this fellow Benedetti, the owner of Rizzo Antiquities, orchestrated the smuggling of the gold pieces. He should be aware of Peralta's whereabouts, even if he left Italy."

"We could start by asking the immigration authorities to verify if he entered the country in Genoa."

"I'm sorry, but it won't work. He was using the name of Feliciano Silva while in Brazil, but he didn't leave the country using that ID. Who knows under which alias he used to disembark in Genoa."

"I see your point."

"Unfortunately, there was not time to check the Porto Velho fingerprints with Eduardo's before I left New York. I don't expect that a match will be found, anyway. Certainly, his Eduardo ID was also fake."

"No doubt," Carlo agreed.

"I need your help, Carlo, to extract from Benedetti the information on Peralta's location."

"I fear I have a problem with that, Alan. We know Benedetti is a crook—rich but a crook. We also know he works with stolen goods. He's a fence, as you call this type of criminal in America, and we believe he is smuggling drugs, as well. Unfortunately, we have yet to prove anything against him. He's a very clever individual, with money to buy good lawyers. My hands are tied. I cannot force him to give me the information you wish."

"But, if he's such a criminal, why have you not caught him at his illegal activities, until now?"

"Here, let me show to you." Carlos stood up, went to a file cabinet, and removed a thick folder. He selected a few documents and came back to sit at his table. He picked his phone and said a few words in Italian. A moment later, a lady came in, collected the documents, and departed. "I've asked the secretary to make copies of the material I would like you to read. It will provide you with a better idea of the man and the type of problem we are dealing with."

"I see."

"Benedetti is the only son of Slovenian immigrants," Carlo continued. "He was born near the town of Udine, in northern Italy, in a small village called Buttrio, to be more precise. His father was a welder, at one of the large equipment factories over there. His criminal career started at a very young age. He was a school dropout and a terrible problem to his parents. His initial contacts with the police involved a series of small crimes and auto theft, for which he was put under probation when he was sixteen. Soon after, he moved to Venice, where he entered a racket of exploiting and robbing tourists. He was finally arrested and served a four-year sentence. After release, he relocated to Rome and entered the service of Dom Enrico Mateo, a former crime boss with activities in prostitution, human traffic, and drugs. A real charmer, Dom Mateo."

"Benedetti too," I confirmed. "I see that he is a really swell guy."

"In the early nineties, we had accumulated enough evidence to allow us to break Dom Mateo's gang. He was arrested and is still serving a long sentence in an Italian prison. Benedetti, however, went free. We weren't able to prove anything against him. He was tried but found not guilty due to lack of evidence."

"Great."

"Anyway, after his scrap with justice, Benedetti decided to direct his interests to less evident crimes. I believe he got the idea to deal illegal art objects from Dom Mateo, who was himself a collector of such items and did not shun away from acquiring them from less reputable origins. Over the years, Benedetti has become very successful in this enterprise. Dealing in drugs is a recent spinoff from his art smuggling."

"I appreciate you telling me all this inspector. Don't take me wrong, but this is not germane to my endeavor and to my request. All I need is you to squeeze Benedetti, to find the location of this Peralta fellow. Obviously, I'll be glad if you can locate and recover the stolen objects. However, my primary obligation concerns my client and fulfilling his wish to find the killer of John Engelhard and bring him to justice."

"I understand you, clearly, Alan. Nevertheless, I cannot squeeze Benedetti, as you say, without firmer evidence."

Always the same police bureaucracy. It was frustrating. "Please, help me, Inspector. I have been pursuing this investigation for months. And now I feel it near its conclusion."

"What I'm going to do is immediately issue a general alarm to find and detain Fernando Peralta, alias Feliciano Silva. I'll inform not only our own police corps but also the Carabinieri and even the Corpo Forestale."

"This will be a long process and probably destined to fail, if he has changed is appearance and is using another false ID," I mentioned, disheartened. "Besides, what further proof do you need? We know this Manaus company, AR Comércio, was responsible for moving Peralta and the objects out of Brazil. We have the name of the vessel they used and that it reached port in Genoa. Benedetti's company was mentioned several times in their files. Isn't this sufficient?"

"Very well, Alan. Let's pay signore Benedetti a little visit," Carlo said after considering my words. "See if we can exert a bit of pressure to try to extract something, shall we? I am not optimistic that it will work, but it's worth a try."

"We should go now," Emmet said. "His shop is in the Trastevere District, and he must leave around five. It's already past three thirty, and with the traffic, it may take us a good half hour to get there."

"Fine, let's go. Leave your car here, Emmet. We go in a police cruiser. It will be faster and more official."

Benedetti's shop was located in a small street in Trastevere. From the street, its appearance was unimpressive, two narrow display windows with a middle entrance door, in a two-floor building. We parked the car in front of the shop, directly under a parking prohibited sign. Well, maybe I was misreading the sign. My Italian was lousy. We all got out of the car and went into the shop. It was narrow but deep. I saw a back wall with a door, probably going into a storage area. There was a long counter to our right, attended by a lady in her thirties. A large man with an unfriendly face was sitting a little to the back. The wall behind the counter was covered with shelves all the way to the ceiling, with an assortment of objects. The lady spoke to us.

"How can I help you gentlemen? Are you looking for some specific item?"

"We wish to talk to your boss," Carlo said.

The big guy got up and came to us with a belligerent air. "Who wants to talk to signore Benedetti? Who are you?"

Carlo exchanged a few words in Italian with the man, too fast for me to follow, showing him his police badge. The man made a sign for us to follow him and proceed to the door I had seen in the back. On the other side of the wall, a stair gave access to the top floor. The man shouted a few words to someone upstairs and indicated we should go up. Arriving upstairs, we saw that a second goon, a pocked-face guy of medium height but strong, was guarding the entrance of Benedetti's office. When he saw us, he made a pretense of frisking Carlo. But both Carlo and Emmet showed their badges and said sharp words. He relented and went ahead to announce us.

"Come in, please, gentlemen," a voice called from inside the office. "To what do I owe the pleasure of this visit?"

We went into the office. Benedetti was a bespectacled, grey-haired, distinguished-looking personage. If he were walking in the street among others, no one except me would take him for a criminal. The worst ones always look least likely.

"I'm sorry I can't invite you to sit. Unfortunately, I do not have enough chairs for all."

"Cut the bullshit, Benedetti," Carlo said. This is not a social visit. We'll stand. Anyway, we are not planning on staying long. We wish to ask you a few questions. First, we want you to tell us where we can find this man."

Carlo set Feliciano/Peralta photo on the table in front of Benedetti, who took a good look at it.

"I do not know this man. I have never seen him before."

"Spare us the lies, Benedetti. We know that you organized the illegal transport to Italy of the items he stole in Peru. We know exactly where and when he landed and the ship in which he traveled. You are only making your situation worse by denying it."

"Inspector Albanese, really, if you have concrete proof of your allegations, arrest me," Benedetti said in defiance.

"I might just do that."

"If you arrest me, I'll be out in a few hours. You know it."

"I'll ask the Guardia di Finanza to go over your inventory to check the legality of your operations."

"Please, do it, Inspector. I run an honest business. I have nothing to fear from the police or the financial authorities."

Benedetti was calling Carlo's bluff who was really powerless to do anything concrete. I knew this approach was hopeless. Sometimes you cannot use the due process of the law to deal with criminals like Benedetti. In his case, unorthodox means were required to ensure success. I could clearly see that Carlo was at the same time fuming and embarrassed with his position, being challenged by a crook. Carlo flushed and became rigid, scantily disguising his annoyance.

"We shall see. You'll regret this, Benedetti.

"Perhaps, but if you do not intend to arrest me, or if you have no mandate to search my premises, I'll have to ask you to leave. I do not have anything else to say to you. Please leave."

"Don't you dare tell us what to do. We will leave now, but I'll come back with a warrant—*a mandato di perquisizione*," Carlo said.

"That's all right, Inspector. I'll be waiting for your visit. But, as I said, I have nothing to hide, and I have never seen in my life the man in the photos you have shown. Never!"

We left Benedetti's shop with a feeling of defeat. Carlo's tactic to put pressure on him had misfired.

"Now what?" I asked. "What shall we do?"

"As I said, this visit had no chance of making Benedetti tell us the location of your man or confessing to a crime. I only agreed to come because he knows now that we are after his ass. I hope he will get nervous and start making mistakes. I'll make Benedetti's life miserable. Every day he'll have to contend with a search by one of the police branches. He'll break."

"He may," I agreed, "but it will take a very long time."

"Unfortunately, for the moment, there's little else I can do. Without proof, my hands are tied."

"I see."

"Give me a day or two to work on Benedetti, Alan. Come see me the day after tomorrow. Let's talk this problem over then and discuss alternatives."

"Fine, Inspector. I'll see you then."

I said goodbye to Carlo after we returned to the Questura. Emmet offered to drive me back to my hotel. There was nothing else I could do today. Inside, I was dying with frustration. The police investigation could provide results eventually. The problem was the time it would take. I was very impatient and didn't see me remaining in Rome for weeks to come. I might have to return to New York and wait for developments there. I could come back if the police found any concrete evidence. I would think of this tomorrow.

CHAPTER 29

Preparations

Carlo had asked me to wait for two days before returning to the Questura. In the meantime, he intended to take a few measures to advance the case. Thus, I was left to spend some idle time in Rome. Emmet had offered to come to the hotel and show me around. I thanked him but politely refused. I knew he had his own problems to take care of, and I couldn't impose on him to babysit me.

I had been to Rome before. I had spent a long weekend in this city when I was still on active duty and my SEAL group was assigned to the Sixth Fleet. This was more than a decade ago. I didn't think Rome had changed much in that interval. However, I did not remember clearly the places I had then visited. I was a lot younger and a bachelor, and I hadn't stayed alone for long. Obviously, my interests then were different. I cannot envisage now another girl having a fraction of the attraction Livy has for me.

I had a few errands to make. I was putting together an alternative plan in the event the police investigation failed or dragged on too long. I just couldn't see myself being bogged down in Rome for an extended period. I had read the material on Benedetti provided by Inspector Carlo. It didn't help me much, aside from confirming him to be a very dangerous person. Benedetti would have no qualms about killing to protect himself and achieving his goals. I might have to drag the information I needed from him by force.

I woke up late to be able to phone home, and I left the hotel immediately after lunch. My first stop was at a shop selling guns and hunting supplies.

I bought a small container of double-naught lead shot, good for hunting boar, according to the salesman. Next, I went to a place that sold security material and police items. This had been trickier to find. My hotel concierge didn't provide helpful information, but at the gun shop, I was able to get better directions. I bought a few plastic hand and ankle cuffs, adding them to my shopping bag. At a hardware store, I got a length of thin cord, the type used for Venetian blinds. Finally, I purchased a pair of strong cotton socks. I had everything I needed. I took a taxi back to my hotel.

After receiving a good tip, the concierge managed to procure me an expensive ticket, most probably bought from the local scalper, for a concert that evening. I didn't much mind the price. It was a good orchestra seat, and I needed something to do. It was better than spending time drinking at a bar. After showering and donning my suit, I still had plenty of time. I decided to visit the fancy shopping area near the Spanish Steps. I wished to buy Italian gifts for my ladies: Livy, Larissa, and Jessica, my sister. The next morning, I would be visiting Carlo again to learn about any new development concerning the case.

CHAPTER 30

Still in Rome

Emmet came in the morning to take me to meet Inspector Carlo Albanese. He was waiting for us with the results of his latest actions, trying to uncover the whereabouts of Fernando Peralta and of the gold pieces. He received us in his office at the Questura di Roma in Via di San Vitale.

"Good morning, Alan. I hope you had a chance to rest yesterday, perhaps also to see a little of Rome."

"Thanks, Carlo. I rested fine."

"Great. Let me tell you what I have found in the same period."

"Please, I'm eager to learn your news."

"After I left you, following our conversation with Benedetti, I called the Genoa Port Authority to inquire about the vessel *The Nemea Lion*, which has brought the Brazil nuts from Manaus."

"Fine, and?"

"Ships docking at Genoa must file the names of all crewmembers with the port authority. After I talked to them, they discovered that one of the crew, a person called Jason Christos, did not return to the ship when it sailed away."

"He must be the fellow we are tracking. Do they take the fingerprints of the crew when they go out of the port area?"

"Unfortunately, unlike in your country, we don't scan fingerprints. I contacted the shipping company in Greece, and they found a discrepancy. The ship had no crewmember called Jason, and furthermore, he was in excess of the regular equipage. The company director I talked to was very annoyed, actually. He said that this couldn't happen without the knowledge of the vessel's captain. They are going to report him to the Greek police, and he will be questioned."

"Good news. The captain must be aware of everything to have allowed this Jason to board in Manaus. This is a very positive development."

"Yes, well, currently the ship is at sea. It's returning to South America. It will take another five days for it to reach port. The company doesn't think it wise, and the Greek police agree to inquire by radio. The captain will be detained as soon as he reaches port. He'll be substituted and sent back to Greece for interrogation."

"I see. Five days is a long time for me to wait in Rome."

"I realize that. While we wait, there are other measures we can take. The cargo of nuts was acquired by a company from Perugia, Fratelli Cataldo Import and Export."

"Excellent."

"Not quite. Such a company does not exist. We checked with the Perugia Commune."

"Damn! We are back at mark zero."

"Don't despair, Alan. These criminals always leave a trace, no matter how well they try to hide their trail. The company doesn't exist. However, the customs broker does. The Genoa police will question him. Also, the port authority is conducting a check of the trucks that entered the port area on the day when the nuts were unloaded. All trucks accessing the port have their license plates recorded. Again, it's regretful that the system is not computerized. The licenses have to be checked by hand and compared with the cargo documentation. This will consume another forty-eight hours. Once we have that, we can go after the trucking company or whoever owns the vehicle in question. Give me a week, tops, and I will find to where the nut cargo went in Europe."

"I don't know what to say, Carlo. You must have dozens of other problems deserving your attention. Obviously, you interrupted other important tasks to give priority to my case. You have done a lot. You have been very kind and accommodating. I must thank you."

"You have been most efficient, Carlo," Emmet concurred. I'll mention your assistance to us and how you supported our job, in my report to Interpol headquarters."

"That's it, gentlemen. I know how urgent this matter is to you, and I do have an official request from Interpol to help find the murderer and the stolen objects. I'm just doing my obligation."

"What will be our next step?" Emmet asked.

"Unfortunately, you shall have to bear with me and wait a couple of days longer, at least until I have news on the trucking company. The matter with the shipping company and the vessel's captain must take a while longer, I'm afraid. I realize how anxious you are to solve this question and return home, Alan. Forgive me. That's the best I can do."

"Absolutely, Carlo. As I said before, your assistance is beyond reproach, more than I could expect. It's actually more than you should be under the obligation to provide." It seemed that my alternative to extract an answer by force from Benedetti was the only viable possibility.

We said our goodbyes and left inspector Carlos. Emmet took me back to the hotel. I was silent in the car on my way back.

"Don't be disappointed, Alan. Spending a few days in Rome is not that bad. There is so much to see. You should profit from it and make the best of your stay."

I was so frustrated it was difficult to express my feelings to Emmet. So I just answered, "right."

"Do you wish me to come back tomorrow, Alan? I could show you some of the sights?"

"I appreciate your offer, but no thanks. I intend to use the day to rest and to write my report to the client. Why don't you call me tomorrow evening? Then we can decide what to do on the following day."

"Deal. I'll think of something to do, and I'll call you," Emmet told me.

Back in my hotel room, I began my preparations. I assembled the items I had bought the previous day. I opened the container from the gun shop and poured a small amount of lead shot into one of the cotton socks and tied the open end with a tight knot. Next, I used the thin cord to make a loop, which went around my forearm and was tied to the sock knot. I had improvised a kind of mace, a thug's blackjack. I put my jacket on and tried to keep the sap hidden, supported by my slightly raised forearm. By lowering the arm, I could drop the sap, picking it on the palm of my hand, or letting it fall further so that the lace loop would catch around my wrist. I practiced this action several times until I was convinced I could do it without failing, with a flip of my arm. I was ready to perform. My plan was risky. There was good chance of failure. I could be hurt or end up in an Italian prison. But I could not wait for the police. Desperate times, desperate measures.

CHAPTER 31

The Second Visit

Next morning, I checked out of the hotel after breakfast. I had no intention of returning. Before leaving my room, I asked the reception to get me a chauffeured car with a reliable English-speaking driver. I would be using the car for the whole day.

"No problem, Mr. Leary. I can recommend you a very reliable man. He's very honest and an excellent driver. If you care to wait, I'll try to locate him and see if he's available. Please, take a seat while I make a couple of phone calls. I'll come for you when I have confirmation. It shouldn't take long."

Sure enough, the receptionist came looking for me, half an hour later, in the company of a short, thin, dark-haired man. "This is Maximo Prieto, Mr. Leary, the person I told you about. We were lucky. He's free today, and he could be your driver for the day."

"Maximo, this is the American gentleman I mentioned to you. He would need your services to drive him around Rome," the receptionist introduced the driver to me.

"How do you do, Mr. Leary?"

"I'm fine, thanks. Please, call me Alan."

I thanked the hotel reception man and gave him a generous tip for his assistance. Next, I discussed compensation with Maximo reaching an agreement that made him apparently happy. "So, Maximo, shall we go now?"

"Certainly, Alan." Maximo picked up my suitcase, and we left to the car. I gave him the address of Benedetti's shop.

When I entered the shop for the second time, the lady behind the counter recognized me. "Bongiorno."

"Hi, I'm here to see Mr. Benedetti," I told her.

She made a head sign to the sitting security guard, who rose and came to me.

"Who are you, and what do you want with Mr. Benedetti?"

The guy was either plain dumb and didn't recall me from the previous visit or he was just trying to be disagreeable.

"My name is Inspector Leary of the New York Police," I lied. "My business with your boss is none of your concern."

He looked at me to decide what to do. Luckily, he didn't ask to see my credentials. He did remember me coming to the shop with the Italian police. Finally, he made a sign for me to follow him, pointing to the door in the back. At the foot of the stairs to Benedetti's office, he stopped, shouted a few words in Italian to the other goon above, and told me to go up.

I let my arm fall. Turning quickly in his direction, I hit him on the side of the head with my improvised weapon. He went down without making a sound. I repositioned the sap on my forearm and climbed the stairs.

The other man came forward to frisk me. I let him approach and start feeling for a weapon. I gave him no chance. Moving quickly, I repeated my previous action with his friend. I swung the lead shot–filled sock. It knocked him solidly in the head. I grabbed him and let him down slowly to avoid the noise of a falling body. I got my plastic cuffs and worked quickly, fastening his arms to his back and his ankles. I removed his gun, a 9 mm Beretta, and a cell phone. I went down and cuffed the other man as well, also collecting his gun and mobile phone.

I returned upstairs and threw open Benedetti's door. He raised his head from the stuff he was reading, alarmed to see me burst into his room. He recovered fast, going for something inside one of his table drawers. I was faster. I shut the drawer on his hand. He shouted with the pain of his squeezed hand. I pointed the gun I had removed from one of his men at him.

"Let go of what you were trying to get," I ordered. "Remove your hand slowly, or I will shoot you."

I eased on the pressure on the drawer, allowing him to remove his hand.

"Get up. Move away from the table!"

Inside the drawer, I found a third gun, which also I took.

"Place your hands to your back," I told him. "And don't make any false move, or I will shoot you."

"What is this?" Benedetti asked, recovering from the initial shock.

"I ask the questions here," I said. "You answer."

I told him to face the wall and fastened his hands. I moved his chair away from the desk and told him to sit down.

"I don't know what you intend, but you will regret what you are doing," he said.

I hit his face with my gun. "Shut up!"

I secured his ankles. I yanked a cord from a Venetian blind and tied him to the chair. I frisked him, but he was unarmed. I removed his cell phone and crushed it with my foot, doing the same with the other two phones I had collected from his bullies. I searched the room and his desk, checking for weapons or other phones, but didn't find any. I pulled his telephone wire from the wall.

"Don't go anywhere," I jested. I'll be back soon.

I went down again, returning to the shop. The lady behind the counter saw me coming and smiled at me. I got close and pulled the gun, pointing at her. She let out a small cry of alarm, looking at my gun with my eyes full of fear.

"Don't do anything foolish and you won't get hurt," I told her. "Raise your hands and come out from behind the counter." She obeyed me. "You are going to close the shop. Lower your arms and go to the front door. Remember, I'm right behind you. If you shout or make any sign to someone on the sidewalk, I will kill you." I hated to be doing this. I had absolutely no intention of shooting or hurting in any way this poor lady in any way. She didn't know my intentions. If she had called my bluff, I would be lost. I realized what I was doing. It was totally stupid and foolhardy, but I was desperate. I had no intention of staying in Italy for several weeks or months. I could not wait for Benedetti to break under the police pressure. By that time, Peralta might be in Timbuktu, for all I knew. I had to do this.

The lady shut the front door and removed the objects from the display windows, closing its doors as well. I told her to turn around and secured her hands with the cuffs. I commanded her to go to the restroom, following behind. Inside, I closed the lid, made her sit on the toilet bowl, and secured her ankles as well. I went out and locked the restroom door. I pulled the shop telephone wire from the wall and returned to the man downstairs, gagging him with rags torn from his shirt. I repeated the same action with the man upstairs. I was ready for Benedetti.

He was looking at me with eyes full of hate. "Nobody fucks with me you sonofabitch American. You will see. I'll have you killed."

I got my sock and hit him on the nose. It broke and started bleeding profusely over his shirt. He passed out. When he woke up, his nose had swelled, and he could only breathe through his mouth.

"Perhaps, now we can talk sensibly," I said. "This is no game, and if you want to continue living, you will answer my questions without dreaming of bullshitting me, as you did with Carlo. Now tell me, where is this Feliciano, Peralta, Eduardo—or whatever what name he is presently using—hiding in Italy?"

"I have nothing to tell, you piece of shit," he answered.

"Very well. I see that you want to make things harder. That's okay with me." I pressed the muzzle of the gun against the fleshy portion of his thigh and pulled the trigger. The noise was loud, but I had noticed during my first visit that his room was soundproofed. With the door closed, I didn't think the shot could be heard by someone passing outside the shop.

Benedetti cried in pain. "You miserable American son of a whore."

"Let me repeat the question. Where is Peralta?"

"Go fuck yourself."

"Fine. This is what I'll do. I'm going to shoot your kneecap. The pain is excruciating, and you'll be lame and forced to walk on crutches forever. No bone surgeon can completely fix it. I've seen such wounds before in war. During the first forty-eight hours, no amount of painkillers will suffice. It's terrible. You wish to try it?" I placed the gun muzzle over his kneecap. Benedetti's belligerent expression had been replaced by one of horror.

"Stop! I'll tell it."

"Good. Wise decision. But let me warn you, don't dream of giving me false information. I'm betting he isn't very far away. He must keep contact with you, right? Likely, you haven't been able to sell all the items yet. If I go and discover you lied to me, I'll come back to kill you. You cannot even begin to imagine what I will do to you before you die."

"He has rented a small farm in a village called Acquaviva. It's near the town of Montepulciano, in Tuscany. The farm has a name, Agroturismo Bella Vale."

"See how easy that was. Now, you just have to stay put for a few hours, until I go to this place and confirm your information. If you are telling the truth, I'll call the police to come save you. But if you are lying …" I didn't finish the thought. "Don't expect anyone to show up in the meantime. I've taken precautions."

I left the shop in a hurry. I had to get to this place Benedetti had indicated as quickly as possible. There was always a chance of something going wrong. All it would take was Carlo or another police officer to pay an impromptu visit to spoil my plan. I returned to my car and told Maximo, "Can you take me to this village Acquaviva? It's near Motepulciano, in Tuscany."

"But Signore Leary, that's outside Rome, and they told me you would only stay in the city."

"What is the distance from here to there, Maximo?"

"Around one hundred and ten miles."

"How much would you charge to drive me there and back?"

Maximo thought for an instant and answered me. "Two hundred and fifty dollars."

"How long it will take you to drive there?"

"Close to two hours."

"Make it in an hour and a half, and I'll pay you five hundred dollars. Deal?"

"Yes, sir. For that much, I'll fly."

CHAPTER 32

Tuscany

Maximo made good on his promise. After we cleared the traffic in Rome and entered the expressway, he floored the gas pedal. The speedometer never went below 105 mph. You could never drive like that on a US freeway or anywhere else, with the exception of Germany, where there is no speed limit. In Italy, we were moving at a totally illegal speed, but we weren't stopped. We arrived at the marked exit to Acquaviva in exactly one hour and twenty-five minutes, after leaving Benedetti's shop in Rome. I was worried during the entire voyage about the things that could go wrong. Benedetti could have lied to me. I could find no farm with the name of Bella Vale. Or I could find the farm but no Peralta. There was a good chance I might find myself in an Italian cell shortly. At this exact moment, the Polizia di Stato or the Carabinieri might be looking to arrest me for the invasion and assault on two Italian citizens. My head was full of potential misfortunes.

After we arrived at our destination, I couldn't help but admire the Tuscany landscape around us. A wide valley of rolling hills, green with olive trees and grapevines, with a scattering of distant lines of tall cypress trees. Acquaviva was a tiny village, its low silhouette barely noticeable on the horizon of the hills. Montepulciano could be clearly seen some distance away, as a fairytale city perched on top of a stony hill well above the surrounding valley. I made a mental note to return with Livy and Larissa to explore this incredible region. It would be lovely to spend a few careless days driving around to the most distant places and cycling or trekking to the closer ones.

Dreams. I had to put those out of my mind for now. I was anxious to encounter the man I had been chasing for so long and over three continents. Then I could end my quest and return home to my family.

Maximo got directions at a gas station and at the village. He had to ask at a few places until finding someone who knew the place we were attempting to reach. He came back smiling with the success of having found our destination. He boarded the car and turned on the motor.

"It's very close," he told me. "They even made a drawing on how to get there. He showed me a piece of paper with lines drawn on.

We drove another ten or fifteen minutes over local unpaved roads and would have never found the farm if not for the drawing Maximo had obtained. We lost our way a couple of times, taking wrong turns at unmarked crossings. I was beginning to get impatient when we finally reached it. Two masonry pillars with a wrought-iron gate marked the farm entrance. A sign saying "Agroturismo Bella Vale" hung from an iron arch supported by two pillars. I could see a house with two levels a short distance away from the gate. The topmost level had evidently the living quarters, and the lower one seemed to be a shed or a granary. I noticed a few bungalows—guest houses, I guessed—far right from the main house. They appeared to be unoccupied.

I told Maximo to wait for me in the car and went on foot. I crossed the gate and walked to the house. I still had one of the guns that I had taken from Benedetti's men. The other I had discarded at a bridge crossing. I released its safety and pulled the action to arm it, placing a round in the chamber. I walked quickly to the stairs leading to the second floor. I hadn't seen anyone outside the house or working in the adjacent fields. When I reached the top of the stairs, I found that the house door wasn't locked. I guessed nobody paid much attention to security in this peaceful area.

I went in as quietly as possible. Stepping carefully, I tried to avoid creaking floorboards or unnoticed obstacles that might trip me up. I saw a medium-size room with a covered porch to my right, giving on to the fields. To my left, two doors gave access to what I supposed were sleeping rooms. In front of me, in the back of the room, another door must have led to the bathroom and kitchen. I was still deciding what to do, which room to examine first.

Suddenly, my quarry, the person I had been chasing, stepped out of one of the doors. He stopped, surprised to see me there. His face expressed alarm with my presence. I had found him. He was not Feliciano, Peralta, or Eduardo Nuñes. We had all been deceived by the true killer. The person I was seeing in front of me was none other than Mr. John Engelhard, the former president of Horizon Mining, the billionaire.

Deville's instinct had been correct from the start. Engelhard was alive after all. I was surprised, flabbergasted, really. I pointed my gun at Engelhard and ordered him to raise his arms. He obeyed me.

"You are supposed to be dead," I said. Then something hit me from behind, and everything went dark.

CHAPTER 33

The Killer

I don't know how long I was unconscious. When I recovered my senses, I was tied to a chair. I tried to free me, but I was firmly bound. Engelhard had taken my gun and was watching me. Standing next to him, to my surprise, was the secretary, Ms. Helen Crawford. She was the one who had hit me, obviously. I winced with the pain in my head.

"I hope Helen hasn't hurt you too much, Mr. Leary. You are Alan Leary, no? I was told you were looking for me."

Engelhard had a clear, firm, and agreeable voice. He was smiling in an almost friendly way. He continued talking to me. "You are cleverer and more ruthless than I thought. You managed to escape two perfect attempts on your life in Manaus—conducted, I should say, by two very efficient assassins. I was amazed. I raise my hat to you, Alan. It's nice to recognize a pro like myself. You are indeed good."

"Thanks for the praise," I said. "It's going to get you nowhere," I managed to joke.

"It's good to see you can keep a good spirit in an adverse situation. I like that."

"What happened to the other man, Eduardo Nuñes or Fernando Peralta, whatever his name was?" I asked.

"His true name was Fernando Peralta. And by the way, you are completely off the mark. Eduardo Nuñes and Peralta are different people. I expect Nuñes to be quite happy in his new job. He had nothing to do with this. Peralta was a geologist consultant with the company. His job allowed him a lot of freedom to travel and move around. He was registered in the company under yet another name: Guilhermo Atrio. I expect he'll be eventually missed, but with his boss, Nuñes, gone, this could take some time. I met him when we were, the two of us, with the Sendero Luminoso, in Peru. He was never a fighter or a soldier, as I was. Fernando was with the administration; he was with the men who made sure we had sufficient money for guns and supplies. The men who dealt with the drug dealers, a disgusting but indispensable activity, a necessary evil, one could say. He was a good geologist, however, and when I started Horizon Mining, I brought him in."

"Why did you kill all those people, to steal the gold? That was nothing to you. You are a billionaire. Then why?"

"Ah, I wasn't interested in the gold. But I had to get the alb, the tunic found in the grave. It represented a new life for me. It was the cancellation of a pact, long contracted, which I had no intention to fulfill. Benedetti got all the gold for himself. The price he paid for it was arranging my safe transportation to this country, providing still another identity, and getting me this villa. He must have told you where I was. I shall have a serious conversation with him after we finish here."

"What about the fingerprint found on the shovel, the one matching Peralta's? What happened? Did you force the poor guy to dig his own grave?"

"No, actually, Peralta was the first one I killed in that campsite. He brought the news and the details of the discovery to me. A geologist who worked with him had found the grave. I cut a deal with Peralta. He would help me steal the grave, and he could keep the gold for himself. I only wanted the tunic. He was greedy. Don't look so surprised. I knew he had been stealing from me for years, selling important information to my competitors. He accepted my offer immediately. But I had intended to kill him from the start of our adventure. He was beginning to know too much about me, and I needed someone to take the rap for the crime to be committed. The native was not part of the initial equation. He showed up at the campsite unexpectedly. I put my documents on him. The fingerprint on the shovel was a nice touch, don't you think. I also placed the ones found in the car." He laughed. "The police, they are so efficient."

I was horrified. He had Peralta's fingertips, and I had never considered he'd used them this way.

"Why did you decide not to use Peralta's assistance? I suppose it would have made your gruesome job easier?"

"You see, Alan, I have been alive for a very long time. When your grandparents were but children, I had already been living for a very long time. I have fought many battles in many wars. I trained and became an expert in every type of martial art you can think of. Some of them, I invented myself, combining techniques from different schools."

"You were confident of being capable of handling the situation by yourself."

"Precisely. I am very good, Alan. I know you are a trained soldier, but I could kill you easily with my bare hands, believe me."

"Would you like to make a go at that?" I asked in defiance. "Just untie me and try."

Engelhard smiled. "I became proficient in handling all kinds of weapons. To me, killing those people was nothing," he continued. "The stupid Peralta thought he could provide help. It was actually ridiculous."

"Why didn't you let him have the gold? Even if he was no help in dispatching those poor souls, he could have still helped you escape."

"As I told you, he knew too much. He was a liability. I couldn't allow him to continue alive. He might have started talking."

"And Helen?" I asked. "Why is she here?"

"We are lovers, Mr. Leary," Helen said, speaking to me for the first time. "I am sorry I hit you. I couldn't let you take John."

Engelhard continued talking. "Now that I have become free of my, let's say, commitment, I can start a normal life. I'll get old and eventually die, like anybody else. Helen loves me and has decided to share my new life with me. My luck. Her timely intervention today saved me from being arrested by you. In former times, I would have had no fear of your silly toy gun. You could never kill me. I was immune to that." He smiled. "But now, I can die. I could not resist you for fear of being shot. You could have arrested me. I would have to obey you. You would have spoiled all my carefully laid plans."

"Too bad she showed up," I said.

"Too bad for you but good for me. But, I'm afraid I shall have to end this conversation."

"Why? I'm enjoying it, actually."

"Time to die, Alan. You should have given up chasing me when you had the chance, when I left you not a trace at Manaus, but you had to persist. I'm sorry, but I cannot let you go alive. You brought this on yourself. You must understand, this is not personal. I even think I like you. Under different circumstances, we could have been friends."

"Hardly," I said.

Engelhard smiled and pointed the gun at me.

"Don't kill him," Helen shouted, trying to interpose herself between Engelhard and me.

"Get out of the way, Helen," Engelhard exclaimed, pushing her out of the way and raising the gun.

I knew I would die one day. As Engelhard had just said, it happens to all of us sooner or later. When I was on active duty, I faced death more than once. On several occasions, I thought I would die. I saw my companions being killed. However, I never expected to die like this, tied to a chair, far from home, far from comrades or family. I could not complain, though. I had lived for more than two marvelous years with Livy and my beloved daughter, Larissa. I wished I'd had more time with them, to see my daughter become a teenager, a young lady as lovely as her mother, but it wasn't to be. I concentrated myself on two of them, the loves of my life. My final thought was for them. I wanted their image to be the last conscious thing in my life. I closed my eyes and rested.

CHAPTER 34

The Encounter

I heard a loud voice in the room.

"What do we have here?"

I opened my eyes. I had heard no shot, but obviously, if I had been dead, I wouldn't remember hearing it, would I? I had been concentrating so intently on the images of Livy and Larissa that I was slightly disoriented, but not so disoriented that I didn't recognize the voice of Anton Deville. What the heck? How could he be here? How had he arrived? He made no noise coming into the house, unless he was part of the other world as well. Engelhard and Helen looked very real and solid to me. She had a shocked expression, but John was positively terrorized. His eyes expressed horror and dread with the new arrival. The gun fell from his hand. Its distinct *thump* hitting the floor was a marked contrast in a room grown quiet, the personages still like static figures in a frozen tableau. Deville was dressed, as I had always known him to be, in a dark black suit with a vest, carrying his cane. Engelhard was the first to break the impasse. He gave an anguished cry.

"Noooo …! You cannot see me. I have the alb."

I understood everything now—the alb, which hid whoever was wearing it from Supay, the Inca incarnation of the devil: Deville, in our case. If you pronounced his name stressing the first syllable, it became the devil, or the "light bringer," as his business card showed. Obviously, Engelhard had entered an agreement with him a very long time ago. Now, the time had arrived to fulfill the contract, which Engelhard was trying to cheat. That's why the alb had become so important to him.

Deville laughed, and it gave me the creeps. I had the feeling of ice-cold fingers grabbing my spine. His laugh was sinister beyond belief.

"Truly, I cannot," Deville replied, "but I can see Mr. Leary. I asked him to chase you down and followed him."

John Engelhard was shaking uncontrollably. For the first time, I noticed a white cloth wrapped around his waist, looking like a thick sash.

"Now, if you permit me, this belongs to me." Deville walked to face Engelhard and yanked the white ribbon from his waist. He folded it carefully and put it in one of his pockets.

"How did you get here?" I asked.

"Please, Mr. Leary, do not ask silly questions. You are more intelligent than that." He turned himself toward Engelhard and spoke to him again. "This wasn't nice John. You were not correct with me. We had a deal. We made a pact. I fulfilled my part, but you tried to deceive me, to trick me out of what was due to me. I couldn't tolerate that. I'm a little mad with you, with the work and trouble you gave me to find you."

"Please, please, my time hasn't expired yet. It's not fair," Engelhard pleaded.

"Yes, it has," Deville contradicted him. "Humans are so pathetic. They have absolutely no notion of the nature of time. Some of your brightest have come up with theories, nearly all of which are idiotic. Some of their ideas, however, are pointed in the right direction, although they never come close to the truth: the arrow of time, the increasing entropy of the universe, parallel planes in coexistence. They are all very colorful and interesting but not real. Still, many of you are all too willing to give up your souls in return for increased *time* in this existence. It's absurd. If they only knew! What are centuries? Nothing compared to eternity, less than a blink of an eye, much shorter than a heartbeat. But it was your choice, John, and now I have come to collect my dues."

Engelhard started to plead again. I knew he was an assassin and about to kill me, but I couldn't help sympathizing with his plight and evident despair.

Deville talked to Helen in a smooth, low, but firm voice, precisely enunciating his words. "Pick the gun from the floor, dear, and shoot John. Do it now."

Helen moved as if she were sleepwalking, in a sort of aloof madness.

I cried her name several times, shouting for her to stop, but to no avail. She walked to the side of John Engelhard, picked the gun from the floor, placed it against John's head, and pulled the trigger.

I had never seen something like that. It was unbelievable to watch. John did nothing to defend himself, stoically accepting his own murder. I was in shock. After I recovered my wits, I told Deville, "That was cruel and very stupid. I'm impressed with your show of mind control, hypnotism, or whatever technique you used to force Helen to murder Engelhard. No matter whether he deserved it or not, it was a crime, and we are all implicated. We shall have to remain in Italy for months or years if we are convicted and sentenced."

Deville had a nonchalant attitude. "Don't worry, Mr. Leary. Helen will confess she did it all by herself, won't you, dear?" He addressed her. "Remember, you are not mine. Not yet, at least. He is," he said, pointing to Engelhard's body. "What you did now doesn't count. It wasn't done by your free will."

He shook his head. "One of *his* rules. So annoying. Anyway, behave, and I won't come back to take you. Besides, the courts are very lenient with crimes of passion in this country. You'll have to serve no more than a few years in jail, probably less than three. And you deserve it for your complicity with John."

He turned to me. "Don't you wish to get up and stretch your legs, Alan? Your position in that chair looks terribly uncomfortable."

"I can't … what the … "

The ropes tying me down had slackened, allowing me to free my hands and release my ankles. I got up, massaging my wrists, trying to reestablish my blood circulation. "How in heaven's name did you manage this trick? Okay, forget it. I don't want to know."

Deville smiled. "You are wise."

"Can I ask you one thing, to satisfy my curiosity?"

"Depends on what you wish to know."

"It's nothing much, I think. What was all that excitement about an alb or tunic?"

"Ah well, the alb belonged to Him. He gave it to me, when we were friends, eons ago. Then, we began to disagree, and He sent me away from His side. We became estranged, but I kept the alb as a souvenir from, you could say, happier times. I lost it—I don't remember how. It was all so long ago. The alb has the property of making its owner invisible to me. One of His friends, an angel, as humans call them, had the alb for a short while. The silly fellow had this absurd notion to help primitive people better themselves. Isn't the behavior of certain people incredible?" He shook his head again in disgust. "Naturally, I took care of that imbecile of an angel, but not before he had the opportunity to hide the alb. The rest, you know. An Engelhard employee found it accidentally. That cheater lying there thought he could get the better of me."

"How old was he? He kept saying he had been alive a long time."

"You are curious, aren't you? Well, you are a detective. I'll humor you. Engelhard was five hundred years old, give or take a few years. My offer to him was to keep him in this existence for five centuries. During that time, he could have whatever he wished—money, women, power. However, at the end of the agreed-upon period, he would come to me. I would own his soul. It was a good deal, don't you think?"

"Absolutely not," I answered.

"Why? Wouldn't you like to live five hundred years, together with the wife you love so much and the daughter you adore?"

"Not in exchange for my soul."

"Forget what I said. This is another of His bothersome rules. I am not permitted to tempt anyone who hasn't shown interest in what I have to offer. Silly, isn't it? However, if you ever change your mind …"

"Not a chance in … the place where you came from."

Deville smiled.

"Are you going to leave that poor lady standing there in a state of stupor?" I asked.

"I'll fix that," Deville said, snapping his fingers.

Helen recovered instantly. She sighed deeply as if waking from a profound dream. Helen appeared to become aware of what she had done and started to cry desperately.

"Why don't you go get a glass of water for poor Helen. She looks like she needs one." Deville told me.

I went past the door I had noticed in the far wall of the room, looking for a glass of water. I came back and offered it to Helen. She was still grieving too much to accept it. I embraced her and tried to give some comfort.

"Now, now, Helen, please do not cry. It was not your fault. That evil man made you do it," I whispered. "I know you loved John and that anything I say will not serve as consolation for his death, but you are still a young woman, beautiful and intelligent. You'll find a decent person who will love you and make you happy. I don't even think you will be in jail. Even if you loved him, you know that John has committed serious crimes. When the Italians learn of his past, they won't treat you with severity."

Slowly, slowly, she began to calm down and stop crying. I offered her the water again, and she accepted it this time.

"Very touching," Deville said. You should be going, Alan. The Italian police have already learned of your exploits at Benedetti's place. I don't believe they are thrilled with you. Go. I'll take care of Helen. Fear not, I'll be kind to her. I have to call the *carabinieri*, and you don't want to be found here. I know how anxious you are to return to your family."

"And you? You shall have to go as well," I told Deville.

"Not an issue, Alan. The police will not find me hear, either. I have my own means of transportation. Ah, and Alan, your company will be fully compensated, according to our contract, and I will add a handsome bonus for your excellent work."

I went back to my car. Maximo was still waiting patiently.

"Sorry it took me so long, Maximo."

"You weren't gone long at all. I didn't keep track of the time, but it couldn't have been more than twenty minutes."

"What? No, I must have been gone much longer than that."

"Not at all," Maximo insisted.

I was confused. After Deville's speech on the true nature of time, I could easily believe in anything absurd, as if time passed differently for two persons separated by a very short distance.

"Very well, Maximo. Can we go now?"

"Where to, Alan?"

"Fiumicino airport. And Maximo, I want to fly in a plane, not in this car. You can take it easy this time."

CHAPTER 35

Going Home

Due to the strange temporal distortion I had experienced in Tuscany, I arrived at the airport with enough time to book a flight to New York, by way of London. The flight left at seven in the evening. I counted five one-hundred-dollar bills from my wallet and paid Maximo, who was exultant with our arrangement. He made a point of giving me his business card and made me promise to call him whenever I was in Italy and needed a chauffeured car.

I decided to pass security immediately and wait in the business class lounge. I owed Emmet a briefing on what had occurred. He had been so friendly and helpful. I couldn't possibly leave the country without at least thanking him. He was surprised when I phoned him from the lounge.

"Gawd blimey, mate, what happened to you? Where did you hide? I called your hotel and was told you had checked out. That chap Carlo is desperately looking for you. In fact, the entire Rome police are looking for you. Everyone, me included, thought you had been killed. That is, until we decided to pay a visit to our friend Benedetti. Then Carlo was pissed off with you. He thinks you overstepped, abused his trust. He's not pleased, I can tell you."

"I'm sorry to hear it, Emmet. What did Benedetti say?"

"He said nothing. He didn't accuse you, if that is what you are asking. The lady, however, gave a very good description of the crazy American who pointed a gun at her. As you must guess, her description fit you like a glove."

"I didn't hurt her. I only locked her in the restroom."

"No matter. She was shocked. Benedetti, however, is going to spend a week in hospital, fixing his nose and a hole in his thigh. His two security men were both treated for severe concussions. You really did a thorough job on them. Care to tell me why?"

"Are we talking as comrades-in-arms or as a suspect to a policeman?"

Emmet sighed. "The former, mate. As friends."

"Fine, this is what happened."

I gave a complete description of everything I had done and how I had found the hiding place of John Engelhard.

"He deceived us all, Emmet. He planted the fingerprints—the one on the shovel and the others in the car. The last body found, outside the camp, belonged to Fernando Peralta."

I told Emmet of my encounter with Engelhard in Tuscany and how he had confessed the crimes. I omitted the participation of Deville and the stranger events, which took place there. I didn't wish Emmet to consider me a loony. I had great trouble myself to understand what I had experienced on the farm. I explained about Helen and her complicity in the story. I lied, saying she had killed Engelhard because, after her involvement and help, he was going to abandon her. I included the fact that she had saved me. If she hadn't killed Engelhard, he would surely have shot me dead.

"Why did he commit those crimes? It's unbelievable that a man so rich would kill all those people to rob items worth a fraction of his fortune."

"The human mind is complicated to gauge," I mused. "Besides, a portion of his former life remains hidden. His identity was false. I know he was a terrorist for some time, fighting in Peru. Who knows? He might have been one of those extreme adventure junkies."

"What will you do now, Alan? Are you going to present yourself at Polizia di Stato and give an account of your involvement in this affair? Carlo would like to talk to you."

"Not a chance, Emmet. I want to go home. I have been chasing this man for more than a month, hopping from place to place in South America and in Italy. I need to go home, to my family. If I show up at the police, Carlo will almost surely detain me for days, even weeks. I can't afford that."

"So you are going to leg it."

"If that's a British slang for taking off, the answer is absolutely."

"You may have trouble boarding the plane, I should warn you. I'm not positive that Carlo has gone as far as to issue a warning to airports, to prevent you from leaving the country. He may well have, as far as I know."

"I'll have to take my chances."

"You may be subpoenaed as a witness if Helen is tried in this country."

"And my lawyers will fight it. That's why I asked you at the start of this conversation under what condition we would be talking. There is nothing connecting my presence at the place of Engelhard's killing. If push comes to shove, I'll have to deny being there at all. I would deeply regret if Carlo became cross at me for not going to talk to him now. I reckon I have already done him a favor of sorts."

"How does that work, Alan?"

"Now he knows, without a shadow of a doubt, that Benedetti smuggled the gold artifacts and John Engelhard into this country. Moreover, he's conscious that Benedetti has kept the gold. If I were he, I would try to hide Engelhard's death for a while, long enough to convince Benedetti that Engelhard had been arrested and was spilling his guts to get a lighter sentence. I would tell Benedetti the police knew everything and his only chance of avoiding a long prison term would be to confess all and reveal where the gold is."

"I really don't expect him to swallow that story, mate, but I wish you luck. I would have liked to know you better. Who knows, if I ever visit the States?"

"I would be delighted to see you there, Emmet. You have been a great friend and a big help to me. I'll always be in your debt. I hope I'll have the occasion to repay the favor."

"Don't mention it, old chap. It was my pleasure. Please give my regards to the two baby seals across the pond. Tell them to visit. I'll show them what good ale is to get pissed on. Not that fruity cold juice they drink over there."

"Leave it to me, Emmet. I'll tell them.

"Cheerio, mate. Come back sometime."

I was feeling like an evaded criminal, fearing not being able to board my plane. It would be miserable to be prevented from embarking. There was nothing I could do other than hope Carlo hadn't issued a warning. It was pointless to worry, but I couldn't stop doing it.

I decided to call home. Livy was still at college, unfortunately, but I talked to Claudia and managed to say a few words to Larissa. A happy family life also has its drawbacks. I missed my wife and daughter. I tried to resist the feeling. In my profession, where I was often forced away from home, it was not wise to be too sentimental.

Finally, my flight was called. I went past the last security inspection, passport in hand, to answer the usual inane questions: *Have you packed your suitcase yourself. Did you receive any last-minute packages*? At any instant, I was expecting a tap on my shoulder and an invitation to follow a policeman away from boarding, but nothing happened. I entered the plane, placed my suitcase in the overhead compartment, and nestled myself into my assigned seat. I waited with impatience for the plane to start moving, and I wasn't totally at ease until it took off. Then I could finally relax. Nobody had stopped me. I was going home.

CHAPTER 36

Epilogue

One month had passed since I returned from Rome. I had written a long, apologetic letter to inspector Carlo, asking his excuse for having departed without warning him. I had to edit the Tuscany story. As in the case of Emmet, I just couldn't tell him about Anton Deville. In the best of cases, he would take me for a liar. The alternative was a lot worse. He would consider me a lunatic. If I ever needed to contact him again concerning a different case, he wouldn't take me seriously. By omitting the stranger details, at least I might be excused of my faux pas with him and given a reprieve. I could never guess when I might be forced to return to Rome, in another case. It's good policy to keep your doors open. In my letter, I tried to be as kind as possible with Helen Crawford. Without providing a full explanation, I mentioned she had been forced into a situation not of her making. Regretfully, she became emotionally involved with John Engelhard, and all her troubles derived from that. I hoped Helen would be able to get off lightly from the charges levied against her. I learned she was going to be tried in Italy after all.

I planned to revisit my friends Paul and Hendricks. I asked Ian to arrange a meeting at his place, and we went back to White Plains a Saturday afternoon. It was a much smaller gathering than the one at the previous barbecue, only the four friends and their wives. This time, we took Larissa with us, to the delight of Agnes and the other two ladies. Paul and Hendricks had introduced me to Emmet. I was under the obligation to recount my adventure to them, once again skipping the less conventional episodes. I transmitted Emmet's message to them and his restrictions regarding American beer.

Hendricks smiled. "That silly Limey. We have to set him straight someday."

"Yeah, teach him a lesson," Paul added jokingly.

The wives had formed a circle of their own, which included the children and were left to exchange idle silly talk, usual in these reunions of male friends. As usual, Livy shined among the other wives. She was not only the prettiest but also intelligent and a good conversationalist. I was amazed at her flair for languages. It was true, she had been living in this city for more than two years, and she had already a very good command of English when I met her. Still, she talked fluently, with a hardly detectable accent. We spent an agreeable afternoon at the McDowells'. However, the time came for us to leave. I thanked them both and embraced my old friends. I wanted to get home early because of Larissa, and we still had a long drive ahead of us.

At work, things returned to normal. Our bread and butter was providing security services. It was actually a boring job, however, opportunities such as the one I had recently completed didn't fall in our laps every day. Years could go by without anything reassembling my last adventure.

Two months went by. Olivia was back to her classes and tried to leave home early in the morning to catch a less crowded subway. I had no need to arrive early at the office. Nevertheless, I fell into the habit of leaving home with her, catching the same subway. I went off at the Fifty-First Street stop, and she kept going south for NYU.

Normally, Livy comes back from college in the early afternoon. Most of her classes are in the morning. I established the habit of leaving my office a few hours earlier, to spend more time with my family. Through the whole period I was back, I couldn't shake a slight feeling of anguish, and I needed the comfort and support provided at home.

I couldn't rid myself of the image of a pleading Engelhard, eyes full of terror. Could he, in his last minutes on this planet, have had a vision of the horrors he would have to face on the other side? I had never paid attention to religion. I have nothing against people who do, but it was not for me. I have always been a little materialistic. This affair with Engelhard and Deville shook my convictions to the core. It was affecting my family life and me.

The joy of discovering Livy pregnant with our second baby wasn't sufficient to offset my down feeling. Livy was six to eight weeks pregnant. I didn't have to be a rocket scientist to determine precisely when and where she had become pregnant. It was in Chivay, in the Peruvian Andes. I was dead tired, still suffering from high altitude effects. Livy, however, had been determined. I now recall with humor the clear annoyance of our travel companions. They were patently pissed with us for making them wait in the morning, delaying our return to Arequipa. Well, once you start, it is difficult to stop. It was still too soon to tell the sex of the baby. It didn't matter: a boy or another girl, I would love either the same way.

We decided to spend a Sunday afternoon in Central Park. The day was lovely—clear bright skies, not cold but not warm either. Larissa loved to play on the grass and to visit the zoo. We enjoyed these careless occasions spent together, and whenever we had the chance, we took it to be there for a few hours. Livy came into the living room, holding Larissa's hand.

"We are ready. Shall we go, Alan?"

I looked them over. "You are both gorgeous. Have you imagined when Larissa becomes a teenager, Livy? The number of heads she'll turn. I bet she'll leave a trail of broken hearts. Poor boys."

Livy smiled. "I don't think so. She's going to be a very responsible young lady, won't you, Larissa?"

"Yes, Mommy. Can we go, Daddy? I want to see the *duckies*."

We decided to walk but took the stroller to give Larissa a lift when she got tired. We crossed Fifth Avenue in front of the Metropolitan Museum and walked south to reach the zoo. The sidewalk was full of people like us, taking advantage of the nice weather. I met a few acquaintances and we briefly greeted each other on our way. The zoo was too crowded, and we gave it up in favor of a less attended spot where we could let Larissa play while we watched.

"Tell me what's bothering you, Alan. You have been different lately. I know you well. Something is not right. Wouldn't you feel better if you told me?" Livy asked.

"Yes," I said pensively. "I believe I would."

"Then go ahead. You trust me, don't you?"

"Do you believe a person could live five hundred years, honey?'

"In the movies yes, but not in real life. That would be impossible, I think."

"What if I told you that I have met such person, one who made a pact with the devil. He would live five hundred years, during which time he would become very rich, powerful, and successful in all fields. There was just one catch. At the end of that period, he would have to surrender his soul to the devil."

"Is this real? Alan."

"Quite real, actually. Remember the conversation we had in my sister's apartment, just after the start of the investigation? The strange fellow who hired us, Deville, gave his business card supposedly from a firm named Light-Bringing Associates. My brother in law was the only person who saw through the charade. He chalked it up to a joke in bad taste. The bringer of light, in Latin, *lux fer*, corrupted to the present name Lucifer. Well, it was no joke. Deville is Lucifer."

"I cannot believe what you are saying, Alan."

"Just try to pronounce Deville with the accent on the first syllable."

"Dev … oh, I see. How awful."

"I hadn't told you this before. My last day in Italy was a nightmare. I had no reason to pity a murderer who sold his soul as Engelhard, but just seeing the fear and the agony expressed during his last moments of life was terrifying. The guy was trying to cheat the devil. This Inca tunic, the alb, was supposed to protect its user from the devil, keeping him invisible. I am sure that you, such as I, hearing a story like that would give it no importance—just a silly fable. Believe me. It is true. Engelhard killed several persons and went through great trouble just to be able to get the alb. With it, he intended to run from Deville. He almost succeeded. His downfall was my perseverance in tracking him down. He had become invisible, but Deville only had to follow me until I found him."

"This has to be the scariest story I have ever heard."

"Imagine the horror of the scene, of being in the presence of that evil being. He even had the gal to offer a similar agreement to me."

"Jesus, Alan."

"Precisely, I obviously refused him. But since that encounter, I haven't been able to sleep well. I keep having nightmares, in which I'm being dragged down with Engelhard."

It made me feel better to confide in someone, to reveal the facts I had been keeping in myself. I should have done this sooner. I felt relieved, like having a weight taken from my shoulders.

Livy was astonished. "I don't know what to say, love. If I had heard this story from another person, I wouldn't have believed it. To witness a dark power, to confirm its existence, it's terrifying. Come here, love." Livy embraced me. "I want to be with you forever, Alan, my love. Don't ever leave me. I believe in the existence of a soul in a life beyond this. Wherever I go from here, I don't want to be without you."

We kissed.

"I think the same, Livy. I want you for always. What happened in Italy changed my way of seeing things. I've been much too concerned with material values. Perhaps I should pay more attention to religion. You might help me with it."

"I would love to, Alan. It would make me even more attached to you, if that's possible."

"We'll then, if it makes you happier, we should try it," I said.

We embraced a long while, watching our daughter, distracted with her toys. I was imagining a long and happy life with my wife, getting old together, educating our children according to our values, following their progress as they grew. Surely, if our love was strong enough, it would endure beyond life.

A WORD ABOUT THE AUTHOR

Dr. Luis Rousset graduated from Stanford University in 1971, with a PhD degree in mineral engineering. During his career, he did fieldwork all over South America, exploring as well as providing counseling to mining operations. He was also on the boards of several prestigious companies, such as BP Mining Brazil. Presently, he is member of the advisory board of a copper mining company in Brazil. Dr. Rousset and his wife have two daughters, born in the United States, currently living in New York, NY, and Boca Raton, FL, respectively. Dr. Rousset and his wife share their time between a home in Rio de Janeiro and their apartment in Manhattan.

Used to technical and scientific documents, he began writing fiction in the last few years, exposing his readers to some of the rugged environments he has experienced during his profession, places difficult to access and not normally visited by tourists.

The Alb is his second work, set in the high-altitude Andes Mountains in Peru, among other places. It is a sequel to the novel *Make It Short, Make It Simple*, in which Olivia and Alan first meet and overcome many difficulties to stay together.

Made in United States
North Haven, CT
01 February 2025

65221345R00133